FULL THROTTLE

JON HARTLESS

Published by Accent Press Ltd 2017
Octavo House
West Bute Street
Cardiff
CF10 5LJ

www.accentpress.co.uk

ISBN 9781786154576

—I pray you, in your letters,
When you shall these unlucky deeds relate,
Speak of me as I am; nothing extenuate,
Nor set down aught in malice: then, must you speak
Of one that lov'd not wisely but too well;

Othello Act 5, Scene 2

PREFACE

By James Birkin, Editor.

Today, Poppy Orpington is hardly remembered at all. Some do know she was a famous racing driver, though only a minority of these are aware that her first car was called *Thunderbus*, not *Thunderbolt*, a mistake arising from her later company of that name. Others wrongly dismiss her as the first of the modern celebrities, working the media for fame and money, while a few will gleefully recall libellous newspaper reports of harlotry in a Parisian bawdy house whenever her name is mentioned.

Most, however, are familiar only with her stained reputation from the Great War – a reputation, I maintain, that is thoroughly undeserved. However, I must not get ahead of myself. I shall explore everything in the right order and put Poppy in the context of her era. Her exoneration, should you wish to grant it, must be given at the right time and with a full understanding of Poppy's character.

This, then, is the beginning of the testimony, taken

from diaries, letters and personal contemporaneous interviews. Some may complain that my shaping of this material into a narrative rather than an academic account will diminish the authenticity of the work; I contest that Poppy's biography is so dramatic in tone, and so rich in style, that it pulled itself naturally into this shape.

Nonetheless, a few disclaimers should be noted. Memory is fragile, and it is unsurprising to see the manner in which events can be transposed, altered and generally misunderstood. Please be assured that I have researched all areas as closely as possible and that everything in this book actually took place, though not necessarily in the order given.

Also, the spoken language at that time was rather more formal than today, especially amongst the upper classes and the well-educated, and this has driven me to lightly edit certain conversations between Poppy, Simeon, Helena and their contemporaries. Please be assured that I have endeavoured to keep the pith of each exchange, sacrificing the semi-archaic speech patterns only for the sake of lucidity.

The reader may ask just why I have devoted so much time to the Orpington archive of diaries, letters and more. Does it really matter what happened to an almost-forgotten woman over a century ago? In my opinion, and simply put; yes. Poppy's life has many parallels today, while her eventual fate in the early years of the twentieth century could – tragically – easily happen again. I will accordingly interpose a series of editor's notes on those aspects of Poppy's life that I feel are relevant to us. I shall endeavour to keep these interjections to a minimum, however, as they serve to illuminate rather than to distract.

Join me, then, as we travel back to when motor sport was still open to amateurs – albeit only wealthy amateurs – who could race their own cars side-by-side with the professionals of the day. Back when the sport still boasted heroic individuality rather than corporate wrangling over fuel consumption and weight limits. Back when cars were designed by hand and built by imagination, and were as much for the public road as the racetrack, unlike today's machine-designed racing vehicles that have no function outside the sport and no individuality within it.

Let us return to an age which is now regarded as a lost era of romance and rugged individualism, but which was also characterised by gross inequality, a rigid social order, casual violence towards women and unthinking submission towards authority. Truly, the past is golden only when viewed from afar.

CHAPTER ONE

'Cripple!' taunted Darren Weldon as he jumped around Poppy, laughing and hooting in the playground. 'One arm! One leg! You're a crip!'

'Leave me alone!' snarled Poppy, swiping at her tormentor. Unfortunately, despite her tall and stocky frame, it was difficult for Poppy to defend herself with just one arm, while her lame leg affected her balance when trying to swing a retaliatory punch.

'Stumpy, stumpy!' screamed Weldon in delight, playing to the crowd of laughing children who had gathered to watch Poppy's pain and misery. 'You're Poppy Stumpington! You're Poppy No-Leg!' High above, a series of airships passed through the bright blue sky, oblivious to the jeering mob of ten-year-olds below.

'I do have a leg,' shouted Poppy, tears running down her face. She tried to spin around and punch Weldon but her weak knee made swift movement impossible.

'You haven't got a leg to stand on,' yelled Weldon before savagely kicking at Poppy's good leg, sweeping it away from underneath her. He laughed in

1

triumph as Poppy collapsed with a howl of pain and misery.

'And you've only got a stump!' screeched Paul Hibbert in spiteful loathing, pointing at Poppy's right arm which only went down to the elbow. 'Stumpy, stumpy!'[1]

'She's Poppy No-Mum,' shrieked a skinny, red-faced girl near the back.

'Yeah, your mum's dead,' said another girl with vicious enjoyment.

'Don't forget her manky leg,' insisted Weldon in glee, kicking Poppy's dress up to reveal the leg brace strapped to Poppy's knee. It was supposed to help strengthen her knee joint, but the brace was cheap and the gears and cogs frequently jammed or fell apart under the pressure of movement.

'You can get a job at the freak show,' crowed Hibbert in delight.

'Yeah, you're a circus freak!' screamed Weldon. Instantly a chant went up around the playground. 'Poppy is a freak, Poppy is a circus freak!'

'What is going on here?' demanded the petulant voice of Miss Godfrey, who had been ignoring the

---

[1] No one is sure why Poppy's arm never developed. What is known is that it was a birth defect – a common one, back then – rather than a workshop accident, no matter what some claim when trying to blacken the reputation of her father.

shouts and screams until they grew so loud they were threatening to disturb the headmaster.[2] 'Poppy Orpington, why are you rolling on the ground? Get up at once.'

'He kicked me,' yelled Poppy, clutching her leg in pain. Both Weldon and Hibbert, however, had already disappeared into the crowd.

'There's no one near you,' snapped Miss Godfrey in loathing. 'I can see through your lies, Poppy Orpington, and I know your sort; didn't God mark you out as sinful from the very start by withering your arm?'

'I'm not lying,' retorted Poppy as she tried to stand up. With an agonising creak, her leg brace buckled under the pressure and various cogs and wheels erupted from the device, spilling out onto the cold, hard ground.

'How dare you answer me back?' demanded Miss Godfrey in outrage. 'You will never be accepted into the Kingdom of Heaven! Now get up, girl, and

---

[2] The mix of male and female pupils was not an early attempt at egalitarian principles; it was simply a result of the poverty of the local council authority, the Dudley Urban Borough, which could not afford to run two separate establishments. This also explains why the school accepted the absolute dregs of the teaching profession.

receive your chastisement.' Godfrey grinned sadistically as she slowly opened her jacket to reveal the slender cane hanging from her belt. The watching children fell silent in anticipation, knowing what was going to happen next, some grinning in violent delight, some staring in horror, all grateful that it was Poppy, once again, who would face the cane.

Godfrey was fond of her cane; its appearance was guaranteed to frighten the most belligerent pupil, thus giving the inadequate teacher a sense of satisfaction that was, in some ways, even more pleasurable than the feeling she got from administrating a good, solid beating.

'Stand up, girl; this is for your own good,' hissed Godfrey. She took a moment to enjoy Poppy's wide, frightened eyes which never left the weaving tip of the cane, following its sweeping movement from left to right. 'I said get up! Or it will be twice the lashes for your wilful disobedience,'

Even before Poppy was upright, Godfrey had pulled the little girl's dress up to reveal the back of her thighs. The cane was raised and held high, so all could see. With a flat crack, the cane dropped, so fast it was nothing more than a blur, and Poppy shrieked as a vivid red weal appeared on the back of her legs. Another crack followed and another weal appeared, but a third and fourth had joined them before

Godfrey was finally satiated.

'Pick up your mess from the ground, girl,' panted Godfrey, her breathing heavy and brutal. 'Pick it all up and do not let me catch you lying again.'

Poppy stared at the collection of cogs, wheels and springs that littered the ground, all blurred by the tears in her eyes from the pain and humiliation. She dashed them away and swore she would never break, no matter what. She would never give them the pleasure. Turning her back on teacher and pupils alike, she picked up the parts from the brace and limped slowly away.[3]

Poppy hadn't gone far when a slim, pretty blonde figure approached her. Although she didn't recognise the girl, Poppy tensed in the expectation of yet more abuse. Lacking the mobility to defend herself, she was sadly accustomed to such attacks from many of the other pupils. The girl's words, however, proved a

---

[3] Scenes like this were unfortunately a regular occurrence for young Poppy. I have it from the diaries and letters of Poppy herself, from Amy and from interviews with some of Poppy's classmates over the years who were always delighted to talk to the press in return for getting their now-forgotten names into the papers. Some journalists even tracked down and attempted to speak to Miss Godfrey herself, but her religious mania had developed to such an extent in her later years that nothing useful could be gleaned from her.

surprise.

'Have you been hurt?' she asked, clearly horrified at what she had just seen.

Poppy was too upset to answer as she hobbled towards a dark corner of the playground, where overhanging bushes cast long shadows. She fell to the ground and fumbled her skirt up over her bad knee, allowing her to view the damage done to her leg brace. Thankfully, the basic frame was still in place, as were the pistons and rods. Once again, it was the gearing mechanism that had let her down. Poppy began to sort the tiny parts and slot them back in place, as she had done many times before. The girl watched quietly until breaking the silence.

'You've got the reciprocal linkage back to front.'

Despite her distress, Poppy couldn't help but be surprised; girls were not meant to know about mechanical objects. Their school education revolved around cooking, household management and the bare basics of English and Mathematics. Had her father not been an engineer, Poppy would have known nothing of gear linkages.

'Can I help?' asked the girl, smiling nervously. 'I like anything mechanical.'

'Really?' replied Poppy, partly in fear that she was going to be attacked again and partly in genuine interest.

'Yeah, my older brothers are always messing about with engines and the like. Mum and Dad keep telling me off for playing with them; "s'not ladylike," they say.' As she spoke, the girl skilfully slotted the intricate parts back into the brace before rummaging around in her school bag and pulling out a small leather tool case, which she unrolled to expose many screwdrivers and spanners.

'My dad has a tool set like that, but bigger,' blurted Poppy, gazing into the timid – yet pretty – face of the girl.

'I asked for this for my birthday,' replied the girl, selecting a tiny spanner and tightening various bolts on Poppy's brace. 'My mum and dad gave me a doll. Huh! Fortunately, my gran bought me this on the quiet.[4] It's only second-hand and it's missing a few bits, but it's mine. My name's Amy, by the way.'

'That's a pretty name.'

Amy coloured as Poppy's green eyes stared at her in open admiration. 'Yours is prettier; like the flower.

---

[4] The casual vernacular of the working class, interestingly enough, is much closer to our own speech today. Poppy's self-education later enabled her to converse equally with Simeon and Helena, but Amy was forever hindered by her lack of vocabulary – as well as the nervous social deference inculcated by the school's hidden curriculum.

My proper name is Amelia. Amelia Abberly. There, all done.'

Poppy glanced down and saw that her leg brace was back together. She ignored the pain from Godfrey's lashes, for even at such a young age she had learned that there were some things that could not be changed. She instead focussed on the brace, flexing her knee gently but then with increasing vigour. The tiny cogs and gears whined slightly as the pistons moved, allowing her free movement. 'Thanks,' she said awkwardly as they both stood up. 'That's a much better job than I could do.'

'That's all right. I've never seen a brace before, so it was interesting to work on it. The principles are quite simple, really. Are you interested in engineering?'

Poppy shrugged. 'I've picked it up from spending time with Dad in his workshop,' she began, but she was cut off by Amy's enthusiastic response.

'Wow! Your dad has a workshop? His own workshop?'

'Yes, just a small one. We live above it and Dad does repairs on anything people bring in. And he can weld, so people bring their old baths and buckets to be fixed if they spring a leak.'

'I wish my dad did something like that,' said Amy, regretfully. 'He works on a farm. The last place he worked at, the cows got sick and they all had to be burnt. It's why we moved here. Sorry about your mum, by the way. I heard what they were chanting over there.'

Poppy shrugged. 'I don't really remember her. You're new here, aren't you?'

'Yes, I only started a few days ago. My name's Amy.'

'You've already told me once,' grinned Poppy.

Amy glanced shyly at Poppy's freckled, pugnacious face, bordered by a wild mane of red hair, and found herself unaccountably blushing harder than ever. 'Does that happen a lot?' she asked hurriedly, gesturing back to the other children.

'Almost every day. If I had two arms and a proper leg I'd show them, but I can't keep my balance with this brace and this, this … ' Poppy angrily gestured at her stump. 'It always lets me down. I hate it!'

'I used to get bullied at my old school because I was more interested in metalwork than needlework.'

'I hate sewing. *And* baking,' said Poppy. 'Not that I can do either properly with one arm.'

'I can't bake either and I've got two perfectly good arms,' replied Amy before blushing again. 'Gosh, sorry, that sounds, um, you know, I mean,' she gabbled. 'I wasn't saying anything about your arm, or not having an arm, or the arm that you've

9

got.' She stopped talking, horrified at the words spilling out of her mouth, but Poppy erupted in a loud, genuine laugh that echoed around the playground, and soon the two girls were both laughing naturally and helplessly, clutching each other for support.

From that day on, Amy could often be found at Poppy's home. She was welcome there and she loved messing around in the workshop, though she was disturbed by how little money Mr Orpington seemed to have. The only reason Poppy and her father had food each day was because they grew their own vegetables and kept several chickens, while Poppy engaged in a barter system with her neighbours to swap the eggs for milk, bread, butter and cuts of meat.

Indeed, Amy discovered that Mr Orpington didn't always have enough work from his garage, so he had to take jobs wherever he could. Sometimes he worked at the local factories, either maintaining the machines or else on the assembly line – both of which he hated – and he'd even shovelled snow one winter when money was very low, just so he could earn a few copper coins. And yet, regardless of his earnings, Mr Orpington spent most of his money on the mysterious project he kept hidden at the back of the workshop, explaining his relative poverty.

Not even Poppy knew what was concealed in the forbidden part of the garage, though one day she did receive a clue to her father's secret. An almighty roar came from the workshop, something Poppy had never heard before. She hurried in and saw flames licking around the wooden doors that separated the back of the building from the front. A few seconds later, the gigantic figure that was her father staggered out, coughing and flapping at a cloud of smoke with a large, dirty towel.

'It's all right,' he coughed. 'Just a slight mistake with the fuel supply line.'

'Is that a dragon in there?' asked Poppy, her eyes wide.

'Don't be silly,' wheezed her father as he patted out a few smouldering embers in his huge beard. 'Dragons don't exist.'

'Are you making thunder, then?' asked Poppy, trying to peer around the door into the gloom of the back workshop. 'It sounds like it.'

'No. If it works, it will be a new form of transport. A new form of transport for everyone, not just the rich.'[5]

---

[5] At this point, only the rich could afford cars which were, without exception, driven by steam. People who couldn't afford cars would keep a horse and cart, and those who couldn't keep a horse would

'For everyone? You mean like a bus? Will it be a thunder bus?'

'Thunder bus?' repeated her father, looking surprised. 'Yes, very good. *Thunderbus* indeed!'

'What was that dreadful racket?' The cacophony had attracted the attention of their neighbour, Mr Jackson, who poked his head through the workshop doors and looked up at the towering form of Mr Orpington.

'It's a new form of transport,' said Poppy, proudly. 'Daddy is making it for everyone!'

'Transport?' laughed Mr Jackson in derision. 'I don't think so! Who would buy any sort of vehicle that sounds as bad as that? Your engine must be broken.' He walked away, still laughing in disdain, leaving Poppy's father frowning after him.

'Blinkered idiot,' he muttered as he strode frantically around the workshop, as though needing to burn off excess energy. His voice suddenly rose as his face darkened. 'I'll show him. I'll show them all. But Poppy, it's a secret; I can't risk anyone knowing about this, in case they try to steal my ideas. You *can*

---

rely on public transport, typically a petrol-fuelled charabanc of dubious reputation, reliability and comfort. Petrol at this time was the fuel of the lower orders and was thus despised by the wealthy. Of course, for the majority below the poverty line, such as the Orpingtons, the only form of transport was walking.

12

keep it secret, can't you? You're not going to tell anyone? You can keep *Thunderbus* a secret?'

'Of course, Dad,' said Poppy, wondering at her father's manic tone.

'You're sure?' roared Mr Orpington, anger suddenly contorting his features as he cuffed Poppy firmly on the side of her head.

'Yes, I'm sure, Dad!' cried out Poppy, her eyes wide.[6]

'Even from Amy? No telling Amy!'

Poppy nodded. She didn't like the idea, but if that was what her father wanted, she wouldn't say anything to anyone; not even to her best friend.

As the years passed, Poppy grew increasingly worried about her father. She helped him more and more in the workshop, fixing anything brought in such as tools and bicycles, and she also visited factories with him when help was required in repairing blown compressors and generators, yet despite this they didn't talk as much as before. Her father often seemed distracted, as though puzzling

---

[6] Unfortunately, Poppy was well-used to very rough handling from her father. What is even more unfortunate is that she viewed this as being quite normal, as did many others at that time, regardless of their social class.

over something bothering him, and he would often disappear into the secret part of the workshop when he wasn't focussed on his work for others. She shared her concerns with Amy one day as the two girls walked to school. It took a little time to get there because of Poppy's weak leg, but it gave them time to talk.

'Maybe it's just something men do,' said Amy with a shrug. 'Your dad disappears into his workshop and you hardly see him, and my dad disappears down the pub or the new Radical Club and I hardly ever see him.'

'What does he do at the Radical Club?'

'Comes home full of radical thoughts, mainly. Last week he said that the Empire is a bad thing because it takes wealth from other countries, and that the steamers hold some responsibility for this. Then Mum told him to stop going to the club after work because it will get us all into trouble, but he still goes. It doesn't half cause some grief between them.'

'I suppose he was just referring to the idea that the original airship crews are to blame for the second wave of the Empire, which of course gives rise to the following supposition that they are morally responsible for the human misery that still continues to this day in less developed countries.'

'You what?' gawped Amy. 'I swear, you

14

sometimes talk like you've swallowed a dictionary.'

'Um,' replied Poppy, puzzled that Amy didn't understand the concepts; they were clear enough to her. Poppy, however, was an avid and advanced reader and she had, to a certain extent, unconsciously adopted the literary rhythms of her books and articles when speaking. And much as she enjoyed Amy's company, she knew her friend struggled with ideas and theories that weren't grounded in machinery.

'I'm surprised the radicals have been attacking the steamers,' continued Poppy, tactfully bringing the conversation down a level. 'They're really popular with everyone. Every kid in school wants to be an airship pilot.'

'Dad said they were living off the goodwill of past deeds,' said Amy, closing her eyes as she recalled the unfamiliar words. 'He also said they protect the sovereignty of their air space. Whatever that means.'[7]

'It just means they run a closed shop. I sit in my

---

[7] In Poppy's day, of course, the airship industry was not yet obsolete, and the descendants of those who had helped forge the Second Empire a hundred years earlier still had an aura of romance about them, fuelled by urban legend and highly romanticised pulp novels in which brave crews travelled the world, delivering their cargo, fighting off air-pirates and living by their own rules.

15

bedroom window and watch the airships flying high in the sky and I dream of escape up there, where my leg brace and arm won't drag me down. They've got real freedom, freedom that even women can share. I wish I could join them and be free.'

'What d'you mean, free?' asked Amy. 'Do you feel trapped or something?'

'No, it's ...' Poppy paused, unable to find the words she wanted. 'I suppose it's just the situation with Dad; I love him, and I know he loves me, but he's always so busy with work so I never see much of him. And I hate school, of course. Sometimes I just feel lonely and ... I dream of being free of it all.'

'I wish I could come over more often but there are always jobs I have to do,' said Amy, her tone slightly bitter. 'I'm expected to help Mum with the cooking and sewing and housework – all of which I hate! I want to work with engines.'

'See, we *both* want to escape!' exclaimed Poppy. The girls smiled warmly at each other, happy in one another's company. 'Wouldn't it be fantastic to get into an airship crew?'

'I love the mechanics of those things but I don't think I'd want to travel in one. Huge tubes full of explosive gases? No thanks. I'd rather stick with engines on the ground.'

'Yes, but the airships can fly almost anywhere,'

said Poppy in excitement. 'We could get out of this place and see the world!'

'No chance we'll ever get that close.[8] Hey, look at that,' said Amy, pointing from under her cheap school cloak as a young man drove past in a car, the steam turbine hissing gently. Cars were becoming a common sight even in provincial towns and cities, which caused many problems for the trucks, charabancs, horses, carriages and carts that already filled the streets. 'I wish we could afford a car. I'd love to take one apart and put it back together. We could do it together.'

'I wouldn't be much help with that,' said Poppy, sadly, looking at her arm. Amy smiled in understanding, took Poppy's hand in her own and the two girls continued on their way to school.

---

[8] Poppy did eventually get to see some of the world, and even went as far as Egypt as part of the famous Bertram Foster expedition of 1914, though almost all knowledge of exactly what she did there is now – frustratingly – lost.

CHAPTER TWO

Two more years rolled by. Poppy grew bigger and stronger, becoming taller than the other girls in the school – and most of the boys. She couldn't fit in her window sill any more, and she had to sit in a chair to watch the airships fly overhead, although she did this less as her love of reading grew, leaving her to explore new avenues of fact and fiction which distracted her from her dreams of flying.

She still helped her father in fixing the various items brought to the garage, but in all that time she was never allowed into the forbidden part of the workshop. She continued to worry as her father grew increasingly remote, as though his secret project was consuming him. His usual robust demeanour was slowly overtaken by bouts of anxiety laced with anger, and he seemed to take very little notice of her presence at all – which thus doubled Poppy's surprise when he presented her with a large, poorly-wrapped parcel one morning.

'Happy birthday, Poppy,' he said, as he pushed bacon and egg around his plate. He glanced up to see Poppy looking at him in puzzlement. 'Er, it is your birthday, isn't it?'

'That was a few days ago,' replied Poppy,

diplomatically. Her birthday had in fact been three weeks earlier, but she didn't want to upset her father. He was increasingly losing track of time, and indeed the outside world in general.

'Oh,' said Mr Orpington, shifting awkwardly in his chair. 'Sorry. I've been, I mean, I've had my mind on, I mean ...'

'It doesn't matter,' replied Poppy with a shrug. 'You finished with the plate?'

Her father nodded and watched as Poppy took the plates to the sink, dropped them in, and poured in a little hot water taken from the steaming kettle over the small open fire. Her movements were becoming ever more graceful as she got older. 'I've got something here for you,' he said. 'Something I saved from the scrap bin while I was working at *Taylor Automaton* last month.'

Poppy decided not to point out that he had worked at *Taylor*'s six months ago; she was far too interested in what her father had salvaged from the factory floor.

'I've been working on this, on and off, whenever I got the chance,' continued Mr Orpington, looking around in puzzlement before remembering the canvas package he had already laid on the table. He opened it and pulled out something covered in a grubby cloth; something attached to a stout backpack by a thick flex, indicating that the backpack contained some form of battery.

'It just needed a good clean and a few extra wires for the new control switch I've built into it. It was silly to throw it out, really, but *Taylor*'s have already invested in a whole new generation of machine arms. It should be about the right size for you – it came from a smaller engine, designed for delicate work – and I hope you like it.' Mr Orpington flipped the cloth away and Poppy saw in shock that the device was a robotic arm made of stainless steel. The top part consisted of a hollow tube which could slot over her stump. There was an elbow joint in the middle and a three-fingered hand mounted on a revolving wrist.

'I know it's nothing like the latest prosthetics,'[9]

---

[9] The new generation of prosthetics, which could be grafted onto nerve endings and function like a natural limb, were very much a novelty at that time. Only the rich could afford them, yet the upper classes rarely engaged in activities that could potentially lose them an arm or leg. The military was the biggest customer for such things, followed by the wealthier industries that needed trained expertise and would therefore pay to keep an injured man on the workforce until retirement, after which the prosthesis was taken back. This, and the enforced deductions from the worker's wage to pay for the prosthetic, often complicated life even more than the original injury, especially if the employee still owed the company money for the limb on retirement – which most of them did.

continued Mr Orpington, examining the arm as though he had never seen it before, 'but it has a neat counterweight pulley for the elbow, so when you move your upper arm the prosthetic should also move. I hope you like it.'

'It's great. Thanks, Dad!' exclaimed Poppy, her eyes wide with the amazement of having a new, working arm, even if it was made of steel rather than flesh. 'Can I put it on?'

'Of course.' Her father helped her into the heavy backpack and then guided Poppy's stump into the top of the prosthesis. He had fashioned the backpack himself, as well as the short tube for Poppy's upper arm. A few leather straps held the new limb in place.

'This is the control box,' said Mr Orpington, holding up a strip of metal attached to the top of the backpack by a long, thin cable. 'The black button causes the hand to immediately clamp tight or to open up, depending on what position it's in, or you can use the green switch to slowly open and close it. Do be careful with that, by the way; I'm not sure what sort of force it can exert.' As he spoke, Mr Orpington fed the switch down the side of Poppy's neck, under her tatty school cardigan, and manoeuvred it down her sleeve until the switch emerged next to her hand.

Poppy eagerly snatched at the dangling control

box, grabbing it at her third attempt. She looked at the controls in her left hand and then gazed at her new robotic right hand, cold and silent, waiting for an order. She heard a click and hum behind her as her father turned on the battery in the backpack and power flooded through the system. She pushed the black switch and the robotic hand immediately clenched, making her jump and release the box.

She pressed the green switch, causing the three long fingers to curl, and she realised that the one finger was actually an elongated thumb. She also saw that the hand was missing the last two fingers to the right, both of which had been broken off at the root, which explained why the arm had been dumped into the scrap bin. She didn't care, though. For the first time ever, she had two hands, meaning she would be able to do at least some everyday things. She lifted her upper arm so it was pointing directly ahead of her and the elbow counterweight system whined slightly as it pulled the prosthetic up into a V shape.

Poppy beamed in pleasure and slowly lowered her arm, making the prosthetic straighten out once more. She lifted and lowered it a few times, rotating her stump around, enjoying the robotic arm as it responded to each movement and slid into a new position of its own. Soon, she could control where it pointed, what position it took, and she could also bring it to rest against the side of her body. 'Thanks, Dad,' she cried, hugging her father tightly. 'It's the best present ever.'[10]

'Good, good, glad you like it,' smiled her father before the familiar look of absent puzzlement took over. 'You'd better get to school. I have things to do.' Nodding vaguely, as though the real world had suddenly melted away, Mr Orpington returned to his workshop and secret project.

Poppy quickly finished her chores before pulling on her school cloak and running out of the flat and down the road to where Amy was waiting for her under the large oak tree.

'Poppy!' Amy exclaimed in surprise, seeing the flash of steel as the wind blew under Poppy's cloak. 'You've got an arm!'

'Dad made it; isn't it great?' shouted Poppy in joy, wiggling her stump and making the arm flex up

---

[10] Today, some disability awareness groups protest against the idea that anyone with a missing limb yearns for a replacement; it is felt this attitude is patronising and assumes that the individual in question feels that they are lacking or incomplete. I should stress that terms such as 'cripple' were common back in Poppy's era, no doubt affecting the way Poppy and others viewed themselves. Plus, anyone with a disability would have found it very difficult to find a job and earn a living, and many were reduced to begging in order to survive.

and down.

'What's the power source? How does it work? What sort of linkages does it use?' demanded Amy, the words tumbling from her in enthusiasm. She spun Poppy around and pushed her cloak aside so she could see the arm and the backpack more clearly. 'Gosh, this is incredible! The power pack has a wind-up recharging facility in it.'

'Is the winding handle in there?' asked Poppy. She felt Amy's hands rummage in the backpack.

'Yes, here it is,' she announced, pulling out a short piece of metal, moulded into a 'T' shape and with a socket grafted onto the end. 'At least you'll never go flat.'

'It will be difficult getting the backpack and arm off each time I need to recharge, though.'

Amy studied the dials on the battery. 'You've got almost a full charge, so I'd guess you're good for a few hours yet. Besides, I'll be around to help you.' She glanced up to see Poppy looking at her over her shoulder, her red hair blowing in the wind, and she blushed as Poppy smiled.

'Thank you, that's sweet,' said Poppy, feeling an odd sensation of warmth seeping through her as she gazed back at her friend's beautiful face.

'What are friends for, if not to wind each other up?' gabbled Amy, stepping away from the intense moment in some confusion.

'You make me sound like a toy soldier,' replied Poppy with a forced giggle, striking out for a normal, safe topic of conversation. 'I bet you wouldn't mind winding up Richard Yardley.'

'Poppy! I told you I liked him in confidence.'

'I've not told anyone.'

'Promise?'

'Promise. Except Dad,' teased Poppy.

'Poppy!' yelped Amy as she playfully squeezed Poppy's sides before dashing away, Poppy chasing close behind. Amy was faster and lighter than Poppy, who was now weighed down with the backpack and steel arm, as well as her bad leg and knee brace. What she lacked in mobility, however, Poppy made up for with sheer tenacity.

'You never give up, do you?' grinned Amy as she fended off another mock blow. 'You just keep on going, ignoring everyone.'

'There aren't many I care to acknowledge,' replied Poppy, panting from the exertion. She and Amy were still unhappy at school, but having each other made it bearable.

'Speaking of which,' murmured Amy as they approached the school gates. Lounging outside was a large group of boys, including Darren Weldon and Paul Hibbert. Age had not improved either for character or appearance. Time, however, had wrought certain changes on Amy and Poppy. Amy, being blonde and slender, was especially pretty to the boys. Poppy was no less attractive, but her remarkable height and broad shoulders made her something of a freak to the rest of the school, as did her disabilities.

Another reason Poppy didn't attract as much attention from the boys was her improved reach and balance. Anyone unwary enough to throw insults at her while standing too close could expect a surprisingly powerful punch to the face, as Lee Stone had found out when he had grabbed Poppy one day and exclaimed, 'You'd be a proper looker if you weren't a cripple!' He had staggered off with blood gushing from his nose. Even so, many still tormented her from a distance, knowing she couldn't move quickly enough to catch them.

'Hello, Amy,' ogled Hibbert, ignoring Poppy completely. 'You want to walk home with me tonight?'

'I'd rather you died in a ditch,' snapped Amy.

'Oh, get her,' and other similar cries went up. Hibbert, who wasn't too bright, took the reply for encouragement rather than as a put down.

'You should consider it; you'll be needing a man to walk you home on the dark nights,' he leered.

'Really? Then I'll have to look for one. I certainly can't see any men around here,' said Amy as she and Poppy walked by. The exchange may have ended there if Amy hadn't added, 'I see only little boys.'

This took several seconds to register with Hibbert. As the meaning sank in, his face flushed an angry red. 'I'm more man than you could ever deal with,' he snarled. 'Come on, I'll show you what a real man is like!' He lunged forward and grabbed Amy around the neck, while his other hand groped downwards.

Amy screamed in shock and fear. Poppy whirled round and her steel prosthetic, hidden under her thick, shapeless cloak, grabbed at Hibbert's hand, the cold open fingers slipping around the warm flesh. Poppy viciously stabbed the black button on the control box and the mechanical hand clenched into a tight fist, causing Hibbert to collapse to his knees, screaming in agony. He was lithe and strong, but no match for the machinery that held him. Poppy's cloak fell off, revealing her steel arm to the group. A shocked silence fell over the gathering crowd.

'Do you know how much pressure a robotic hand is capable of applying?' snarled Poppy, furious that the lout in front of her, who had bullied her mercilessly for years, should try to molest her dearest friend. She pushed the green switch forward, increasing the compression. 'Do you think it can squeeze enough to splinter the bones in your hand?'

Amy looked at the scene in horror tempered with malicious satisfaction; she was well aware of the anger her friend carried, borne out of frustration at her disabilities and the limited nature of their lives. Poppy could talk for hours on how the workers were kept down by a variety of social and legal methods. Was it all now breaking out from her control?

'You're crazy!' shouted one of the boys, his face blanching.

'Remember all the times you hit me and tormented me and kicked me over the years,' hissed Poppy in rage at both Hibbert and the group behind him. 'Well? Do you remember?' The group muttered and backed away from the glare, which was as frightening as the implacable mechanical fingers crushing Hibbert's hand. 'Come near me or Amy ever again, for any reason, and this will happen to you.'

She released the control switch and the mechanical fingers sprang open. As Hibbert swayed back and forth, keening in pain and fear, Poppy balled her left hand into a fist and drove her punch, powered by years of misery and torment, deep into his stupid, grimy face, knocking him unconscious. Poppy picked up her cloak as she and Amy strode away, the boys flinching as they passed. No one dared to say a word until the two girls were well out of earshot.[11]

'Slow down, Poppy,' gasped Amy as they made their way to their classroom, unable to keep up with Poppy's longer strides. Poppy turned her head and Amy faltered at the blazing fury in her friend's eyes.

'I should have finished him,' growled Poppy. 'I should have crippled his hand for the way he's treated us over the years.'

'I think you did finish him,' replied Amy meekly. 'He looked to be out cold.'

'He'll be able to get up, though, and that's something he doesn't deserve. Scum like that do nothing but pull us all down to their level.'

'Poppy Orpington!' barked a voice immediately behind them. The girls turned and saw the unwelcome figure of Miss Godfrey striding towards

---

[11] Hibbert subsequently claimed that he got his hand caught in the engine of a car he was trying to hotwire, but privately I suspect he could never erase the shaming memory of what really happened. Certainly, his friends were always happy to tell the story to the press, exaggerating it wildly over the years; some even claimed that Poppy already had her Turner-Casbach arm fitted at this point, which is of course nonsense. I am fairly certain that my description, taken from Poppy and Amy's diaries, is as accurate as possible.

them, surrounded by a group of excited pupils all staring at Poppy in horror and fear. Most of them, over the years, had contributed to Poppy and Amy's misery, through direct or indirect means.

Poppy stared with fresh loathing at Godfrey; she hated the bullying, foul-tempered crone and considered her to be the worst teacher at the school – which was quite an achievement, given the competition.

'What is the meaning of these outrageous accusations I've just heard, girl? How dare you assault a fellow pupil?' demanded Godfrey as she strutted forward.

'It's true, Miss Godfrey, she's got a claw under her cloak!' exclaimed one of the girls.

'Yeah, she hit him with it!' smirked a male pupil who hadn't even been at the gates at the time.

'What the hell is it to you, Godfrey?' exploded Poppy in fury. The advancing group stopped so suddenly that the pushing students at the back collided with those ahead of them. Poppy advanced towards the crowd, her eyes dangerous, causing those nearest to take several nervous steps backward. 'What have you ever done to stop any of the filth here from tormenting me over the years? Nothing!'

Godfrey stared at the unexpected rebellion to her authority. She was accustomed to submissiveness, at least from those she could safely bully, and the crippled girl had always been the easiest of targets. Until now. 'How dare you shout at me?' she squawked, shoring up her dwindling courage with the belief that the pupils should defer to her at all times. 'This is monstrous behaviour!'

'What, monstrous that I'm answering back?' snarled Poppy as she continued forward without breaking her step, forcing Godfrey to scurry backward until she found herself trapped against a wall. The crowd of pupils melted away to either side, some appalled at Poppy's behaviour and looking forward to her punishment, others simply enjoying the drama.

Godfrey, confronted with a girl she could no longer terrify with words alone, fumbled at her belt for her slender cane, expecting Poppy to cringe away in fear, yet all she saw on Poppy's face was savage disgust.

'Stay away, Orpington, or I shall punish you!' she cried in alarm but still the girl advanced until Godfrey, with a scream of fear and fury, swung the cane directly at Poppy's head, losing all sense of finesse at the blazing hatred in Poppy's eyes.

Poppy jerked her mechanical arm up and blocked the clumsy blow. Before Godfrey could move, Poppy reached out with her free hand and grabbed the cane.

31

'You'll never do that to me again, Godfrey,' she hissed as she slid the cane into the fingers of her mechanical hand. Then, slowly and deliberately, she twisted the end of the cane upward, using her prosthetic as a base for the leverage until the cane splintered in two and fell to the floor with a sharp sound that echoed in the utter silence of the long corridor.

'There's the headmaster!' exclaimed one of the pupils in horrified enjoyment. Several heads swung round as David Bainbridge appeared around the corner and hesitated at the scene ahead. He would have hurried away in the opposite direction had he been aware of the confrontation, but on being observed he had to step forward in all his inadequate authority.

'What is going on here?' he squawked, swallowing nervously at the fierce expression of Poppy Orpington, whom he disliked for being highly intelligent, and the white-faced hatred of Miss Godfrey, whom he feared owing to her forceful character.

'Poppy Orpington is threatening me!' squealed Godfrey, her faith in the authority of the headmaster's office – though not the man himself – redoubling her bravery.

'I haven't made a single threat or touched you,

you lying toad,' snapped Poppy, looming over her adult tormentor. 'Yet,' she added, making Godfrey flinch before glancing in contempt at her headmaster. 'Do you really want to know what I'm doing, Bainbridge? I'm challenging the behaviour of this evil-minded witch. For years, she has told me that God hates me and he withered my arm because I'm evil. For years, she has enjoyed caning anyone she can, just for the pleasure of it. What have you got to say to that?'

Bainbridge squirmed. He was well aware of the failings of his staff but he lacked the character, ability and inclination to do anything about it. In desperation, he resorted to school convention; a pupil was lacking in respect, so she had to be reprimanded. 'It's "Mister Bainbridge", or "Sir,"' he bleated, feebly.

'Answer the question,' snarled Poppy.

'Errrhhh,' squealed Bainbridge, his breath hissing from his body as he writhed in apprehension.

'I demand you call the police in, immediately, for assault!' screeched Godfrey, her face twisted in hatred and malicious revenge against the girl she could no longer bully.

Bainbridge, despite dreading the publicity and official attention which would inevitably arise, knew he had no choice; Godfrey was clearly on a crusade of righteousness. With a sense of foreboding, he despatched a member of staff to run round to the local police station before hiding in his office until they arrived.

Unfortunately for Poppy, the sergeant who answered the summons, Nathan Thacker, was a man of social rectitude; he believed in God's ordained society and he was industrious in obeying his betters while bullying his supposed inferiors. He also respected education inordinately, being a man of very little learning, and thus he found himself deferring naturally to the headmaster and teacher when listening to their highly-coloured version of the morning's events. It was clear he had made up his mind on the matter long before summoning Poppy to the headmaster's office.

'Now, then, girl,' began Thacker, immediately annoying Poppy who hated the condescending term. 'You got anything to say about this?'

'About what?' asked Poppy, challengingly.

'You know full well what,' snapped the sergeant, looming over Poppy. He was a big man; not much taller than Poppy but far wider, and experienced in using his bulk to intimidate witnesses.

'No, I do not know what,' snapped Poppy. 'I've not been told what I'm accused of, so how can I say anything in reply?'

'Don't you use that tone on me, my girl,' snarled Thacker. 'You know full well what you've done. I have a complete account of it here in my official notebook.' He waved the small notebook in the air, as though the writing inside had the authority of Holy Writ.

'So, you've already decided on what happened, have you?' retorted Poppy, her voice rising in anger. 'Do please tell me when you took the witness statements of everyone who was in the corridor to come to that conclusion.'

'I'll have none of that backchat,' glowered the sergeant. 'You used that metal arm of yours to attack Miss Godfrey, didn't you?'

'There's not a mark on her and several witnesses will tell you I never touched the old boot,' snapped Poppy, glaring in hatred at Bainbridge and Godfrey who were both seated behind the headmaster's desk. Bainbridge did not like having Godfrey at his side, and he disliked even more the fact that she was slowly pushing him to one side. Even with the bulk of Sergeant Thacker to support him, he was still hampered by his lack of personality and force.

'One more bit of backchat and I'll arrest you,' threatened the policeman. 'You own up to what you did or you'll be in more trouble than you can guess at, girl.'

'I didn't attack her,' repeated Poppy in anger.

'So, that's your version, is it?' replied the sergeant, his face locked in a sneer.

'Oh, so you treat my statement as a version, but hers is taken as fact, is that it?' demanded Poppy.

'You hold your tongue,' said Thacker, his face going even redder as his casual assumptions were exposed. 'I have a duty to perform and your duty is to assist me in every way.'

'Your duty should be to the truth, not to simply agree with that lying vermin on the other side of the desk, or is that beyond you?' shouted Poppy in fury.

'You see how unbalanced and dangerous she is?' spat Godfrey, venomously. 'She pushed me into the wall and threatened me with that steel arm of hers! And this was after attacking another pupil outside the school!'

'Really?' said Thacker, making a careful note in his small book and glancing unfavourably at Poppy.

'He attacked a friend of mine and I was defending her,' hissed Poppy. 'Or do you think I should have let him molest her outside the school gates? Well?'

'We'll come to that in due course,' said Thacker, turning a page in his notebook but writing nothing of Poppy's words.

'Due course?' echoed Poppy. 'I've just told you

about a sexual attack and you do nothing about it?'

'Sexual attack? Don't you go exaggerating and flinging accusations around like that, young woman, or you'll be in serious trouble,' snorted the sergeant.

'Flinging accusations?' bellowed Poppy, but she was cut off by the sergeant.

'Yes, accusations. I know the way it is at school; there's a fair bit of horseplay and it's all part of growing up, but there's always one who wants to find some offence in it somewhere, so don't you go smearing people's reputations or you'll be in trouble.'

'You haven't even investigated and yet you've made your mind up, haven't you?' yelled Poppy in fury. 'God, you're just as bloody useless as those two incompetents!'

'There's no call for foul language – what will your parents think if they hear of you using words like that?' demanded Thacker. 'And I'll thank you not to blaspheme, either.'

'And I'll thank you to do your job and investigate properly what actually happened,' snarled Poppy, her words spitting from her in hatred at the three smug faces ranged against her. She turned on Bainbridge. 'What will you tell the local council when they hear of this?'

Bainbridge stuttered in horror, but was rescued by

the sergeant. 'The council does not need to be troubled; I think I have seen enough,' he said, snapping his notebook shut. 'I'm giving you an official caution for assault. Maybe in the future you'll act more like a respectable young woman instead of some lout.'

'You've done nothing to investigate and now you're just brushing it all under the official carpet!' raged Poppy.

'You watch your mouth, or I'll watch it for you!' snarled the sergeant, flustered by Poppy's accurate assessment. He resorted to force to impose his lost authority. 'Get out of this office and I don't ever want to hear of you again. Get out, now!' he roared, suddenly grabbing Poppy and propelling her towards the door.

'Get off me!' yelled Poppy in shock and anger, but the sergeant was used to physically restraining drunks and hooligans and he already had a painful grip on Poppy's arm and neck. She found herself powerless against his sudden, unexpected attack and his superior strength.

'And I'll have that arm off you as well,' crowed the sergeant, yanking the prosthetic savagely from Poppy's upper arm. The straps holding it in place snapped as the arm came away, while the cable to the backpack let out a spark as the connection was severed from the power source. Poppy was jerked almost off her feet and she screamed in pain as the hot end of the broken cable lashed against her upper arm.

'Out!' bellowed the policeman, yanking the door to the office open and bodily hurling Poppy through the frame.[12]

'Give me my arm back!' screamed Poppy in fury as she staggered several steps under the force of the shove, but the door was slammed in her face. 'Give me my arm back!' she shouted again, but the door remained shut.

'You're expelled!' bleated Bainbridge's voice through the door, his bravado amplified by the wooden barrier.

'As if I care!' yelled Poppy in impotent fury as she gave the door a savage kick.[13]

---

[12] This, then, was Poppy's first police encounter and her first official caution, and sadly it was fairly typical of what lay ahead. The law at that time would rarely take any woman, indeed any working-class person, seriously. The press, of course, would later use Poppy's criminal record as a weapon when attacking or belittling her to their readers.

[13] Poppy's expulsion was officially for attacking the staff. I can only assume she escaped punishment for what happened at the school gates for the simple reason that the incident was

The following day, Amy waited somewhat nervously at their usual meeting point under the big tree, hoping Poppy would be there. She breathed in relief and happiness as she saw the familiar figure of her friend appear, her left leg limping slightly as always.

'Hello, Amy; I hoped you'd be waiting for me.'

'I shouldn't be. I've been forbidden to see you by my mum.'

'Why? You're not in trouble with the school, are you?'

'No, but I got a slap round the ear from Mum when she heard you'd been. She assumed I must have had some part in it. Thank God she didn't hear about the police being called in to the school, or it would have been worse.'

'I know she's never liked me but that's ridiculous. I hope you explained you didn't have anything to do with it?'

'What's the point? She never listens,' muttered Amy, glossing over the screaming match that had resulted. Such occasions were the norm between Amy and her mother. She swiftly changed the subject. 'How did your dad react to you getting expelled?'

---

technically off the school grounds and was therefore ignored by the ineffectual headmaster.

'I got a clout as well,' said Poppy with a grimace. 'Nothing new there. Though I think it was more for getting involved with the police. Dad's very deferential to authority. I suppose he knows his place,' she added, with some bitterness. 'Come on, let's get to school.'

'Er, why? You can't go to school anymore.'

'I know, but I'm going to get my arm back from Bainbridge. Then I'm going to visit the police station and lay a formal complaint against Sergeant Thacker.'[14]

'Poppy! You'll get in even more trouble.'

'Good.'

'You seem ... different,' said Amy, gazing at Poppy's face. Her red hair was billowing in the breeze and her expression was somehow defiant against all of creation.

'In what way?'

'I don't know,' replied Amy, suffering her usual difficulty in expressing herself. 'There's just something different.'

Poppy looked directly at Amy and cocked her head to one side. 'How, exactly?'

---

[14] Despite much searching, I have been unable to discover any internal investigation by the local police in respect of Poppy's complaint.

'Just different,' muttered Amy, wishing she had never said anything. Poppy had dropped into the slightly demanding tone Amy knew and rather disliked; it fed into her growing inferiority complex over Poppy's intelligence as compared to her own.

'You must have seen something different otherwise you wouldn't have said anything,' insisted Poppy, a smile of exasperation on her full lips.

'Um,' muttered Amy, uneasily aware that they were still standing under the tree, barely inches apart. She gazed at Poppy's face and realised anew that there was indeed something different there. Lacking the vocabulary to explain, Amy looked down and muttered again. 'You look, I don't know, like maybe you've got a devil in you.'

'A devil? Have I grown horns?' laughed Poppy.

'Oh, I don't know how to explain it. I suppose you'd be able to, with your long words,' said Amy, looking slightly cross, uncomfortable and apprehensive.

'Maybe I *have* changed,' replied Poppy with a shrug. 'What happened with Bainbridge and Godfrey and that oaf of a sergeant all just confirmed what I've read in my books – that the world runs on the assumption we should know our place and respectfully defer to our betters. From school to family, to employers to the police; we're sold the same lie every damn day. Well, no more.'

Someone with a more enquiring mind than Amy may have wondered how Poppy's new philosophy would actually work in the real world, but Amy's world only extended as far as her own immediate well-being. 'What does that mean for me? For us?' she asked, nervously, but Poppy was already striding away.

CHAPTER THREE

Unfortunately, the problems afflicting Poppy's school days were superseded by a new set of complications at the start of her working life. Her first concern was trying to find a job, which proved to be impossible; quite apart from having no school exam results, no potential employers could see beyond her disability.

'How did the interview go?' demanded her father as she returned to the workshop after a typical encounter with the world of commerce.

'Badly, like the others,' replied Poppy, bristling at her father's brusque tone. 'I did all the tests along with the other fifty applicants and got the highest scores in grammar and comprehension, but I was last in typing and shorthand.'

'Last?' raged her father. 'Are you even trying?'

'Of course I'm trying!' snarled Poppy. 'I only have one arm! It makes me slower at loading paper in the machines and it makes it damn near impossible to hold the writing pad to take dictation. My artificial arm is too clumsy for work like that.'

'Damn it, Poppy, we need the money!' roared Mr Orpington in frustration. 'You should be getting a regular paying job, not making excuses.'

'Having one arm is not an excuse,' yelled Poppy in reply. 'And if you want to talk about the lack of money, you can explain why you spend all your spare time in the back of the workshop instead of taking on more work out here!'

'You needn't think I'm going to keep you,' snapped her father, stung by the truth of Poppy's observation. 'I've no place for passengers here.'

'Passengers?' hissed Poppy, shocking herself with her fury; she had never before raged at her father in such a way. 'I help out here every day for no money or thanks, and we wouldn't even be here now if I hadn't started doing odd jobs with the neighbours for extra money to buy food. And it was me who suggested the chickens out the back; left to you, we'd have starved years ago.'

'Don't flatter yourself, girl; all you ever did was buy a bit extra!'

'That bit extra kept us above the starvation line, which is more than you ever did. You'd rather spend all your money on whatever the hell it is you keep hidden in the back of the workshop instead of feeding your own family.[15] When is that thing out

---

[15] Poppy's criticism was not just about her father's parenting; in bringing up the issue of his failure to provide, Poppy was questioning his basic manliness, it being a belief then – and

there ever going to start paying back?' Poppy took a step back as her father flushed angrily and raised his hand. 'Go on, then, take the easy way; it's the only way you know how to respond, isn't it?' she shouted. 'That's all a woman is to you, isn't it? A punch bag for when things go wrong. Did you ever give Mum a slap as well?'

Mr Orpington swayed back slightly and slowly lowered his hand. 'Your mother never gave me any call to,' he eventually muttered, his voice oddly subdued.[16] 'And the project I'm working on could make us rich. It's an escape from … from … from all this!' He gestured angrily around the workshop, though it was clear he was actually indicating their lives and lowly place in the world. 'But I need money to make it work. Don't you understand that, Poppy?'

'Yes, I do understand,' replied Poppy, forcing – as much as she was able – the anger out of her voice. 'I

---

indeed, even now – that a large part of a man's worth lies in his effectiveness as a provider.

[16] Another sad indictment of the social era; neither Poppy nor her father saw anything wrong in his supposition that a woman could indeed give a man a genuine reason to strike her. A husband or father's right to physically chastise "errant" family members was simply a part of life.

know our lives are curtailed. I know we are trapped within a socially predestined life of limited prospects. I do read, you know. I read every worker's paper and magazine and book I can get.'

'Yes, and that's why Amy always says you talk like you've swallowed a dictionary,' said her father, smiling slightly to try to defuse the anger between them. 'Look; you know your way about an engine, and you can weld. Why not help me out here officially? I'll give you some pocket money, and between jobs I can carry on working on my project. Deal?'

Poppy nodded miserably and said 'Deal,' acutely aware that she did not want to spend her entire life trapped within the poverty of the workshop. But she also knew with chilling certainty that her chances of escape were blighted by a dearth of genuine opportunity. As such, it would take something unexpected and special to save her now.

Almost a year passed by with Poppy working for a pittance with her father. Amy had taken her final exams and failed most of them, but this was not an issue as her parents had already obtained a post for her as a maid at the house of a prosperous cutlery manufacturer. As such, the two girls saw little of each other except for the occasional evening and every Sunday; most people in the neighbourhood attended church on Sunday, though Poppy and Amy's reason for doing so had little to do with moral salvation.

'How's life with the spoons?' asked Poppy after quickly and discreetly embracing her friend.

'Hard and dull,' muttered Amy, looking tired as she spoke. She had to get up every day at six to clean the sitting rooms, hallway and staircase before the family got up, after which her duties involved dressing the mistress of the house, cleaning all the bedrooms as and when the family vacated them, and helping the cook in preparing the family's breakfast, elevenses, lunch, tea, dinner and supper. It was little short of slavery by another name. 'How are things working out with your dad? You still arguing?'

Poppy shrugged. 'Sometimes. He left me alone again last Wednesday when he disappeared into the back of the workshop, despite us having a motorbike to repair. I know what to do, but I can't do it alone. I kept calling him but he just wouldn't answer.'

'You tried knocking on the door?'

Poppy pulled a face. 'Once, years ago, and I'm not doing that again; it cost me a partial black eye. Now when the customer returns I go up to the flat and wait. Dad comes out, realises the work hasn't been done, and he has to deal with it all.'

'My God, Poppy, do be careful,' breathed Amy. 'What if your dad blames you for the work not being done? He could black your eye again.'

'Sometimes he tries, but I put a wedge under the door to my bedroom. Sometimes he's reasonable and realises he's in the wrong, but when that happens he'll often burst into tears and beg for forgiveness.'

'Tears? Your dad? Actual tears?' exclaimed Amy, mockery and disbelief mixing in her voice at such unmanly behaviour.

Poppy shrugged. 'He's getting worse, I swear. Mentally, he swings from exquisite delirium to the lower slopes of absolute despair.'

'I can't believe he cries,' sniggered Amy. 'But never mind that.' She shyly produced a small box and thrust it towards Poppy. 'Here,' she mumbled, going slightly red. 'This is for you. Happy birthday.'

Poppy felt a surge of pure happiness at having Amy in her life. She took the small home-made box with a smile of genuine delight. 'Oh, Amy, this is so kind of you. No one has ever given me a birthday present before, except for Dad.'

'That's ok, hope you like it,' mumbled Amy, going even redder. 'It's nothing much, just something I made for you.'

Poppy fumbled with the box with her one hand. She no longer wore her artificial arm as she had experienced another growth spurt and it no longer fitted properly. Her father had promised to enlarge it but had never done so. She finally managed to flip the lid open and gasped as she saw a pendant crafted from tiny cogs laid out in an intricate pattern, with a small red stone set in the middle. 'It's wonderful,' she said, admiring it in the early morning sunlight. 'It must have taken you months to make.'

Amy smiled, happy that Poppy liked it. 'It took a few attempts to get right. Connecting all the cogs so they won't fall apart and getting the shape and everything.'

Poppy gazed at the pendant, admiring the elaborate craftwork. Amy was very talented with anything mechanical, but here she had created something beautiful as well. 'Wherever did you find the jewel? It's a lovely colour.'

'Yes, red, like your hair. It was in a big piece of jewellery that belonged to my gran, but it fell apart and she divided the stones between me and Mum, to use any way we wanted. Mum got the biggest stone and she had it cast in a necklace. I got the smaller ones. That's the first one I've used for anything.'

'Thanks, Amy, it's perfect,' smiled Poppy before spinning around with a happy laugh and lifting her thick mane of hair. 'Can you do it up for me?'

Amy placed her hands around Poppy's neck,

conscious of the perfect shape of her friend's head and shoulders, and drew the cord up around the back of Poppy's neck. Amy fumbled at the latch, her normally skilful fingers suddenly heavy and clumsy.

'You're all fingers and thumbs today,' giggled Poppy before falling silent. She was suddenly aware of the warmth of Amy's body against hers, of the gentle tickle of her breath, her lips close to Poppy's ear, almost touching as the world drifted away.

'Come on,' blurted Amy, suddenly taking a step back, 'We're going to be late.'

After the service, Amy accompanied Poppy to her home and the workshop. The girls didn't speak about the moment in the lane; neither was entirely sure how to talk about the strange mood that had overtaken them, or how to deal with it.[17]

'Hello, Amy,' boomed Poppy's father as the girls walked in. He was striding around the workshop as though too excited to stay in one place. 'I've got some old compression units there in the corner, if you want them.'

---

[17] Given society's taboo against anything other than heterosexual marriage, it is not surprising that neither Poppy nor Amy knew how to handle or even understand their feelings at this point.

'Cor, great! Thanks, Mr Orpington,' beamed Amy. She often took old machine parts home with her and spent her scant free time stripping them down in her tiny attic room, learning their secrets.

'Look what Amy made for me, Dad,' said Poppy, proudly drawing the pendant out from under her frayed blouse.

Mr Orpington grabbed hold of his workbench as though needing to anchor himself to the world before leaning over to look at the pendant. 'That's nice. A friendship charm, is it?'

'It's Poppy's birthday present,' replied Amy, happily sifting through the compression units.

Mr Orpington's face fell, dimming the manic glee in his eyes. 'Is – is it your birthday? So soon?' he whispered in anguish. 'No, it can't be!'

'Poppy's sixteenth,' laughed Amy, unaware of the expression on Mr Orpington's face.

'Sixteen?' gasped Mr Orpington, staring at Poppy as though in shock. 'Already?'

Poppy shrugged, uneasy at the wild expression in her father's eyes. 'Yes, Dad, sixteen.'[18]

'I ... I'm, sorry, I didn't ... I shouldn't,' muttered

---

[18] Thus setting this auspicious day as the 20th September, 1903. Poppy rarely recorded dates in her diaries, making this chronicler's job ever more difficult.

Mr Orpington incoherently. He shook his head, looking sad and bewildered as he stared at Poppy and her new pendant. Finally, he spoke again. 'That is a very fine, delicate piece of work. If you ever give up on the engineering, Amy, you could always go into jewellery design. Perhaps it would be better to do so. Don't waste your life on engines and miss what is important.'

'It's engines all the way for me, if I ever get the chance,' replied Amy, still absorbed in the compression units.

Poppy put her hand on her father's arm and he grasped it tightly. 'Are you feeling ill, Dad?' she asked, concerned at his strange mood.

'It's too much, Poppy. Sometimes I think it's all too much,' groaned her father, bitterly, shaking his head. 'Sometimes I wonder if it's been worth it, but what else is there? The work must go on. When there is nothing left, there is always the work.' His mood suddenly lifted as excitement surged through him. 'Yes, the work. It's finally ready! My secret project. It's ready to show to the world.'

'*Thunderbus*?' asked Poppy, intrigued despite her concern for her father. 'Is it ready? What's it like? How fast does it go? Is it actually a bus?'

'What's *Thunderbus*?' asked Amy in surprise. Poppy had followed her father's instruction to never mention his project to anyone, and she had kept the secret ever since.

'Despite Poppy's name for it, it isn't actually a bus, though it could be,' said Mr Orpington. 'In fact, it could be anything. The shape is not important. It's what is inside that is significant. And magnificent!' He grinned feverishly and began pacing around the workshop again, breathing deeply as the smell of the garage and the bright sunlight pouring through the windows filled his senses almost beyond endurance.[19]

'Now,' he continued in wild exhilaration. 'We all know what powers most engines, don't we?'

'Steam,' said both girls together. Trains, airships, cars, motorbikes, warships; all ran off the same power source, though the designs varied considerably depending on the manufacturer and size of the vehicle.

'And what are the specific problems with a steam-driven car engine?' asked Mr Orpington.

'They can't be run at full power for very long,' said Amy. 'They won't take the strain, so you have to

---

[19] It is clear from various accounts that Mr Orpington suffered from manic depression. At that time, of course, no one had identified the condition, and society certainly had no proper treatment for it, or indeed for any other form of mental illness.

keep easing off the throttle so they don't boil over.'

'That's why cars have to travel in spurts, gaining speed and then losing it before regaining it,' added Poppy. 'And the durability of car engines is a constant issue.'

'Exactly,' beamed Mr Orpington. 'All these are indeed problems facing steam-powered cars. Now, do you know what the solution is?'

'Better designed engines?' asked Poppy uncertainly. 'Some foreign cars are reckoned to be much better than ours.'

'No, ignore steam; think of a different type of engine altogether.'

'You're not thinking of petrol, are you?' asked Amy suspiciously. 'Petrol engines are too unreliable. And dangerous.'

'And petrol is viewed as being fit only for the lower classes,' added Poppy in a scathing tone. 'That's why petrol engines only get used in trucks and public transport rather than private cars. If you're rich enough to drive, you're too rich for petrol.'

'I see you've been reading your socialist literature again, Poppy.' Her father grinned. 'You're both absolutely right. A few dominant steam manufacturers have a virtual stranglehold on the market, so no one has ever invested serious time and effort into eliminating the flaws in petrol engines. Or in steam engines, come to that. My petrol engine is smoother, more powerful and far more reliable than steam. Once people know about it, the old snobbery about petrol will be swept away. Everyone will want to buy one.'

'Really?'

'Really. Do you want to see it?'

'See *Thunderbus*?' asked Poppy. 'Of course we do! Have you dropped the engine into a chassis already?'

'I have. I had to modify an old charabanc chassis, which was the only thing I could get that was wide enough, long enough and strong enough to hold the engine in place. After that, I took the panels from an old limousine, adapted them, made some new ones to fit the gaps, and then scrounged an old driving seat from another scrapped limousine.'

'Cor, limo seats?' said Amy. 'It must be luxuriant.'

'Well,' coughed Poppy's father, 'it *was* a very old limousine. You must remember *Thunderbus* is home-made, so the suspension doesn't quite work properly and all the rivets are on display. Do you still want to see her?'

'Yes!' shouted the girls, jumping up and down.

'Very well. Open the outer doors as far as they can go and wait in the road.'

The girls did as they were told and ran excitedly onto the quiet road. Behind them, Poppy's father pulled open the inner doors and disappeared into the rear section of the workshop, where a faint outline of something tall and wide could be seen. After several moments' silence, there was a faint whine of something mechanical waking up in the shadows. Small flashes of light, some red, some green, pierced the darkness. A second, deeper whine joined the first, while the red flashes disappeared. There was a pause of absolute calm, as though the world was holding its breath, before it abruptly exhaled with the ear-splitting roar of a huge engine bursting into life.

This was no quiet cough and hiss of a steam-powered vehicle, no refined hum of a copper boiler releasing power into a turbine. This was a brutal, elemental roar of pure anger and power. Spurts of flame erupted on each side of the mysterious vehicle, the red fire briefly illuminating the outline of a huge radiator grill – a snarling mouth of aggression – almost as wide as it was tall. Two enormous headlights, like the eyes of some primeval monster glaring from its dark nest, were also briefly illuminated by the hellish flames.

Amy let out a yelp of pure terror and leapt over a garden wall opposite the workshop. Poppy fought back against the impulse to flee, determined to see the beast, alarmed but also intensely curious at what lay in the darkness. The tone of the engine changed, became louder and deeper, and with a fresh burst of flame on each side *Thunderbus* roared out from its nest, belching smoke and fire.

Poppy gaped at the car; it was *huge*. She knew that limousines and continental touring cars were long and wide, but *Thunderbus* could eat them for breakfast – assuming it didn't just melt them with the continual jets of flame coming from the exhaust ports on each side of the bonnet. Or shake them apart with the vibrations from the engine, which was causing the ground to tremble underneath Poppy's legs.

Poppy walked unsteadily all the way around *Thunderbus*, mesmerised at the sight. The car was black, open-topped, with two large but battered seats in the cockpit, and a huge curved rear end. Everything about the car seemed oversized, from the enormous electrical lights, larger than Poppy's head, to the bumpers attached by twelve-inch steel bolts. And inside, grinning like a lunatic, was her father, built to the same huge scale.

Poppy moved forward but another burst of flame made her step back. Mr Orpington held up a warning hand and pulled some levers on the dashboard, with the result that *Thunderbus* settled down to a good long grumble. The flames erupting from the side also diminished until they were nothing more than glowing tips visible through the bonnet vents.

'Well, what do you think?' roared Mr Orpington.

'It's … it's …' stuttered Poppy, fear and amazement holding her in equal parts. The amazement won. 'It's *brilliant*!'

Amy popped up cautiously from behind the wall. Her eyes were huge and unbelieving, as were the faces of the neighbours who had come out to see what was causing the incredible noise.

'What is that terrible sound?' demanded Mr Jackson redundantly, given that the huge car was blocking the entire lane.

'Is it Judgement Day?' shrieked old Mrs Wright, holding her hands up in hopeful supplication.

'Not to fear; it is merely a revolution in transport that you see before you,' bellowed Mr Orpington, theatrically flinging his arms out in stark contrast to his anguish in the workshop.

'A revolution?' repeated Jackson. 'Not bloody likely; I can hardly hear myself think!'

'And it stinks,' added another neighbour, wrinkling up his nose. 'Who is going to drive in that smell all day?'

'And it's too big,' added Mrs Wright, who was under five feet tall even when wearing large boots.

'That is the noise of tomorrow,' snapped Mr Orpington. 'As for the smell, steam lets off vapours but no one complains, and finally, madam, it has to be this size to win at the Purley racetrack.'

'Purley?' echoed Jackson. 'You're going to enter this *thing* into a gentlemen's race?'[20]

'I am. And, such is the power of *Thunderbus*, it will romp home the sure and certain winner,' replied Mr Orpington.

'More likely it will blow up,' snapped Mrs Wright, looking smugly satisfied at her own prophecy of doom.

'*Thunderbus* will compete and win,' replied Mr Orpington. 'Then the world will beat a path to my door for the secret of a reliable and powerful petrol engine.'

'Ha!' exclaimed Jackson. 'Who in their right mind would want something that loud and smelly? People like steam. You mark my words; no one will be interested in this monstrosity. It will never catch on. Never.' The neighbours drifted away, laughing disdainfully and shaking their heads.

'I think it will win, Dad,' said Poppy. 'It's amazing.'

---

[20] Purley was the biggest, best known racetrack in the country. It was frequented by wealthy men with time on their hands looking for danger and publicity.

'So do I,' said Amy, loyally, who had been edging her way back towards the car. Now she was over her initial shock, she too was intrigued by the vehicle.

'I'm glad someone appreciates it,' said Mr Orpington, scowling ferociously at the departing neighbours. 'Right, jump in; we'll go for a drive.'

'But, Dad, there's nowhere for Amy to sit.'

'Yes, there is,' replied Mr Orpington. He climbed out and walked to the curved back end of *Thunderbus*, undid a strap, and pulled up a section of the bodywork to reveal the bare frame of a double seat. Padding had been added by strapping old pillows and cushions onto the frame with ropes and old belts. 'She can go on the dickey seat.'

'Brilliant,' exclaimed Amy, vaulting up the side of *Thunderbus* and settling herself down. Poppy climbed rather more awkwardly into the passenger seat – which was actually half an old sofa welded into place – hampered as always by her weak knee and missing arm.

Mr Orpington settled himself back in the driver's side and pushed a lever into the dashboard, and the engine sound quietened again to a gentle purr. 'There, she's not that loud once she's warmed up,' he asserted.

Poppy looked at the dashboard and the bewildering layout of dials, levers and switches.

'What was that you just used?'

'It regulates the flow of petrol. As the engine warms up, less fuel is needed to keep it running smoothly. You girls holding on? Yes? Then off we go!'

Mr Orpington engaged first gear before cautiously releasing the brake lever mounted outside the car on the right-side running board. *Thunderbus* jolted forward with a violent snort. 'Steady, steady,' he muttered, easing off the accelerator pedal. *Thunderbus* moved forward again, much more smoothly this time, and growled up the lane towards Wollaston village.

The way ahead was clear. Mr Orpington didn't stop as he heaved the huge, heavy steering wheel round to his left, turning the long nose of the vehicle onto the road. He pressed down on the accelerator, building the speed and quickly changing up through the gears. *Thunderbus* hurtled forward, clearly enjoying the long road and the many exciting curves. On the sharper bends, Mr Orpington would slow and change down to second gear, causing *Thunderbus* to grumble in frustration, but on the straights the car was allowed to do what it had been built for – to roar and eat up the road.

Trees, hedges and the occasional house zipped past Poppy's head. Pedestrians and cyclists on the road looked left, right, and even upwards upon hearing *Thunderbus*' engine, all reacting with horror or astonishment as they realised that the deafening sound wasn't an oncoming storm. Some stood and stared while others leapt out of the way, perhaps fearing they would be devoured by the huge black monster.

Poppy glanced at her father and saw he was sweating with the effort of keeping *Thunderbus* on the road. The steering had to be incredibly heavy for her father to struggle with it, yet she envied his position in the driving seat; even the secondary thrill of controlling the huge power of the car was exhilarating, as was the sheer joy of travelling at such high speeds.

Eventually, Mr Orpington turned the car and started making his way back. He had avoided entering the Black Country as he hated the heavy industry that generated the permanent thick smog hovering overhead, a black shroud by day and hellish red at night. They rounded another bend and before them were the final few miles of road to Stourbridge and its glass industries. And just turning onto the road ahead of them, heading in the same direction, was a large, steam-driven car.

The driver was a young man, accompanied by a young woman. Both were fashionably – and expensively – dressed. They heard the roar of *Thunderbus* and turned in their seats, both astonished at the sight behind them. The young man quickly checked the road ahead was clear all the way into town and stopped his vehicle, meaning that Mr Orpington would have to stop also or else go around.

'Look!' shouted Amy, her voice almost lost in the wind and the excitement. 'That's a Webley Roadster. They are incredibly fast!'

'And that is a challenge, if I am not mistaken,' Mr Orpington replied as the young woman waved a brightly coloured handkerchief in the air while the man pressed on the accelerator of the car, making the steam engine hiss ever louder. 'He wants a race to town!'

CHAPTER FOUR

Mr Orpington's grin was almost a demented snarl as he brought *Thunderbus* to a halt alongside the Webley. He and the young man nodded at each other but exchanged no words. The woman lifted the handkerchief over the side of the Webley and held it for several seconds over the road.

Both cars seemed to sneer at each other as they stood immobile, the Webley hissing steam in a disdainful manner, *Thunderbus* snorting with proletariat impatience. The woman dropped the handkerchief and the Webley Roadster leapt forward, the wheels spinning momentarily until the young man regained control and accelerated away, leaving *Thunderbus* growling and stationary behind.

'Damn cheek!' roared Mr Orpington. 'You're supposed to wait for the hankie to hit the ground.' He stamped hard on the accelerator while bringing the clutch up, crudely balancing the engine with the gearbox.

Poppy had thought she'd got used to the noise but now, with the engine revving at near maximum, she realised the true power of *Thunderbus*. The roar was probably heard for miles around, and if it wasn't heard, it was surely felt. The power seemed to smash down into the road as the huge tyres dug in and kicked away.

Thunderbus accelerated, the noise of the engine growing ever louder as the car surged forward. Just as they were catching up with the Webley Roadster, the young man changed gears and his vehicle leapt ahead. Mr Orpington pressed down even harder on the accelerator, building the revs until it seemed the engine could take no more and would tear itself apart before he thumped the gearstick into second.

As the gearbox re-engaged with the engine, which was still running at the upper end of the tachometer, *Thunderbus* shot forward with such a kick of speed that all three of the occupants were slammed backward. Poppy grabbed onto the dashboard in terrified delight, fearing they would crash yet wanting to go even faster. Behind her, Amy clung onto the numerous belts and straps that held her seat down and turned green in the face.

Thunderbus hit third gear and again the force of the acceleration was almost like a physical blow. The Webley Roadster was still ahead but it had reached its top gear and was almost at maximum speed. In contrast, *Thunderbus* had barely warmed up. As the nose of the huge black car drew level with the Webley, Mr Orpington changed to fourth gear, releasing more speed and power. Flames roared from the side of the bonnet as *Thunderbus* blasted forward, streaking past the Webley with a contemptuous snarl, marking its territory and announcing its presence to the sleeping world.

The young man, his face white with shock, tried to coax the last drop of power from his car but he already knew it was too late; *Thunderbus* was moving so fast, it was as though the Webley was standing still. The wind tore at his driving hat and buffeted the car, reminding him of his high speed, and yet it was nothing to the enormous vehicle that had just kicked dust at him from its fast-disappearing rear end. The race was over, and in truth had never really begun.

Mr Orpington slowed *Thunderbus* at the edge of the town, where a curious crowd had gathered on hearing the ferocious sound of the approaching petrol engine. The long road was a popular place for vehicles to race each other, a fact that irritated the older citizens but delighted the younger. Now, all ages were united in shock at what they had just seen and heard.

'I've never seen anything so fast!' gasped a young boy in astonishment.

'Or so loud!' shouted a girl in delight.

'What is it, Mum?' asked another boy. 'What's it called, can I have a look at it, can I, can I, can I?'

Mr Orpington grinned at the reactions, though his smile faded as a policeman pushed his way through the crowd and pointed sternly to the side of the road. *Thunderbus* appeared to snigger in disdain as it slowed and then stopped in front of the policeman, burbling in defiance. Mr Orpington closed off the flow of petrol, turned off the electrical system and shut down the engine. With a last snap of flame, *Thunderbus* fell silent.

'What's all this, then?' demanded the policeman, indignantly. 'What sort of speed was that on a road into a populated area?'

'I don't know; the speedometer blew up,' replied Mr Orpington, to much laughter from the crowd.

'Here's the other car now!' shouted one of the spectators.

'About time, too,' said another voice, causing another ripple of laughter. The Webley Roadster pulled in behind *Thunderbus* and the young couple climbed out, removing their leather goggles to reveal their faces. The crowd fell silent, recognising the young man as Lord Simeon Pallister – though neither Poppy nor Amy had seen him before.

'Is there a problem, officer?' asked Simeon cheerfully as he strode forward through the crowd.

'Er, that is, um,' said the luckless policeman, realising he would not be doing his career any good if he arrested the son of a retired magistrate and the wealthiest man for miles around. 'I'm afraid we have had some complaints about racing on this stretch of road, my lord.'

'Really? Do tell me more.'

Lady Helena Pallister smiled in private amusement at her husband; she was a beautiful woman, with soft auburn hair and kindly eyes. She glanced at the huge black car and observed the stunning girl with the red hair in the front was looking worried, while the blonde in the back seemed rather queasy after the race. 'Perhaps I should give these young ladies some tea while you sort matters out with the police, my dear,' she said. 'The poor things must be chilled to the bone.'

'An excellent idea,' Simeon replied, looking fondly at his wife. He turned back to the policeman, a gleam of pleasure in his eyes.

'You come with me,' whispered Helena. 'Once he starts talking, Simeon can persuade water to flow uphill and charm snakes into biting themselves. He'll sort this out. Oh, my dear, are you able to get out unaided?' she added in genuine concern as she saw Poppy's half arm.

'I'm fine, thanks,' mumbled Poppy, ashamed of her deformity in front of such beauty and elegance. She clumsily lowered herself down to the ground, her

Sunday School dress catching on part of *Thunderbus'* frame and briefly revealing her leg brace, embarrassing her further and triggering a spurt of habitual anger at her disabilities.

'Let's leave the men to it while we partake of a light snack. This little place will do,' said Helena, guiding the girls with a friendly arm towards an unobtrusive side street.

Poppy blinked in surprise. She had lived close to Stourbridge all her life but she had never known a restaurant was hidden down the alley. She was also amazed it was open on a Sunday, given the restrictive trading laws. She glanced back at her father as she was ushered through the door; he was loudly insisting that *Thunderbus* was indeed a new type of car, and in proof he had opened the huge bonnet to show the engine to the crowd, which gasped and shoved in wonder.

'Lady Helena,' murmured the head waiter, smiling deferentially as they entered. 'Your usual table?'

'No, the small table close to the fire, please, Clarence. These girls need warming up. And a large pot of tea and a plate of muffins, if you would be so good. Sit down, girls, and relax. I'm Helena, by the way, Simeon's wife.'

'I'm Poppy, this is Amy, and that's my father

outside,' replied Poppy as they sat, openly watching their hostess. Helena moved with an easy charm that made both girls quite envious. Poppy especially felt clumsy in comparison; she moved by simply stomping from point A to point B via the straightest line possible, whereas Helena was graceful and light as she shook out her hair, slipped off her large, cumbersome driving coat, and seated herself delicately at the table, swishing her long dress to one side.

Helena discreetly examined the two girls as she removed her outer garments and settled herself in her chair. Superficially, there was little similarity between them. Of the two, the redhead was the more intriguing; she carried a lot of anger, probably from her disabilities and the restrictions they imposed upon her, yet her build was truly Amazonian and Helena found herself wondering …

'I do a lot of physical work in my dad's workshop,' said Poppy, breaking into Helena's thoughts.

Helena blushed slightly, startled at the girl's perception. 'Not many can read me so well,' she said, reappraising Poppy accordingly.

'I could see the way you focussed on my missing arm and then my shoulders,' explained Poppy, a slight hint of belligerence in her tone.

There's the anger, thought Helena, *but not actually breaking out. So, she has control.* Aloud, she said, 'I do apologise. You're an interesting study and I'm something of a people watcher.'

'And good with people, too, if you can flatter them so easily,' replied Poppy.

The two looked at each other for several seconds before Amy nervously tried to smooth the atmosphere. 'Thanks for bringing us in here; it's very kind of you.'

'Amy is very good at diplomacy,' said Poppy, warmly. 'She often has to apologise for me when I open my mouth.'

Helena's own mouth trembled as she bit down on a smile. 'That's quite all right; there is nothing to apologise for, except my own rude prying.'

'Do you often do that?' asked Poppy as she gazed with deep interest at Helena.

'Do what?'

'Stop yourself from smiling.'

Helena paused, a slight frown on her forehead. 'I suppose I do; it's not seemly for a lady to demonstrate too much emotion. I suppose I've got into the habit of hiding anything that shows too much feeling.'

'Habit or training?' asked Poppy.

'Poppy, don't be rude,' muttered Amy in

affectionate exasperation. 'I'm sorry, she doesn't mean it; she just says things as she thinks them.'

'I rather think Poppy *did* mean it,' said Helena with a genuine laugh. 'What do you mean by training?'

'People of different backgrounds are trained for different roles by society. I read about it in a book from the *Radical Press* and now I see it everywhere; the lower classes are taught by society to accept orders, while the upper classes are taught to give the orders. The book also argued that women are trained to be discreet and gentle, and to never put themselves forward, while men are encouraged to be strong and logical – the decision makers. What do you think, Helena?'[21]

Helena saw that Poppy was not being confrontational; she was simply asking for her opinion. More than that, she was genuinely interested in the answer. Poppy was clearly a girl who drank in knowledge, examining concepts and ideas before

---

[21] Poppy's precocious prescience here is still true today, alas. We may think we live in a world of freedom and equality, yet what true opportunities exist for us outside of social convention? School, college, job, mortgage, family, retirement, death; behave, save, and repeat. This is the pattern to which we are still enslaved, with the rich at the very top and everyone else below.

packing them away for future reference.

'I think that after such an invigorating ride, my husband and your father will be some time explaining themselves to the policeman, so we can take our time with the muffins and tea until they arrive,' replied Helena with a slight air of challenge.

'Is this where I'm supposed to discreetly accept that I haven't had a proper answer and make small talk?' asked Poppy.

'Yes,' exclaimed Amy, 'but how many times do I have to tell you, you're only supposed to *think* things like that, not say them out loud!'

The tension dissolved with the arrival of the muffins. All three felt as though some sort of test had been passed and they could relax.

'It's true, you know,' said Helena as she nibbled delicately, 'We are trained to occupy the space we are born into. I have been taught from birth what is acceptable and what is not. I just never really put words around it.'

'Some would say you were indoctrinated with those concepts,' replied Poppy. 'There is a definite set of rules within all levels of society on what is acceptable and what isn't. And yet you have defied your society in bringing us in here – two working-class girls. And you let us use your name, not your title. Would your peers approve of such a thing?'

'This is a basic human kindness, available to anyone,' countered Helena.

'You're not answering the question again.'

'No, many of my peers probably wouldn't,' replied Helena thoughtfully, 'but thankfully I am in a position to be able to exercise my own choices somewhat, which I would imagine is a luxury denied to many. Hmm, you are a strange girl. I've only known you two minutes and already you have me dissecting my life.'

'She often does that. It really annoyed the teachers at school,' said Amy from behind a muffin. 'They didn't like it when they were questioned about things.'

'I'm assuming you have both left school?'

'Yes, months ago. Thankfully.'[22]

'And what are you doing now?'

'I work with my dad in his workshop,' said Poppy, keeping her answer brief. She had an aversion to being questioned about her private life, though she was uncertain as to why.

---

[22] The 1897 Education Act raised the school leaving age to sixteen, but left a loophole that pupils could leave earlier if they found a job. The Government claimed this was to improve educational standards. Critics believed it was more to do with keeping as many people as possible off the unemployment lists.

'And you, Amy?' asked Helena, recognising Poppy's discomfort. She decided to give the girl a little time to compose herself before asking any further questions.

Amy gurgled down some tea and sighed. 'I'm working as a maid at a local toff's house but I want to go into engineering, if I can. It's my parents who wanted me to go into service but I love engines, so why shouldn't I do what I'm good at?'

'Why indeed,' replied Helena, sympathetically, 'though it will be difficult to find a company willing to take on a young woman. What about you, Poppy? Are you happy where you are?'

Anger flashed over Poppy's face before she damped it down. 'Not much else I can do,' she said with a bitter shrug. 'I can't work properly because of my arm and knee. I understand engines but I can't fix them efficiently with just one hand, so no one except family would employ me. I'm too slow for any sort of secretarial work and there is nothing else a woman is allowed to do, except teaching or being a governess, and I doubt anyone would hire a cripple anyway. My options are somewhat limited.'

'Oh, Poppy,' said Helena, gently, laying her hand on Poppy's. She wanted to say more but she knew there was nothing she could add; Poppy was right in her assessment of her future prospects. If only the girl had a wealthy family – but if her family were wealthy then Poppy would simply have been corralled into the marriage market. Assuming any man could be found to take on a crippled wife …

The door to the restaurant opened and Helena's husband walked in, accompanied by Mr Orpington.

'Have you got it all sorted with that policeman, Simeon?' asked Helena, waving gracefully to attract their attention.

'Oh, yes,' he replied, airily. 'Officer Macintosh insisted, nobly though unhappily, that his orders were to arrest the drivers of any steam-powered vehicles found racing along the road. That, fortunately, gave me some wriggle room, as I pointed out that Mr Orpington's vehicle is not driven by steam and hence there was no steam-powered race, merely two cars driving far too quickly, for which we both apologised profusely. The poor man was happy to accept that and merely advised us against excessive speed on the public highways. Quite right of course, but I really could not resist challenging such a vehicle. I've never seen anything like it!'

'Very kind, my lord,' mumbled Mr Orpington, suddenly looking like a twelve-year-old despite the fact he towered over Simeon.[23] Waiters appeared with two chairs and they sat down, Simeon next to his wife and Mr Orpington next to Poppy.

'Tell me, how large is that engine? And where do you get the petrol from?'

'It's three and a half litres. The petrol comes from *Jenkins Charabanc Company*. They usually have a little surplus at the end of each month.'

'I see. And what are your plans for your vehicle?'

'I want to sell the designs to the highest bidder,' replied Mr Orpington. 'To do that I need people to know about *Thunderbus*, so I'm going to enter it at the final motor race of the season. The Purley Cup.'

'Purley,' said Simeon with a look of distaste. 'You might consider shifting your sights there, old chap. A nasty little clique has developed with the organisers of that track. And racing in general.'

'It's the biggest racing event in the country, so it carries the maximum publicity. And there's the prize

---

[23] Simeon was the heir to the extensive Pallister's Sticking Plasters and Home Medicine fortune, and a keen motorist. What are the chances that on the very day Mr Orpington took *Thunderbus* out for its first run, he should meet someone so well placed and knowledgeable in the world of motor racing? Someone who would have a huge impact on his – and Poppy's – life? Strange are the ways of chance.

money. Over a thousand pounds[24] last year for the winner! With money like that, we'd be free of worry. Poppy could have a new arm, one of the latest models, and I can retire and do whatever I want for the rest of my life.'

'I quite see that,' responded Simeon, 'but have you considered the problems facing you? No one has ever won the Purley Cup on the first attempt. To my knowledge, no one has won a race without having some experience beforehand.'

'I understand, but what I lack in experience I make up for in superior speed, braking and reliability.'

'How so?'

'The top speed of a steam car is about seventy to eighty miles an hour, yes?'

'Ninety, if the publicity for the new Carralago Grand Tourer is to be believed.'[25]

'*Thunderbus* will surpass one hundred miles per hour.'[26]

---

[24] Somewhere over one hundred thousand pounds in today's money.

[25] The publicity was *not* to be believed; the Carralago Grand Tourer topped out at eighty-one m.p.h.

[26] Also something of an exaggeration, at least with *Thunderbus* in its original shape.

'You must be joking!' exclaimed Simeon.

'Not at all. And, more importantly, it can sustain that high speed for hours. How long can a steam car maintain its top speed before having to be cooled by easing off the throttle? About fifteen minutes? Not even that, sometimes. And they're fuel inefficient. And they have relatively small water tanks, unlike my larger petrol tank, so you don't have to stop so often to refuel.'

'You mentioned something about the brakes, too, I believe?'

'Indeed. Steam-powered cars usually only have one set of brakes at the rear, and they tend to be rather weak and feeble. I have far more powerful brakes on each wheel which will allow me to brake later and more efficiently, meaning I can get around corners far more rapidly. So, what I lack in skill, *Thunderbus* will more than make up for.'

'I see,' said Simeon thoughtfully. 'If the car is truly as advanced as you claim, you may well do the impossible and win, though I suspect your lack of experience will still tell against you. But there is another problem I fear you have overlooked; the expense of motor racing. Do you know how much it costs just to enter the race?'

'There's a cost?' exclaimed Mr Orpington, suddenly looking anxious. 'I thought it was free entry.'

'Not anymore. The clique I just mentioned brought in an entry fee; partly for genuine reasons of covering the race costs but also to keep out the "wrong" sort of racers. I'm afraid it's getting awfully snobby of late.'

'How much is it?' demanded Mr Orpington, looking as though he didn't want to hear the answer.

'One hundred pounds.'

'One hundred pounds? That's well over a year's pay!'

'And it's not just the entry fee,' said Simeon in sympathy, feeling bad for breaking Mr Orpington's dreams. 'The costs of running a car are considerable. You need spare engine parts, steering components, and spare tyres and brakes. You need a pit crew, you need money to stay at hotels during the race – there are all sorts of extras that build up. It really is a sport for the wealthy only.'[27]

'I-I never thought about that,' stuttered Mr Orpington. 'It was so simple when I was building the engine; make it, race it, done. And now everything is

---

[27] In order to give some context for the costs involved, at that time a farm worker could expect a yearly wage of approximately £55, while a miner could bring in £85. Mr Orpington averaged anywhere between £50-£70, though some years were much worse than others. Simeon's Webley Roadster would have cost him about £650.

ruined.'

Poppy looked in concern at her father as he slumped down in his chair, his face tired and grey. She was even more alarmed at the look of despair in his eyes. 'We can do it, Dad,' she said. 'If we save hard for a few years we can raise the entry fee. And Amy and I can be your pit crew. We know enough about engines to do that.'

'You don't know *Thunderbus*,' replied her father, his voice quiet. 'No one does. It's a whole new approach to engineering.'

'Then we can learn,' said Amy, eagerly, seeing an opportunity not only to follow her dream job but also to escape from scrubbing floors and cleaning fire grates at six o'clock every morning. 'I want to help. Mum and Dad always say I can't work with engines but I know more about them than my eldest brother, and he's got an apprenticeship with Wilson Mechanical! We can do it, Mr Orpington, we really can.'

'Simeon, can we not help?' asked Helena, placing a hand on her husband's arm. 'We could perhaps sponsor Mr Orpington and his car.'

'We certainly could, my dear,' said Simeon, warily, 'but there is the issue of experience. Without that, you really have very little chance of finishing the race, never mind winning. Would you be willing to let another driver take *Thunderbus* out onto the track?'

'Impossible,' said Mr Orpington.

'I understand your reluctance, but a skilled driver has far more chance of winning.'

'No, I mean it is literally impossible,' clarified Mr Orpington. 'The steering is heavy, far heavier than any other car, because there is no power steering unit. There was one originally but I had to remove it to fit the engine within the chassis. And then I had to bodge the steering assembly back together in the available space, which means the driver has to turn the wheel with his own strength. I can manage it – just. No one else would have a chance.'

'I see,' replied Simeon, looking at Mr Orpington's huge frame and enormous arms.

'We could enter for the smaller Sussex Race, just over a month away,' exclaimed Helena as the idea hit her. 'Heed my advice, Mr Orpington; enter *Thunderbus* in the Sussex and gain the experience you need. After that, you will have a greater chance of success at Purley.'

'What do you say, Mr Orpington?' asked Simeon, nodding his head. 'We'll deal with your running costs as long as they are reasonable. We have the contacts and we can get you there, in return for a percentage of any sales made on the back of

Thunderbus' designs.'

'Do say "yes", Mr Orpington,' said Helena, as he hesitated. 'I know you had the dream of doing this by yourself but it just won't happen. You have to spend money to get anywhere near the race, and you have to spend even more money to compete.'

Mr Orpington looked at Poppy, unsure what to say. Poppy put her hand on his and smiled.

'Let's do it, Dad,' she said. 'It's our only chance.'

Mr Orpington sighed. His dream, which had long ago turned into a mania that had motivated him for years, had been wrenched apart with a few words, leaving a terrifying emptiness inside. He could see no other way of keeping alive even an echo of his obsession.

'Very well,' he said. 'It's a deal.'

CHAPTER FIVE

After verbally agreeing to do business, Simeon and Helena became frequent visitors at the workshop, often in the company of their solicitor, Mr Pippin. Simeon and Mr Orpington haggled over the exact terms of the contract until eventually all was ready for signing. Simeon ran his signature over the required areas with a flourish. Mr Orpington wrote far more slowly and laboriously; his schooling had been limited, so he had to concentrate over his words and letters.

'Thank you, Mr Orpington, and the duplicates, please,' said Mr Pippin, dexterously flipping away the top contract to reveal the bottom copies. He glanced at the signed copy and paused. 'Excuse me, but what is this you have put here?'

Poppy's father squinted in puzzlement at where the lawyer's finger was pointing. 'My name.'

'P. Orpington? I thought your name is Robert?'

'My given names are Peter Robert, but I never liked Peter, so I don't use it. But of course official forms have to be signed for properly, don't they?'

'Indeed they do,' said Mr Pippin through a tight smile.

After the visitors had gone, Mr Orpington looked

at his daughter and said, heavily, 'Well, that is that. We're locked in now, Poppy. No longer our own masters, bound to no one. From now on, we have partners to please.'

'At least Simeon and Helena are nice and fair, Dad,' said Poppy in return. She had been worried afresh about her father. Although he had engaged with Simeon over the contract, he seemed to have lost some of his focus and energy since the revelations in the restaurant. 'And Amy and I are definitely going to be on the pit crew?'

'Yes, I held out on that; only you and Amy can work on the engine. Not that Amy's mother is very happy about it. Or her father, come to that.'

'They're not going to stop her coming along, are they?' asked Poppy in fear; she couldn't imagine being separated from Amy.

'No, Simeon talked them round. He's got a silver tongue, that man, and of course his title helped. No matter how much Amy's dad considers himself a radical, he still goes weak at the knees when in the presence of a toff.'

'Don't call Simeon that, Dad, he's been really good to us,' said Poppy, sighing in relief. 'So, are we the only mechanics?'

'Simeon plans to employ a pit crew to look after the rest of the car, like the wheels and suspension.'

'When are you going to start training Amy and me?'

'We'll start tomorrow and get in a few days tuition before we leave the workshop.'

'Leave the workshop?' echoed Poppy in surprise.

'Yes, we're moving to Simeon's country estate, a few miles from Worcester. He has a complete, fully-fitted racing workshop there, with far more facilities than we have.'

'Where will we live, though? Actually in Pallister Hall itself?'

'We're being given accommodation somewhere on the estate. Simeon used to house a racing crew there, so it's all sorted.'

'Oh, right, sorted,' echoed Poppy, suddenly nervous at the huge change that had overtaken her life.

A few days later, Poppy, her father and Amy packed their few possessions into *Thunderbus* for the journey to Pallister Hall. Poppy still wasn't sure how to react. Her entire life had been lived in the workshop and the small flat above, and now they were simply locking the door and walking away. The existing lease had a few months to run so they weren't abandoning the small garage, but it felt like it.

They climbed into *Thunderbus*. Poppy sat in the front surrounded by bedding and clothes. Amy, who had said goodbye to her parents that morning before walking over, was squashed in the dickey seat between boxes of tools and the many books Poppy had scrounged from various sources over the years. Just as her father could not leave his tools, so Poppy could not leave her books. Amy's possessions consisted of a much smaller tool collection and a few pieces of clothing.

The journey to Pallister Hall was oddly subdued as they drew closer to their new life. Poppy's father finally broke the silence when he flung out his hand and pointed. 'There you are, girls. Our new home.' The hall was a huge eighteenth century building, somewhat grim and forbidding with its grey stone walls and high tower.

Somewhat incongruously, modern attachments such as a huge antenna could be seen at one end of the building. Poppy had never even seen a Rotational Telecasting Retriever, never mind watched one; telecasting was a luxury only the wealthy could pay for, enabling them to watch news and cultural entertainment for the few hours each evening the signal went out. The working class could, if lucky, just about afford to hire a cheap radio set. Poppy had never seen one of those, either.

Another oddity was the snaking road cutting through several large fields at the back of the hall, spoiling the green landscape. After squinting at it for several seconds, Poppy realised she was looking at a home-made racetrack. Simeon had mentioned being an enthusiast, but she didn't know he had churned up his own land to practise on.

Mr Orpington consulted a scrap of paper as he approached the hall. He went past the front gates and continued to the trade entrance, halfway around the estate. He turned carefully through the narrow gate, the long car only just making it through, and accelerated up the drive until they reached a fork in the road.

As they turned onto the left-hand lane, an elderly man, well-dressed and leaning heavily on a cane, appeared at the top of the road and stared at them with malignant ferocity. Neither Mr Orpington nor Amy seemed to notice the old man, but Poppy somehow made eye contact. She shivered under his gaze, glad the lane was taking them away from the figure that stood outlined against the trees like a totem warning them to leave.

Normality only returned as they reached the end of the lane and arrived at what looked like an old stable block. Mr Orpington drove in through the open doors and cut the engine. 'This is it,' he said, his voice loud in the sudden peace. 'This is the workshop. Our quarters are just behind.'

'This is amazing,' gasped Amy as their eyes adjusted to the darkness. The stables had been gutted of any trace of horse riding, making way for tools and machinery. In the middle of the floor was a rectangular pit, allowing the crew to work underneath a car. The garage held everything a racing driver needed to keep his vehicle running. Except, of course, everything in the workshop was designed with steam power in mind; *Thunderbus* was a different type of car altogether.

'The grooms used to live in the old cottages behind this building,' said Mr Orpington, glancing again at his notes. 'That is where we are to live, as will the rest of the crew. We can get all our meals from the servants' quarters. Presumably,' he added with a touch of acidity, 'we are not allowed anywhere near the main house. Come on, let's find our lodgings and get unpacked.'

The cottages were spread around in a square formation, small but charming to look at. The largest, with three bedrooms, had been put aside for their needs. It even housed a small indoor bathroom complete with flushing toilet, shower and bath, rather than just the privy in the garden and metal hip bath Poppy had grown up with.

'I could get used to this,' said Amy in a stunned tone, looking in amazement at the luxury of the cottage. 'There's a carpet in each bedroom. Actual carpets!'

'Let's hope we win; then we can keep living this way,' replied Poppy, before she was cut short by a shout.

'Did you hear that?'

'Yes,' said Poppy, looking around. 'I think it came from the garage. It must be Simeon. Come on, let's get down there.'

Poppy was right; Simeon was in the workshop, gazing happily at *Thunderbus*. With him was a group of men that Poppy assumed to be the pit crew.

'Ah, there you are,' said Simeon. 'Gentlemen, this is Robert Orpington, the creator of *Thunderbus*, as the car is known. I'm glad you got here in one piece, Robert. I was afraid you'd have an accident on the way over.'

'All was fine, my lord,' rumbled Mr Orpington in reply.

'Well, I don't want you to risk damaging *Thunderbus*,' said Simeon. 'I'll loan you a little steam runabout for day-to-day use. Now, let me make the introductions. This is the head of the pit crew, Jack Talbot, who has many years' experience of racing, so what he doesn't know is not worth knowing. Next to him are Mason and Palmer, who have responsibility for the steering and suspension, then we have Carter and Swindon, who will take care of the wheels, tyres and the chassis. Young Dale is the apprentice, and the large gentleman at the end is Tully, who acts as a general factotum.'

Poppy looked over the men as they were introduced. She had already noticed that Dale was the only one close to her age. He was tall, good-looking and winked brashly at her and Amy when no one was looking. She was also aware that she and Amy were drawing some puzzled – and hostile – stares from the rest of the pit crew, who were clearly wondering why the two girls were even there.

'You say that Mr Orpington is both driver and mechanic?' asked Talbot, looking concerned. 'If I can say so, that won't work for a start. The driver needs to focus on one thing – the driving. We need to get another mechanic for the engine. I don't know anything about petrol. I suspect no one does on the racing circuit.'

'I do hope not; this is our secret weapon,' replied Simeon. 'Don't worry about the engine, though. That is the exclusive preserve of Robert, assisted by his daughter, Poppy, and her friend Amy.'

Poppy wasn't certain she was happy with the way Simeon spoke; he was scrupulously polite but his voice was a little too careful and controlled. She suspected he didn't think they were up to the job. She was also now convinced of the ugly undercurrent from the pit crew. On being informed that the engine was off limits to them, their scowls deepened; on finding out that two females were the official mechanics, their expressions became belligerent. All this went unnoticed by her father, Simeon and Talbot, who were more absorbed with *Thunderbus* and the problems of getting the car ready for racing.

'The tyres are no good,' said Talbot, his Yorkshire accent breaking out as his emotions rose. 'And the wheels look like they're off an omnibus! It will take Carter and Swindon an hour to change those. They need to be removable in under a minute if we are to compete. I bet the suspension is all wrong as well. And how heavy is this thing?'

'The basic chassis *is* from an old charabanc,' replied Poppy's father, looking quite discouraged at Talbot's words. 'As are the wheels and suspension. And it weighs about two tons.'

A gasp of incredulity and contempt went round the pit crew. Talbot glared at them and they hastily modified their expressions, but Poppy found herself increasingly concerned about the sort of men she and Amy would be working with every day. She turned her attention back to Talbot, who was speaking again and looking increasingly mournful.

'Two tons? The heaviest car I've ever seen in a race was the Webley Roadster Mark II, which weighed about a ton. And it lost, as I recall. Lord Dunnage raced one for a while. The best he ever managed was third place on the Dublin track, which of course has lots of straight roads so the power of the Webley compensated for the bulk.'

'My Mark III Webley is faster than the Mark II,' replied Simeon with a grin, 'and you know what? *Thunderbus* left me standing! The acceleration and cruising speed have simply never been seen on the road before.'

'From a petrol engine?' queried Talbot. 'They're good for nothing but trucks and buses.'

'This one is better at everything,' said Poppy's father, grumpily. He strode to the side of *Thunderbus* and unstrapped the huge side bonnet. A hush fell on the pit crew as they stared at the engine inside the car. Even standing still, it looked like a machine built for speed.

'What's the top speed?' asked Talbot.

'I don't know,' admitted Mr Orpington. 'I've never found a long enough stretch of road to find out. I did once get it up to about seventy and it had much more to give.'

Talbot hummed in grudging astonishment. 'I can

94

see why you think you can win, with that sort of power. But you won't. Not on those wheels and tyres.'

'Then we have four weeks to find wheels and tyres that will do the job,' announced Simeon, briskly. 'Four weeks to adapt *Thunderbus* for racing. We need quick-release wheels, quick-release filling caps and better components. Oh, and we need to replace that sofa in the cockpit with a proper passenger seat. That is why I have hired you all. We are going to enter the race, gentlemen, and we are going to win. So, make it happen!'

For Poppy and Amy, the following weeks were filled with hard work and stress. Not only were they now learning about petrol engines in general, and *Thunderbus'* secrets in particular, but they were also being taught about motor racing itself. There was a lot to take in, especially as no one could be sure how well *Thunderbus* would perform on the racetrack. Fuel consumption, for example, was an unknown factor. Although petrol-driven charabancs and trucks had been commercially produced for years, none had ever been used for racing, meaning no one knew how much petrol *Thunderbus* would consume on each lap.

Simeon therefore demanded that *Thunderbus* be tested repeatedly on the long track around his family's huge estate, which caused some disagreement as Mr Orpington wanted *Thunderbus* to remain a secret, hidden away from any prying eyes for as long as possible. Simeon, supported by Talbot, insisted that their only chance of winning would come through finding and eliminating problems before the race, and this could only be achieved through rigorous testing.

'Time?' bellowed Simeon as *Thunderbus* roared past, having completed a lap of the home-made racetrack. He, Helena and the pit crew were gathered to watch *Thunderbus'* performance after an improved suspension system was fitted, along with new wheels and tyres.

'One minute, twenty-five seconds,' answered Talbot as *Thunderbus* turned awkwardly and returned.

Simeon shook his head. 'It's fast, yes, faster than anything I've known, but look at the way it handles. The turning circle is awful. It needs a field to complete a simple three-point turn!' Mr Orpington's assertion that no one except him would be strong enough to drive had been proven beyond doubt when Talbot had tried to take *Thunderbus* out for a lap. He barely managed half the course before giving up in agony. 'It has to be more manoeuvrable on the corners or we will lose. How are the redesigns coming for the new steering rack?'

'Not good, my lord,' replied Talbot, shaking his head. 'We just can't find any way of fitting in a new system because of the position of the engine within the chassis. We need to chop the front end off to accommodate the power steering unit but that, of course, is impossible. Ideally, we need to re-build from the ground up, with a special chassis designed for the engine and with a bespoke steering system that will fit properly, and not use bits and pieces salvaged from an old charabanc.'

'Can't you drop in the steering mechanism from the old Sylvestril Roadster?' asked Helena. 'That is significantly larger than most other cars. We could cannibalise that for parts.'

'Afraid not, my lady; it's still too small. So, we keep coming back to the problem that the driver has to be able to turn the steering wheel himself, with no mechanical help, using a bodged-up steering system barely adequate for the job, and all built into a car that weighs two tons and which will be travelling at anything up to a hundred miles an hour.'

'Dad has managed so far,' pointed out Poppy.

'Your father is the strongest man I've ever met,' conceded Talbot, brusquely, 'but not even he can steer such a heavy car for an entire race, even a short one like the Sussex. It's impossible.'

'What is?' asked Mr Orpington as he parked *Thunderbus* and cut the engine, thus overhearing the last part of the conversation. Poppy, Simeon and Talbot explained between them, frequently overlapping each other as Simeon spoke, Talbot shook his head, and Poppy supported her father.

'If the Sylvestril steering rack will not fit, we will have to do without,' said Mr Orpington, finally. 'I'll handle the driving.'

'You'll never last an entire race, man,' exclaimed Simeon. 'Fifteen laps, each one a mile long? You'll never be strong enough. No one would be.'

'Then it is clear that it is not just *Thunderbus* that needs to be prepared for racing,' replied Mr Orpington, 'but the driver also. I shall need to start a training course to prepare me for the rigours of the race. Something to build my stamina as well as my muscles.'

'It's still impossible,' said Talbot for the second time.

'Finding room to insert a power steering unit is impossible,' said Mr Orpington. 'Compared to that, preparing this body for racing is merely difficult.'

Simeon sighed. 'Very well; we'll organise a suitable training and fitness plan for you. I just hope it will be enough.' He noticed Poppy grinning as she and her father walked away and he sighed again. For all her intelligence and acumen, she still had a blind spot where her father was concerned. If he said he could do it, then he could do it.

'This is ludicrous,' muttered Talbot in a low tone. 'No one can race for so long in such a heavy car. I remember Lord Foulkes, back in the nineties, doing an endurance race in a car with no power steering. It nearly crippled him, and his car was nowhere near as heavy as *Thunderbus*.'

Simeon shrugged. 'We have no other choice. We don't have time to redesign the car and we have now entered for the race. We must turn up and do our best.'

'Is it going to be worth it?' asked Talbot, dubiously. 'Orpington's driving skills are pretty limited. The chances of him winning are not good.'

'The gamble we are taking is that the sheer power of *Thunderbus* will be enough,' pointed out Helena.

'I realise that, my lady, but I still can't see him winning. I'm afraid you're going to lose a lot of money on this deal.'

'Fortunately for us,' said Simeon, an innocent expression on his face, 'a new rule has been brought in for the Sussex track that may help to offset the financial issue. Given that even amateur racing is increasing in popularity, the sponsors are now offering prize money for each leader of the lap.'

'Leader of the lap?' asked Helena.

'Indeed; if you lead the race for a complete lap, you get twenty pounds. So, if you lead the pack for five laps, you'd get one hundred pounds. Of course, the prize money is higher for whoever takes the chequered flag, but every little bit helps.'

'Hmm,' murmured Helena, suspiciously. 'Sir Trevor Baxter is in charge of the Sussex Race, isn't he?'

'Well, more of an advisory capacity, really.'

'Your old friend, Sir Trevor Baxter,' persisted Helena, refusing to be deflected. 'Who you were at school with, and Cambridge thereafter, and who you took out to a very fine dinner last week. You didn't by any chance encourage him to bring in this new rule, did you?'

'Helena!' said Simeon, looking shocked and hurt. 'You are taking a mere coincidence and overlaying an imaginary set of circumstances upon it.'

'So, you had nothing to do with it at all?'

'No.'

'Nothing at all?'

'No.'

'Simeon Pallister, you look me in the eye and tell me you had nothing to do with that new rule being introduced!'

'Well, maybe I did possibly hint at the suggestion

that it would be marvellous publicity and would increase the excitement for everyone. And somehow the media have found out about it. They were chatting about it in the London papers when I left.'

'So, if *Thunderbus* leads the race even for a few laps, which it may well do given its sheer power, then you can recoup some of the money you have invested *and* capitalise on the publicity?'

'*We* can capitalise on the publicity,' corrected Simeon. 'After all, we are all working to the same end: to get *Thunderbus* noticed and to make money from the designs. Which, of course, will have the knock-on effect of giving a better standard of life for both Orpington and young Poppy.'

'Simeon, you are the most deceitful yet caring of men. How you fit all this into one personality is more than I can fathom.'

'It's amazing what marriage can teach you.'

CHAPTER SIX

In the run-up to the race, Mr Orpington worked all hours on both *Thunderbus* and his own training programme. Outwardly, he was now in better condition than he had ever been. He ate regularly and well, chopped and carried wood several times a day, did calisthenics to build his physique, and raced *Thunderbus* as often as possible around the estate to improve his strength, skill and endurance.

Poppy accompanied her father on his training each day and, like him, she was benefiting from the exercise; even the limp in her left leg had diminished considerably as her muscles toughened under the new exercises. She was oblivious to her own changes, however, as she was increasingly concerned about her father's mental state. He was focussing purely on *Thunderbus* and the race to the extent that he hardly spoke about anything else. His determination swept aside any human warmth, leaving behind a machine with but one purpose: to win.

Time and again Poppy tried to draw him out and interest him in other subjects, to find some hope that her father was still there. 'Amy and Dale seem to be getting on well,' she said as they chopped wood one morning. The muscles on her shoulders, torso and legs moved sinuously as she swung her axe in a circular motion and split her log with one clean movement.

'Ah,' said her father as he single-mindedly put a thick length of wood on the tree stump that served as a chopping board, swung his massive axe around, split the wood, cleared it and started again with another piece.

'Yes, they spend a lot of time together in the workshop,' said Poppy, busy with her own axe. She wasn't quite sure how she felt about Amy's friendship with the young mechanic. 'She seems happy when she's talking with him,' continued Poppy, speaking as much to herself as her father, 'but I don't know if Dale is the right sort of friend for her.'

She paused. Dale was good-looking but it was his cocky swagger that really seemed to attract Amy; Poppy found Simeon's charm and knowledge rather more appealing. 'After all,' she continued, decapitating another log, 'Dale and the rest of the crew don't think women should be allowed to do any sort of engineering work. Apparently, we'd be happier in the home. I told him exactly where to put his attitude. How could Amy ever be close or happy with someone who holds that sort of opinion? What do you think, Dad?'

Mr Orpington paused, wiped the sweat from his brow, gazed into the far distance and finally spoke. 'I think the timing belt needs to be replaced. If that breaks, it would be a disaster.'

'What do you think about Amy and Dale?'

'Dale? Seems to know his way around the suspension.'

'Yes, Dad, but what of him and Amy?'

'Yes, I think so,' muttered her father.

'You think what?'

'We definitely need to replace that timing belt. I'll do it now. Then I'll have an early run in *Thunderbus*.' Mr Orpington strode away, seemingly oblivious to Poppy, who savagely split a small tree in two with an angry swing of her axe. She turned to follow but stopped short. Standing against one corner of Pallister Hall was the gaunt figure who had stared at her from the driveway on the day of their arrival. She now knew who the old man was: Simeon's father, the Duke of Shalford. Every few days he would appear, usually in the distance, glaring maliciously at her or the pit crew. Poppy stared back, letting him know she was not afraid, before turning away.

Poppy also accompanied her father on the practice laps in *Thunderbus*, again in the hopes of getting through to the man she knew. Unfortunately, when in *Thunderbus*, Mr Orpington's obsession reached its zenith; he would mumble frenziedly about the race and the car, quite often starting a monologue on how *Thunderbus* was handling, how to change gear and how to approach a corner the correct way. 'When approaching a sharp corner, don't ease off the throttle; brake hard and late, change down, but keep the revs under the red counter,' he intoned, recalling all he had learnt through continual practice. 'Then, as you turn into the corner, accelerate hard. Don't wait until you've cleared the corner, by then it's too late. You need to be speeding up before you see the next straight, otherwise you have lost. Lost everything!'

During the hectic days of maintaining *Thunderbus*, trying to stay close to her father and worrying about Amy and Dale, Poppy found just one solace. When her father needed to leave the estate, Poppy would take him out in the steam car lent to them by Simeon, so her father could conserve his strength. She enjoyed driving the car and was surprisingly talented at it. The steering was light enough for her to control with her single arm, and the drive shaft ran directly off the turbine which meant there were no gears to worry about, unlike on many other vehicles.

Unfortunately, there was a far darker issue facing

both Poppy and Amy. Although Jack Talbot, as the head of the pit crew, tolerated them for the sake of his job, and Dale had learnt to keep his mouth shut in Poppy's presence, the rest of the crew resented not being given access to the engine – and they positively hated having two women on the team, a previously unheard of and outrageous state of affairs. And with each passing day, the animosity was turning into open hatred.

The hate finally broke out when Simeon, Talbot and Mr Orpington were away visiting an engineering works which was fabricating some spare engine parts. In their absence, Simeon left instructions for Poppy, Amy and the rest of the crew to rehearse for the single pit stop *Thunderbus* would have to make when racing. Various levers had been fitted to the oil, water and fuel caps, as well as the four wheels, so that all could now be released quickly and effectively. Practice was required, however, to ensure the crew could perform their allotted tasks without impeding each other or *Thunderbus*.

Although Amy and Poppy were the only people allowed to check and repair the engine, it was Tully, the largest, tallest man, who had the responsibility of topping up the oil and petrol, for the simple reason that he could best lift a heavy tank to shoulder height to release the feeder pipe down to the car. Unfortunately, Tully was careless in his work. The fresh oil sloshed out of the pipe and doused the metal engine.

'Be careful,' warned Amy, sharply. 'If that gets into the electrics it could short-circuit the system!'

'Oh, get out of the way, girl, I know what I'm doing,' snarled Tully.

'No, you don't,' Amy snapped back. 'If you did, you wouldn't be so slovenly. If you spill that oil in the wrong place, the electrics will get clogged and they'll start to burn.'

'What the hell do you think you know about engines?'

'We're in charge of the engine because we know how it works.'

'And that's a mistake!' hissed Tully as his anger and resentment at having to work with two women erupted. 'What the hell are you going to do if the engine breaks down on the racetrack? Go out and fix it? Don't make me laugh!' The rest of the pit crew sniggered at the confrontation. It was their habit to make snide remarks and innuendoes each day when Simeon and Poppy's father were absent. Amy had worried about this, knowing Poppy's temper would not stand such behaviour for long, yet it was Amy herself who finally snapped when Tully's slapdash attitude threatened *Thunderbus*.

'I've stripped it down and rebuilt it with more skill than you can even pour the oil in,' responded Amy, her voice rising in anger.

'Only because your friend's daddy is too paranoid to share his precious secrets,' yelled Tully, hurling the now-empty oil can to the ground. 'I bet we could learn more about that engine in one day than you could in a lifetime!'

'You shut your stinking mouth, Tully,' snarled Poppy, her hand clenching in fury as the two people most dear to her were insulted.

'Or what?' snapped Tully. 'What are you going to do? Stump me? At least you've got an excuse for pretending to be interested in engines – no man's going look twice at you. But what excuse does this slag have for interfering with men's work? She ought to get back in the kitchen where she belongs!'

Poppy strode forward, her face flushed and dangerous. The sniggers of the pit crew disappeared as they realised that Poppy, despite her limp, was moving with a strong, deadly purpose, powered by anger, hard sinew and bone. What working in her father's workshop had started, sharing his training regime had finished; Poppy was tall, her shoulders broad, and her limbs long and strong, despite her weak knee.

Tully instinctively backed away before realising what he was doing. His face went red with embarrassment as he stopped and folded his arms, hastily assembling a sneer at the advancing figure. He clearly expected Poppy to stop and thus he was completely unprepared as she hit him with a savage punch to the face. He staggered back and fell, only his substantial bulk saving him from being knocked cold.

Rage swept through his disorientated mind, fed by his many insecurities concerning his ability, class and attractiveness to women. And now one of them, a mere girl, was challenging him in what should have been his domain, acting as though she had some right to be there. He staggered to his feet and charged at Poppy, semi-conscious but with vengeance stamped clearly on his face. He never reached her. Amy leapt between them, hefting a large wrench which she swung into Tully's stomach. He couldn't even cry out in pain as the wrench expelled the air from his body and he collapsed in a tight ball.

Palmer snarled and leapt towards Poppy, his hands reaching out. His head jerked back as Poppy drove her elbow deep into his face, causing him to stagger back a few steps. He rushed forward again with a scream of incoherent rage, his eyes streaming in pain and humiliation. Poppy dodged to one side

109

and slammed her left knee up into his stomach, her brace adding to the force of the blow and sending Palmer down in a heap, but under the impact the brace broke and the tiny cogs and pistons exploded over the ground.

'You stupid cow,' spat Mason as he and Carter advanced on Poppy and Amy. 'We're going to show you what real men are like.'

'Yeah, let's see you move faster than us now, cripple,' smirked Carter, gesturing in contempt at the cogs and pistons from Poppy's brace that lay scattered on the ground.

'I don't want any part of this,' said Dale, looking terrified.

'Me neither,' grunted Swindon. 'I can't afford to lose this job.'

'Then get out,' snarled Mason. 'Keep watch while we teach these little girls not to go messing in men's work.' Swindon and Dale hurried out. Dale glanced at Amy on the way, but he said and did nothing to help.

'Yeah, you deserve this, always flaunting yourselves,' grunted Carter, sweat glistening on his face.

'And sitting around in your nightdresses,' leered Mason as he advanced, his eyes flicking manically from side to side. 'You've been asking for it ever since we started work here.'

'Nightdresses?' repeated Poppy in terrified disgust. 'Have you been spying on us in the cottage?'

'Lord Simeon will be back soon,' snapped Amy, unable to hide the fear from her voice.

'Nah, he'll be ages, yet,' giggled Carter, his voice suddenly high with excitement. 'Plenty of time for all of us to enjoy ourselves. *Plenty* of time.'

'Yeah, we'll teach you a thing or two,' grinned Mason, his teeth overhanging his blood-red lower lip. 'Make women out of the girls.'

'And what do you think Lord Simeon will say when we tell him about this?' demanded Amy.

'You never will,' growled Mason. 'Not if you know what is good for you.'

'By the time we've finished with you,' gasped Palmer, heaving himself off the floor and staggering forward in fury, 'you'll regret ever coming into this workshop – taking our jobs and driving cars around like it's a normal thing to do.'

Poppy silently cursed her weak leg, her missing arm and her stupidity in not backing down when she had the chance. Why had she let her temper get the better of her? Why stand up for herself when the consequences could be so dire? All she had done was provoke the situation and put Amy and herself at risk, and if anything happened to Amy …

'Get ready to run,' whispered Poppy in a low tone. 'I'll hold them off; you just get out of here.'

'I'm not leaving you,' gasped Amy.

'This is my fault; I will not have you hurt because of my bad judgement,' retorted Poppy. She was still scared, but growing within her was an intense feeling of anger; Tully and Palmer could only view women as homemakers, while Mason and Carter saw them simply as sexual objects. And both viewpoints led inevitably to marginalization and violence.

'Up the side of the car, quick,' she commanded, realising that none of the advancing men were covering the exit from the workshop. 'Get help from the house staff.' She snatched up a large spanner, ready and willing to defend herself even if it meant killing one of her attackers.

Mason jumped forward, intending to cut off Amy's escape route, but he hesitated as he saw Poppy swinging the spanner wildly at Carter and Palmer. He was unable to decide between catching the tart or helping his two friends subdue the hysterical woman, but on seeing Amy outlined in the door against the clear blue sky beyond, he realised they were doomed if she escaped and he followed after her.

Poppy bellowed in defiance and hurled the spanner at him. It left her without a weapon, but if it saved Amy it was worth it. The spanner flew through the air and caught Mason on the shoulder. He screamed in pain and staggered to one side, allowing Amy to sprint out through the doors. Carter and Palmer stopped in horror, fearing they were exposed, but there was a muffled cry and Swindon appeared, dragging Amy back in with him. 'Get in there, girl,' he snarled while Dale, almost chalk-white with fear, followed behind, looking in silent appeal at the rest of the pit crew.

'Keep hold of her,' croaked Palmer. 'If she gets out, we've all had it!'

'You've had it anyway, Palmer,' snarled Poppy as she leapt up onto *Thunderbus*' running board, gaining extra height and hopefully some control of the situation. 'You think you can keep this quiet? Three of you injured – how are you going to explain that away? And when I tell Lord Simeon what you tried to do, it will be the courts and jail for all of you.'

'Christ, what do we do?' moaned Carter. 'The little cow is right. How do we explain away all of this? We've had it!'

'You stupid cow!' spat Palmer in terrified anger, but he seemed unable to think of anything else to do or say.

'I'll tell you what we do with them!' screamed

Mason in furious agony, clutching his shoulder where the spanner had hit him. 'We finish them, that's what we do!'

Carter went pale. 'You don't mean,' he gasped, unable to complete the sentence.

'We tie them to that car and we torch the whole garage,' continued Mason, his voice shaking hysterically. 'It's not our fault they fiddled with the engine while we were outside having a break. They ignited the petrol and burnt to death. We tried to help but the fire spread so quickly, we couldn't get them out and we got injured trying. That explanation covers everything!'

Silence fell. The men seemed frozen, their thoughts turning over Mason's words. Then Carter nodded, as did Swindon and Tully, who was still lying where had fallen, though he was trying to get back to his feet. Dale looked horrified but still said nothing. The silence wrapped itself around them, the outside world adrift from the horrors within the garage, separate and unknowing.

'That explanation covers nothing,' roared Poppy in contempt as she stared down at the faces beneath her. 'How do you think a fire will successfully explain away two deaths and all your injuries? How would you ever have the intelligence to get away with it?'

114

'W-we can do it,' stuttered Mason. 'If we stick together.'

'We do it,' hissed Tully in fury, clutching his belly where Amy had struck him with her wrench.

'So, wounded pride wants revenge,' sneered Poppy. 'How about the rest of you?' She held her breath, willing the men to see sense. The silence was finally broken by Carter.

'We've gone too far now. If we let them go, we're for it.'

'It's their fault anyway,' snarled Tully, heaving himself to his feet. His stomach was on fire and his legs felt weak enough to collapse at any moment. All that kept him upright was his desire for revenge, not just against the blow to the stomach but against the very existence of Poppy and Amy.

'Then take us down, Tully,' challenged Poppy, silently cursing the stupidity and injured pride of the pit crew. Her best chance now was to remove the dominant personalities of the group. 'Come over here and kill me, just you, with your bare hands, if you think you can. If you think it's the right and proper thing to do.'

Tully lurched forward. The rest of the men stood watching. No one moved forward to help or to hinder. It was as though they were waiting to see who would win before choosing sides.

'Come on, Tully, come and murder us!' shouted Poppy. 'Show how much of a man you are by murdering two young girls. Come and kill us, Tully, kill the women and be a man!'

'I … I don't want no part of this,' blurted Dale again.

'Your followers are thinking for themselves, Tully,' taunted Poppy as the large man shuffled sideways, breathing heavily, clutching his stomach with one hand. His other hand groped along a workbench and found a small hammer. 'What's the matter, Tully; can't you deal with a girl with your bare hands? Not man enough? Not strong enough?'

'What on earth is going on here?' demanded a voice from the doorway. The group looked round and saw Simeon and Poppy's father staring in at the scene.

'Your men have just attacked us,' snapped Poppy.

'That's a lie; they've been flaunting themselves!' shouted Palmer, fear sharpening his wits.

'Then why is Swindon restraining Amy?' challenged Poppy. 'She tried to escape and was caught and dragged back inside.' Swindon hastily let go of Amy, who ran towards Poppy and flung her arms around her friend's waist.

'You, you were here to work on *Thunderbus*, nothing else,' snarled Poppy's father, his face turning red. Poppy looked at him, trying to read his expression. His reaction revolved around the car, not her. Was he simply expressing himself badly because of his anger, or was that all he was thinking about?

Simeon walked to the door of the workshop and called out. Poppy heard running feet and three of Simeon's groundskeepers appeared, holding a variety of tools in their hands. They must have been working only a short distance from the garage all the time.

'How long have you three been working on the fruit grove?'

'Ever since lunch, my lord,' answered one promptly.

'Did you hear or see anything unusual going on here?'

The three men looked puzzled. 'Thought I heard a bit of shouting,' said one of them, 'but I was absorbed in the work so I didn't look up straight away. I glanced up just after we finally got that dangerous branch cut off and saw two of the pit crew outside the door, but when I next glanced up, they'd gone. That was just a few minutes ago.'

'I saw them pacing about like they were worried, in as much as you can tell from that distance.'

'That's right,' said the senior of the three. 'I thought I heard a faint yell or something about that time, but as Ted says we were all concentrating on

117

hewing off a tricky branch and we were worried about it falling badly. When I looked over there was no one there. Thought I'd imagined the shouting but if the other two heard it as well, clearly not.'

'Right,' said Simeon grimly. 'You three stay here and watch these men. None of them are to leave this garage or try to talk to each other in any way. Girls, you go to your cottage. Robert and I shall go fetch the local inspector.'

Ignoring the baffled looks of the groundskeepers and the apprehensive expressions of the pit crew, Amy and Poppy walked out. 'Oh, Poppy, you were amazing,' whispered Amy. 'The way you took control of the situation.'

'What about the way you took down Tully? That was astonishing!'

'That was just a reaction to him threatening you. You were the one who used your wits to fight, not just your muscle. You were so brave!'

'Brave?' echoed Poppy in relief. 'If I'd known the gardeners were just a few feet away, I'd have screamed the roof off to bring them in!'

Later that day, Helena rushed in to see Poppy and Amy in their cottage. 'Oh, my dears, are you hurt?' she asked as soon as she had entered.

'We're fine,' replied Amy. She and Poppy were

relaxing in the large, sagging easy chairs provided by Simeon. Amy was curled up modestly in hers, while Poppy preferred to sprawl. Both girls made to rise but Helena waved them back with a soothing gesture and a worried expression.

'Are you certain?'

'Yes, honestly,' replied Amy. 'It was a horrible experience but it could have been much worse.'

'We're fine and ready to get back to work as soon as possible,' confirmed Poppy. 'Probably the best thing for us; get back to normality. And we do still have a race to win.'

'I can't begin to apologise enough, and please believe me when I say that neither Simeon nor myself had any idea the pit crew would react so badly to your presence. It is unbelievable. Why, I have spoken to them many, many times over the past few weeks and never once have I felt there to be any danger.'

'Possibly you were protected by your title,' said Poppy, thoughtfully. 'Whereas we come from the same background, so perhaps they viewed us as obtainable and within their rights?'

'Yes, I believe you are correct. Unfortunately, such attitudes are present at all levels of society,' said Helena, her face clouding before she quickly spoke again. 'I'm afraid I was only told what occurred when Simeon and your father returned from the police station.'

'How's Dad taking it all?' asked Poppy in alarm. 'Why hasn't he come in to see us?'

'I'm not sure; I just know that, when they got back, Robert returned to the workshop. The last I saw he was stripping down part of the engine.' Helena saw the pain in Poppy's face and tried to reassure her. 'I think it's his way of dealing with the trauma, especially after what happened at the police station.'

'Why, what's happened?' asked Amy. 'Are the police charging the pit crew?'

'There are charges, but for attempted assault only,' said Helena quietly.

'What? Why?' demanded Poppy and Amy simultaneously.

'As best as I understand it, Inspector Pilbeam's definition of anything ... more serious involves a respectable woman being attacked by someone from the lower classes.'

'And I suppose we are not respectable, being working-class?' spat Poppy, her anger at the situation fuelled by the continuing relationship problems with her father. Was *Thunderbus* more important to him?

'There were other problems also, I'm afraid,' continued Helena. 'Apparently, there is an official caution on file about you, Poppy?'

'I'd forgotten about that,' gasped Poppy. 'That was back when Amy was attacked outside school.'

'Unfortunately, having a previous conviction seemed to make you, in the inspector's eyes, a suspicious and untrustworthy witness. I'm afraid any police record prejudices officialdom from the very beginning, no matter what the circumstances.'

'That caution shouldn't exist anyway,' fumed Poppy. 'What else did he say to get out of actually doing anything?'

'I'm afraid Inspector Pilbeam was sympathetic to the claims of the pit crew that you both acted provocatively,' murmured Helena, closing her eyes as though in pain.

'They were going to kill us!' exclaimed Amy.

'I know, my dears, but proving it is next to impossible. Simeon really tore him off a strip for that and he demanded that a more experienced officer should question the men individually, before they could concoct a story and hold to it. The inspector grudgingly agreed to bring in his superior, but he then proceeded to lock the men in adjoining cells where free communication is all too easy. I fear by the time they are questioned they will have created a plausible story, and shaking them from it will be next to impossible. Not that the inspector will try very hard.'

'So, they'll be free to do the same thing again in the future?' demanded Poppy.

'Please be assured that the pit crew will never work here again, and indeed, they will find it difficult to procure employment with any other pit crew across the country. These things travel fast.'

Poppy leapt up and limped around the room in agitation. 'And that's it? One assault charge which will probably result in a month inside – if that – and we don't even matter? We're just dismissed as working-class slags?'

Helena bit her lip, deeply distressed. Her voice, when she spoke, trembled slightly. 'I'm sorry, Poppy. Simeon did his best, believe me, but the police are reluctant to prosecute men accused of such crimes. We have very little protection, despite the law.' She looked away, her body shaking. Neither Poppy nor Amy noticed.

'Little protection?' raged Poppy. 'We have none at all. In future, we'd better do it ourselves. We'll make sure we always have something to use as a weapon hidden away in our clothing – something like a sharp screwdriver; that would work.'

'I'm sorry, I really am,' murmured Helena as she stood up. She didn't look at the girls as she walked to the door, so neither saw her tears as she hastily slipped through. 'I know how you feel, truly I do, and I am sorry.' Then she was gone.

Simeon had to move quickly to find and hire a new pit crew. Introducing them at such a late stage, with the race barely a week away, would have been bad at any time; given the behaviour and dismissal of the previous team, it made the transition even more fraught.

Amy brought the matter up with Poppy one evening after everyone else had left for the day. It was late and the electric lighting had been turned off in the workshop to save money, so the place was lit only by the old gas lamps which flickered and spat out long, oddly-shaped shadows. Poppy and Amy had stayed to paint the team number onto *Thunderbus*. 'It doesn't have to be artistic,' Simeon had explained. 'Just large and clear enough to be seen from a distance.'

'What do you think of the new team?' asked Amy casually as she painted the numbers onto *Thunderbus*. She glanced up at not receiving an answer and saw that Poppy was removing a small satchel from the old desk that stood at the back of the workshop. 'Poppy?'

Poppy shrugged as she opened the satchel. 'They can't be any worse than the last lot.'

'They're not as experienced, though. Clive and

123

Michael haven't even worked in a crew before.'

'Neither have we, if it comes to that, but they understand their duties well enough.' Poppy pulled out various small items from the satchel and began slotting them together. Amy peered at them in the gloom, trying to guess what Poppy was building. Poppy was extremely dexterous with her one hand and had developed coping strategies to compensate for her missing arm when performing many tasks.

'Michael seems nice enough,' continued Amy.

'Yes, I noticed you like him,' said Poppy in a flat tone. 'A tall and well-built frame seems to be your thing.'

'I was only saying he seems nice,' muttered Amy as she glanced at Poppy's tall, well-built frame.

'You said that about Dale.'

'You're not saying all men are the same, are you?'

'Maybe. They all think the same way, that's for sure.' An uneasy pause descended; Poppy was still hurt over her father's actions after the attack, and his subsequent refusal to talk about it. There was little she could do about that, however, and so she returned to the topic now bothering her considerably. 'Do you like him? Michael, I mean. Really like him?'

'I just don't know, Poppy. He makes me laugh and he is good-looking, but sometimes I feel …'

'What?'

'That I'm not ready, or it isn't right, somehow; not right for me, I mean, but I don't know why. Do you think he's good-looking and nice?'

'Yes to the first, not sure about the second.'

'Well, don't you like any of the crew?'

Poppy shrugged. 'I don't know. Well, I do think Christopher is nice,' she said, mentioning the young man who had special care for the suspension, 'but I feel … odd thinking about him that way. I'm not sure about anything, really.'[28]

'It's all so confusing,' agreed Amy. 'We were always told at school that you grow up and marry and have children, but then you get … odd feelings and you just don't know what to think or where you stand.' She glanced over at her friend and saw the uncertainty in Poppy's face. 'Let's not worry about it yet,' she added. 'After all, we have the race to complete first.' She turned back to *Thunderbus* and finished her painting. 'There. What do you think?'

Poppy backed away towards the rear wall, looking at *Thunderbus* which now had a large white number six on each side. 'Interesting number. When you turn

---

[28] In the privacy of her diary, Poppy opened up on her confusion from being attracted to male and female alike. The social pressure on a woman to become a wife and mother was all-encompassing and almost impossible to resist, given that this lifestyle was – and is – seen as "normal" while absolutely anything else is deemed "unnatural".

it upside down, it becomes something else.'

'I hope *Thunderbus* isn't going to finish the race upside down,' exclaimed Amy as she put the lid back on the paint pot and wiped her hands on a cloth. She looked at Poppy and saw she was once again working on the mysterious bits and pieces taken from the satchel. 'What have you got there?'

'A new leg brace. It's larger than my old one and far more powerful.'

'Where did you get it?'

'I designed it and asked the local blacksmith to make the parts.'

'I would have helped you, if you wanted,' said Amy, her voice revealing her disappointment that Poppy hadn't asked.

'I know, but we've been busy with *Thunderbus* and I didn't want to distract you from that. We can't afford to lose any time. That's why I asked the blacksmith.'

'How can you afford it? I mean, it's not as if we're getting paid that much. We get our keep and a roof over our heads, of course, but the actual money is negligible.'

'He did it for free when I smiled at him. I think he's sweet on me.'

'Poppy! You say men are all the same, yet you use them to get what you want!'

Poppy shrugged, though she did go red in the face. 'I never said I wouldn't use that to my advantage. Besides, the entire village is behind us, or at least they're behind Simeon and *Thunderbus*. That probably had more to do with it.'

'Oh, give over,' exclaimed Amy. 'It was Wednesday you went down there, wasn't it? I wondered why you were wearing your best dress that afternoon – the really short one that stops just above your ankles. The one that's really tight around that huge bust of yours!'

'Can I help it if nature compensated for the missing arm and weak knee by blessing me in other ways?' asked Poppy, jiggling her chest under Amy's nose and making her friend blush. 'And what nature missed, technology can fix. Hence the new brace.'

Poppy quickly assembled the last few pieces of the brace. It looked like a piece of tiny scaffolding, a gantry of cogs and gears designed to support and assist Poppy's knee movements. There was even a tiny motor incorporated into the design to help move the linkages, powered by a series of flat round batteries embedded in a garter-like belt that lay on the table next to the brace. Any good smith needed more than a passing knowledge of electrical engineering to stay in business, and the village blacksmith was very good indeed.

'There, that should do,' said Amy as she helped tighten the nuts and bolts into place.

'Excellent.' Poppy pulled her dress up to her knee and stripped off her existing brace, aware of Amy blushing as she did so. She slipped her foot though the brace and pulled it up and around her knee before hitching her dress up even higher to fix the battery strap around her solid thigh, connecting the batteries to the brace by a few wires. Amy wordlessly handed over a small screwdriver so Poppy could tighten the connections.

'All done,' said Poppy, looking up directly into Amy's face and grinning wickedly.

Amy started, as though waking from a dream. 'Er, good, right. Um, how are you going to test it?'

'A simple walk should do it,' replied Poppy. She pivoted and strolled around the workshop. In the silent evening air, a slight whine could be heard from the new brace as the gears moved in smooth precision. Poppy wobbled slightly as she walked, getting used to the tension and reaction of the brace, but within minutes she was striding around the workshop with long, graceful movements.

'Poppy,' exclaimed Amy. 'You're not limping anymore!'

Poppy smiled and looked at a heavy, empty oil drum in front of her, waiting to be taken away by the local garage when it delivered the new batch of drums. She balanced on her left leg and pushed against the drum with her right foot. It wobbled slightly under the pressure but was too solid to be moved any further. She swapped legs and pushed again. The brace whined ever louder at the increased pressure and work required of it. Poppy hitched her dress up so she could see the brace working, revealing the perfect movement of the gearing system as it responded to the forces acting upon it. With a sudden, unexpected thump, the drum was shoved backward before toppling over.

'What do you think?' asked Poppy.

'Very impressive,' coughed Amy.

'Do you mean the brace or the leg?' asked Poppy, moving closer. They were alone, the gaslight flickered gently, and the moment was suddenly heavy with an indefinable, warm pulsing sensuality.

'Have either of you seen the spare throttle cable?' barked Mr Orpington as he strode into the garage.

'No, yes, I mean, er, what?' gibbered Amy, jumping a good six inches into the air.

'It's over there,' hissed Poppy, feeling she could quite cheerfully use the cable to throttle her father's neck.

'Good. I want to get this fixed tonight.'

'But it doesn't need replacing,' began Amy,

before Poppy nudged her.

'Then we'll leave you to it,' replied Poppy. 'We'll go back home. Alone,' she added in an undertone to Amy.

'You may as well stay and help, as you're here,' said Mr Orpington, striding around *Thunderbus*. 'It should only take an hour or two.'

'Yes, right, fine,' muttered Poppy, the mood completely broken. She wasn't entirely certain what would have happened had her father not walked in, but she was certain that she wanted to find out. At the earliest opportunity.

CHAPTER SEVEN

Race day drew ever closer, spurring the new pit crew to work even harder to perfect their roles and to ensure *Thunderbus* was mechanically sound. Finally, on the day before, *Thunderbus* was loaded onto the back of a flat-bed truck, ready to be taken to the track. Mr Orpington supervised the loading himself, fretting all the while in case the car slipped and fell from the truck. 'Easy now, easy!' he shouted to the loaders as they operated the winch.

'They know what they're doing, Robert,' admonished Simeon gently. 'They have loaded my racing cars several times in the past.'

'Yes, but they were lighter steam vehicles; they have no experience of this,' retorted Mr Orpington, staring manically at the truck. 'Is there sufficient clearance at each end for *Thunderbus*? You know steam cars are a lot shorter; are they accounting for that? If the exhaust gets ripped off, or the front end is damaged, we're finished. You hear that? Finished!'

Simeon looked in appeal at Poppy, who walked around the trailer. 'It's fine, Dad,' she said, soothing him as best she could. 'I can see right through to the other side of the garage. *Thunderbus* has room to spare at both ends.'

'Are those straps strong enough, though?' demanded her father. 'Are they strong enough to take the heavier weight? If they snap and *Thunderbus* falls off, it will be ruined. Ruined!'

'The load-bearing weight is two and a half tons, Dad,' said Poppy, as patiently as she could. Her father was becoming unbearable. 'More than enough for *Thunderbus*.'

'More than enough? More? That only leaves a tolerance of half a ton! That isn't enough! Are they new? Have they been used before? If so, they could have been weakened!' He paced back and forth, his eyes never leaving the back of the truck.

'They're brand new, bought especially for this job,' said one of the men as he eased the winch up another notch.

'You hear that, Dad? Brand new. There is nothing to worry about.'

'Have they been tested, though, have they been tested? Sometimes the factories make mistakes and they knowingly pass out shoddy goods! Has anyone tested the straps?'

'It's on, it's safe,' said the man in irritation, knocking off the winch. *Thunderbus* stood immobile on the truck, looking even more imposing than usual with the added height. Mr Orpington continued to worry as a large tarpaulin was laid over *Thunderbus* and strapped down with ropes, though what he feared from a large sheet being draped over the car was uncertain at best.

'Right, everyone, are you all packed?' asked Simeon, briskly rubbing hands. 'Yes? Good. We meet at the racetrack tomorrow at one o'clock. Your charabanc taking you to your hotel leaves from the side gate in ten minutes, so go and get your things and don't be late. See you all tomorrow!'

A chorus of respectful replies wafted out as Simeon left the garage, with only Poppy and her father not answering. Mr Orpington was still staring intently at *Thunderbus* on the back of the truck, while Poppy was looking puzzled. Talbot noticed her expression and asked what the problem was.

'Aren't we all going to the hotel together?' she asked.

'Of course not,' replied Talbot, impatiently. 'We go to our hotel, Lord Simeon and Lady Helena will go to theirs.'

'Oh, we're at different hotels?' asked Amy, creating a ripple of amused laughter in the rest of the pit crew.

'You want to stay at the best hotel in town, be my guest,' smirked Talbot in an unpleasant manner. 'I'm sure it will only cost you more money than you'll earn in two years.'

'Oh, of course,' mumbled Amy, going red.

'Thank you for explaining in such a pleasant manner,' said Poppy, the sarcasm dropping like boulders in a landslide. 'I do appreciate, in my weak and womanly manner, how we are too stupid not to know things that have never been explained to us. It must be so wonderful to be a man and to be born with all this knowledge already in your heads. Truly, you are gods amongst us.'

'That'll do Poppy,' snapped her father, his face tetchy as he continued to stare at the truck.

'Come on, let's get our gear before the charabanc leaves,' said one of the pit crew, hoping to defuse the situation before an argument could start. It was no secret that Poppy and her father were getting increasingly irritable with each other, and the relationship between Talbot and the two girls was also brittle.

'Don't you move,' commanded Mr Orpington to the truck driver, who went by the nickname of Digger.

'You what?' asked Digger, his face flushing in anger.

'I'm coming with you, to keep an eye on things,' replied Mr Orpington.

'Like hell! This is my rig, hired to take one vehicle to the hotel, and after that to the track.

Nothing was said about passengers.'

'It's my car so I'm travelling with you,' insisted Mr Orpington.

'No, you ain't,' said Digger. 'Here, what's your game? You keep away from me!'

Poppy had to stifle a gasp as her father strode towards the driver, lifting his hand. She sighed in relief as he reached past Digger and pulled the truck's key from the ignition barrel in the cab. She had enjoyed a quick joke with Digger earlier in the day and she suspected it was purely her father's attitude which had made the driver protest against a passenger. She remembered her scripture lessons at Sunday school, and the proverb that a gentle answer turns away wrath. It was a lesson her father could do with learning.

'You give those back,' demanded Digger, striding after Mr Orpington, who stopped so suddenly that the driver bounced off his immovable bulk.

'You'll get them back when we leave, and that will be in ten minutes sharp.'

Digger looked ready to protest again but he shrank back as Mr Orpington loomed over him, intimidating him with his size. 'Lord Simeon will hear about this,' he muttered, but it was clear there was nothing he could do.

Squirming in embarrassment, Poppy pulled

Amy's sleeve and they slipped out to grab their own bags from their shared house.

'Your dad's getting nervous,' whispered Amy once they were out of earshot. 'He seems to be getting worse each day.'

'I know,' said Poppy, miserably, as she opened the door of their cottage and walked in. 'I just don't know what to do.'

'Not much you can do, except wait and see what happens tomorrow,' replied Amy as they picked up their packs. 'Hopefully everything will be fine and he'll be back to normal after the race.'

They rushed to the hall's side entrance and boarded the waiting charabanc, which quickly filled up with the rest of the pit crew. They set off, followed by a truck containing the tools and spare parts, while bringing up the rear was the truck carrying *Thunderbus* itself. Poppy's father rode in the double cab with the driver and driver's mate, determined to never let *Thunderbus* out of his sight.

Poppy wasn't sure what to expect from the hotel as she had never been in one before, but she was surprised when they disembarked next to a long line of rather shabby houses. Looking at the various signs hanging from chains or painted onto posts, she saw they were actually guest houses. *Bide-A-Wee* sat next to *The Jolly Traveller* which abutted *Mount Pleasant*.

Their home-away-from-home was advertised by a rusting, tetanus-coated chain as *Alpine Air*. Amy opened the front door and a gust of putrid wind covered them. With some trepidation, the pit crew entered.

The small lobby they found themselves in was as shabby and cracked as the exterior. A tiny reception desk lurked in one corner, behind which a greasy, stained door rattled on its hinges as it was buffeted by the passage of violent air currents which blew continually from the back of the house. A door immediately on the left had a cheap, corroded tin sign nailed to it, announcing it to be the visitors' lounge. The next doorframe along was missing the actual door, revealing within a dining room that looked as warm and welcoming as a crypt.

'No drink, no food, no women visitors allowed in private rooms,' snapped a voice, causing the group to jump. An elderly woman had somehow materialised behind the grubby reception counter. She was wrapped in several layers of dirty clothing, while her lank grey hair uncoiled down her dingy brow like strands of greasy rope. She glared at the pit crew and breathed out an enormous quantity of gin-soaked cigarette smoke, reminding Poppy of a pile of burning tyres she had once seen in a scrapyard.

'No men visitors in private rooms, neither,' she

wheezed again, realising there were women in the group. 'This is a high-class establishment.'

'Oh, first rate,' replied Poppy, staring in horror at the walls stained yellow with years of nicotine poisoning. The faded and grubby carpet looked as though it was dissolving into the fetid floor, while the stink of the woman's cigarettes, powerful as they were, barely smothered the persistent background smell of old cabbage and damp feet.

'Sign here,' coughed the woman, hacking up a gigantic lump of phlegm which she chewed on with relish before swallowing it back down. 'And make it quick; I have to get back to the dinner.'

'Is that smell the dinner?' asked Talbot in revulsion.

'Aye; it's included in the price, take it or leave it, and payment is in full, up front, no refunds,' snapped the owner of the *Alpine Air* as she honked into an overflowing handkerchief which she then stuffed up the sleeve of her grubby cardigan with an audible squelching sound.

'We'll leave it,' said the entire pit crew with one voice.

That evening, after a meal found in a cheap café that at least had the attraction of not being prepared by their revolting hostess, the crew returned early to the

Alpine View to ensure they were not locked out. The owner had made it clear that the front door would be bolted promptly at nine o'clock and anyone arriving after that time would find themselves spending the night huddled under the front porch.

The crew was too depressed to stay up chatting in the damp and mouldering lounge, and one by one they found their rooms in the confusing rabbit warren of cracked, uneven extensions built onto the back of the original building. Behind them, the old woman hacked and coughed and glared as she made sure each guest shut their door and turned the key in the lock, thus preventing any outbreak of immoral behaviour.

Amy found her room, turned to say goodnight to Poppy, and leapt back as the old woman surged down the corridor as though floating on a cloud of righteousness to physically interpose her body between the two young women. 'Goodnight,' squeaked Amy as she fled inside her room. The crone nodded in satisfaction as the key turned in the lock.

'No immorality here,' she coughed, giving Poppy a direct glare. 'No opening your door to anyone, especially men, until the maid knocks in the morning with your towel.'

'You have a maid?' queried Poppy in disbelief as she was ushered down the corridor by the woman's cloud of tobacco and gin, which seemed to be a physical entity in its own right.

'You'll have a towel in the morning,' repeated the woman, ignoring the question. 'This is yours. Now lock your door.'

'What if there's a fire in the night?' asked Poppy.

'No chance of a fire here, this is a safe place,' snapped the woman, her cigarette quivering in outrage and scattering mounds of hot ash in a wide vicinity.

Poppy decided she had no energy to argue; the old woman seemed to be sucking the life and hope from her. Or maybe it was the *Alpine Air* doing it? The decrepit, stinking building and the decrepit, stinking owner seemed to be in an eerie parallel relationship with each other; did one affect the other, or were they both degenerating independently?

Poppy walked in and locked the door behind her before looking around. The room was sparsely furnished with a narrow bed, a single hook for clothes on the damp wall, and a single kitchen chair that wobbled under the persistent draught blowing in from under the door. She decided against the risk of actually sitting in it and instead sat on the edge of the bed, which sagged with a long, damp sigh which almost obscured the mutterings of the old woman as she wheezed away up the corridor. Silence fell. The room was at the very back of the house, well away from the main road, and yet there was no peace in the quietness; the air had the uneasy stillness of a recently filled shroud.

A strange gnawing sound came from the window. Poppy went across and opened the cheap curtains which were so transparent as to be almost invisible. The feeble light from her gas bracket fell on something just below the window, something brown and wet, with a long tail and sharp teeth. Poppy looked down at the rat chewing on the rotten wood of the window ledge. The rat glanced up at the human.

'You can bugger off,' said Poppy. 'I don't know why you're trying to break in, anyway; you're better off out there.' The rat's nose twitched as though in agreement. Turning gracefully on the window sill, it jumped a few inches into the darkness and hurtled away as though flying through the air. Poppy stared, taken aback at what seemed to be a remarkable act of levitation by her rodent visitor until she realised the ground level outside her room was unusually high, or to put it another way, the entire back extension was sunk into the ground rather than having been built on top of it. Probably the owner had viewed proper foundations as being an unnecessary expense.

'Sod it,' muttered Poppy. She had been told not to open her door until daylight and she had no intention

141

of breaking the injunction. Instead, she grabbed her pack of clothes, opened the window, swung her leg out onto the high concrete walkway outside, and wriggled out. Amy's room was the next but one. Poppy slipped by her neighbour's, which seemed to be empty, and stopped at the next window along. She tapped it gently and hissed Amy's name.

After a few seconds, the curtains opened and Amy's astonished face peered out. 'Poppy! What are you doing out there?'

'I'm waiting for a number seven bus,' answered Poppy, rolling her eyes.

'You what?'

'Open the window, will you? I want to come in.'

'You know we're not allowed to have people in our rooms,' whispered Amy.

'Amelia Abberly, if you think I'm sleeping alone in a moist mausoleum with rats trying to eat their way in, you can think again,' exclaimed Poppy. 'Now open the bloody window!'

'Do you really think Dad will get better after the race?' asked Poppy after she had settled on the edge of the bed.

'I don't know,' said Amy. 'He's getting ever more agitated each day. Some of the crew have been complaining about it amongst themselves.' Amy braced herself for a protest from Poppy, but none came. 'Are you all right, Poppy?'

Poppy shrugged, looking uncertain in the dim light. 'I don't know, Amy. He's changing. He's drifting away each day, obsessed by the race and the car. He keeps pushing me away whenever I try to talk to him about anything not related to *Thunderbus*.'

'Maybe he'll be back to his old self after the race,' mumbled Amy, who suspected the father-daughter relationship had deteriorated past anyone's ability to fix it, though she didn't want to upset Poppy by saying so.

Poppy sighed, blinking tears from her eyes while looking at her friend. 'As long as you're always there, that's all I ask.'

'You, too.' Amy smiled, her own eyes glistening. She doused the spluttering gas flame and the two girls snuggled down together, their noses brushing each other, until Poppy moved forward and kissed Amy fully yet gently on the lips.

'Poppy!'

'I've wanted to do that for a long time.'

'I've wanted you to do that for a long time,' replied Amy, happily. They kissed again, their bodies pressing together, Poppy's hand slowly moving Amy's nightdress aside at the shoulder until Amy broke away and buried herself in Poppy's chest. 'Just hold me, Poppy; I'm too scared to do anything else tonight.'

Despite feeling amorous enough to ravish half the hotel, Poppy kissed Amy's forehead in gentle affection and did as Amy asked, cuddling her under the cover of the blanket until they fell asleep.

Early the next morning, the *Thunderbus* team left for the race. The journey to the Sussex track took over three hours because of heavy traffic, so they were late arriving and the whole area was already busy. Originally, the racetrack had been for horses but it had been adapted and extended for cars as motor racing increased in popularity.

Simeon's limousine had caught up with them on the road and it now led the way to their paddock through the melee of cars, racing drivers, manufacturer's representatives and mechanics. Around them, the other teams had already unloaded their cars and were checking over every part of them to ensure they were ready for the race. The sound of hissing turbines filled the air, while steam periodically rose in small jets from various radiator grills.

'Damn that delay,' muttered Talbot as he jumped out of the charabanc. 'We've barely got time to unload the car, never mind prepare it properly.'

'Don't forget; the advantage of petrol is that you just start and go,' said Simeon, looking sick with worry, though he tried to disguise it under a wide smile. 'It takes far less preparation than a steam engine. And on a small race like this one, we don't really need to warm the engine too much. We'll just have to rely on Robert's engineering.'

'Er, explain again how the race actually works?' whispered Amy as the pit crew swung open the side of the maintenance truck to reveal the spare parts and tools. 'Does everyone just line up on the track and go?'

'Weren't you listening to the briefings?' asked Poppy in surprise.

Amy shrugged. 'Not really. I ignored the details about the race itself except for when it related to the engine and the pit stops.'

'Amy has always been happiest when tinkering with the engine, I suspect,' observed Helena. She was keeping slightly to one side as she had no practical role in the paddock.

'The race itself is quite simple,' explained Poppy. 'There have already been practice laps done by most of the drivers over the past few days, and those with the fastest times are allowed at the front when the race starts. It's then simply a case of first over the line after completing all the laps is the winner.'

'But we haven't set a lap time in *Thunderbus*,' objected Amy.

'No, we've entered on a wildcard,' said Helena. 'That means we just have to turn up and compete, though of course we must start at the back behind those who posted the slowest lap times.'

'Are there many other wildcard entries?' asked Poppy, scanning the flowing crowd of spectators who were now pouring into the stands, eager for the race to begin.

'Not as many as there used to be. It was a good way of getting your foot in the door at one point, but the racing world is something of an exclusive club for the wealthy and idle. Even the wildcard entries cost a lot of money, now. Simeon had to call in some favours to get one for your father.'

'You're not saying Simeon is idle, are you?' asked Poppy, looking at Simeon as he fussed around the truck holding *Thunderbus*.

Helena hesitated before answering. 'I do sometimes feel he could be doing more with his gifts than playing with his cars and whatever else takes his interest.'

'Has he got many other interests?'

'Yes, but they come and go. In fact, he hasn't been particularly active in the racing scene recently. I suspect it was *Thunderbus* and its possibilities that drew him back in so firmly.'

'Do you mind about that?'

'As I say, he could use his talents more wisely, for the greater good. But men are all the same; nothing more than small boys underneath it all. You don't look convinced, Poppy?'

Poppy shrugged. 'I was just thinking of something I read in a magazine article not long ago. It said the traditional gender roles are being challenged by modern life as more women are going to work in factories and offices, taking on the roles usually done by men.'

'Huh,' muttered Amy. 'Try telling my parents that.'

'There have been a few female pioneers, like the aviatrix Lady Daphne Mandeville,' said Helena.

'She could afford to be a pioneer,' replied Poppy. 'She had a rich father, and because she was titled all her anti-social behaviour was excused as upper-class eccentricity. I'm talking about those women from poorer communities and the middle classes taking up new roles. Unfortunately, one aspect associated with this change is the growing idea that if women can do any job, then men are irrelevant. A consequence of this is the growing trend in treating men as nothing more than overgrown schoolboys. And if men are continually told by society that they are stupid and adolescent, then they will increasingly *become* stupid and adolescent.'

'Doesn't sound very likely to me,' said Amy.

'Why do most little girls play with dolls and prams? Why do most boys go running about and climbing trees? Because this is what society demands of them, and as we develop we pick up on what sort of behaviour is expected and then we usually conform to it. Very rarely can you rebel because you don't even realise there is anything to rebel against. It all becomes a self-fulfilling prophecy.'

'Your reading material is rather ... wide-ranging,' observed Helena. 'I must make an effort to read more myself. It seems I am missing out on quite a lot of new ideas.'[29]

'Now then, everyone, stand back,' barked Simeon in excitement. 'We are about to reveal *Thunderbus* for the very first time! Exhilarating, isn't it? Make a space at the back end of the trailer, please.'

Poppy looked around. A few drivers from rival teams were idly observing them, but most continued

---

[29] Unfortunately, we still experience today this same cultural conformity in which boys and girls – as well as different classes, ethnicities, etc. – are treated and moulded, all of which sustain the unfair status quo. Despite my best efforts, I have been unable to identify the specific article Poppy mentions. A great shame, for clearly it had a profound effect upon her.

to work on their own vehicles. She turned back to the trailer and watched as two of the crew finished unlashing the tarpaulin that covered *Thunderbus* and rolled it back in quick, economical movements, revealing the car. This caused a few more people to take an interest as *Thunderbus* was far larger than any of the other cars at the track. In fact, when compared to the sleek two-seater sports cars purring around them, it seemed rather brutal. The steam-powered cars were aerodynamic darts, built low to the ground in order to slice through the air. *Thunderbus*, with its huge bodywork and harsh edges, had enormous ground clearance and simply swatted the air aside.

'What's that, then?' shouted a voice from the crowd as the winch on the truck was activated and *Thunderbus* eased down from the trailer, watched by the fretful crew. Nerves were beginning to affect all of them.

'This is the future,' replied Simeon to the unknown voice in the crowd. 'Be proud you were here to witness history in the making.'

'With that thing?' asked another voice. 'It's like a brick on wheels!'

'All competitors to the starting line, all competitors to the starting line,' announced a voice from an automated loudspeaker fitted in a nearby tree.

'Start her up, Robert,' said Talbot, having released the straps that secured *Thunderbus* to the winch.

'Last call for all competitors; if you are not at your allocated place in five minutes you will be disqualified,' shouted the loudhailer from the tree.

'You'll never start that in time,' shouted another voice from the crowd. 'You need a few minutes to let the turbines warm up.'

The voice, and indeed the crowd, was silenced as Mr Orpington started the car, *Thunderbus* giving its customary roar as it woke. The engine noise deafened the spectators and caused the line of steam-powered vehicles flowing past to stutter as each individual driver jumped at the unholy sound.

Thunderbus' pit crew grinned at each other, their anxiety gone as they saw the reaction from the crowd; some were startled, some turned pale and a few even sprinted away in fright. Even the seasoned drivers, used to the danger and drama of racing, stared in astonishment and apprehension at the flames and thunderous noise coming from the huge black car.

Mr Orpington hastily pulled on his leather driving helmet, goggles and thick leather gauntlets before backing out of the paddock and onto the track, joining the line of cars heading for the starting line.

Poppy watched the incongruous black vehicle, longer, taller and wider than anything else on the road, snarling its way along. It was like watching an alligator swimming amongst a school of beautiful silver fish. Sooner or later, something was going to be devoured.

'Come on, everyone, up to our observation point,' said Simeon, giddy with excitement. The entire group rushed up to a stand that had been built on top of a small rise, giving a reasonable view of most of the course. From here, each team could watch the race and be ready to rush back to their paddocks ready for the pit stops.

'All competitors are now lined up,' squawked the loudhailer. 'At the front of the grid is Lord Harry St Simon in car number fourteen. Next is the Honourable Peter Honeycombe, car number thirty-eight.' The voice continued, listing each competitor, until only one was left. 'At the back, on its debut, sponsored by Lord Simeon Pallister, driven and owned by Robert Orpington, we have *Thunderbus*!'

Poppy and the pit crew cheered while Simeon waved at the crowd. Puzzled, frightened and outraged faces were swinging from *Thunderbus* to Simeon and his group. No one had ever seen or heard a car like it, and no one knew how to react.

'This is it,' muttered Poppy to Amy. 'Everything

we've worked for, everything Dad has wanted.' She looked at the distant cars waiting at the starting line and almost found herself praying to a God she didn't believe in for protection during the race, for she couldn't shake a sense of foreboding that had suddenly settled on her like a black shroud.

Poppy squinted into the distance and watched a tiny figure unfurl a large flag, wave it theatrically, and then drop the flag down. The cars surged forward, those at the front sprinting ahead while those at the back weaved around each other, trying to overtake and keep the leaders in sight.

A few moments after the cars began to move, the sounds of the race drifted over. This mostly consisted of the hissing noise associated with a steam turbine working at full capacity, from which racing tracks derived their collective nickname of the snake pit. The sound of tyres on the road, the changing of gears for those vehicles that had gears rather than a turbine drive shaft, and the occasional tapping from the engines, completed the eerie soundscape.

Behind these traditional racing noises, however, was the dull rumble of *Thunderbus*. Poppy saw a few people in the crowd look up in puzzlement at the bright blue sky, wondering if they were in for a storm, confused by the lack of dark clouds. No one had ever heard a noise like it from a car before, but to Poppy and the rest of the pit crew, it meant *Thunderbus* was snorting impatiently for a clear road. It wanted to run.

Before it could, however, it needed room to manoeuvre. The pack of cars was dense and tight at the back, and already the leading vehicles were almost out of sight on the first curve of the racetrack. Most of the cars at the back were older and slower than the leaders, though there were also a few powerful roadsters and sports cars caught in the crush, driven by novices or those who just weren't very good at racing.

Thunderbus growled its way through the throng, the enormous nose snarling in contempt. Many of the rival drivers swerved in surprise and apprehension at the ferocious rumble coming from behind them, clearing a path that *Thunderbus* could prod its way through, but a line of four cars driving abreast of each other at the front were made of sterner stuff and refused to yield any space.

Mr Orpington slammed the clutch down to disengage the engine from the gearbox and then pressed hard on the accelerator. The engine roared in anger and one of the cars ahead wobbled madly at the fearsome noise before veering off to one side. Mr Orpington quickly re-engaged the gears, the revs

153

tickling the higher end of the scale as *Thunderbus* surged forward and claimed the new space for itself. This left five cars running equally to each other as they entered the first long, gentle corner of the track, a bend that could only accommodate four cars running abreast. One was going to have to drop back, yet none were going to give way.

'Come on, Dad, come on,' whispered Poppy in apprehension. There was a shriek and clank of something mechanical as Mr Orpington clashed the gears, making Poppy wince. She didn't want to think what would happen if her father made a bad gear change. The damage could rip the gearbox and engine apart, and that would be the end of everything; her father's dream, his patents, their life as it was. Everything depended on how he performed in the race and how well *Thunderbus* could hold its own, yet already, right at the start, panic was setting in and *Thunderbus* was falling behind, unable to compete, her father unable to hold on, the mental and physical pressure too much …

With a grunt and a roar, the gears engaged properly and *Thunderbus* launched itself forward, outpacing the other four cars in the line. By the time it reached the middle of the long, flowing curve, *Thunderbus* was more than two car lengths ahead of its nearest rival. As the curve straightened, Mr

Orpington changed gear again and *Thunderbus* pulled effortlessly away, increasing the distance between itself and the back of the pack.

There was now almost half a lap between Mr Orpington and the race leaders, and past experience decreed that this sort of a gap was too much for any car to overcome. *Thunderbus* sneered at past experience, the engine now singing rather than snarling, though it was still a song of power and menace, a mechanical opera of war.

The gap between *Thunderbus* and the leaders grew ever smaller, the huge black car eating up the straights and gentle curves despite being hampered by the awful steering system. It took several laps to do it, but eventually Mr Orpington had gained on the leaders of the pack and was approaching the rear bumper of the last car in the group.

'He's almost there!' yelled Amy in excitement.

'Yes, but he's got to come in now,' fretted Simeon. 'It's time for his pit stop.'

The pit crew turned and rushed back down the bank, Poppy slightly behind as she paused to look for her father on the final bend, to make sure he was all right. By the time she reached the paddock, the crew members were organizing themselves for their appointed tasks.

'Ready, everyone!' called out Simeon as he stood

at the side of the track with a scarlet flag, the signal for *Thunderbus* to come in. He waved the flag energetically before running to one side as *Thunderbus* turned off the road and entered the paddock. Within seconds, William and Clive had jacked up the vehicle and were quickly but methodically checking the steering and tyres. At the back end of the car, Michael released the petrol down the long pipe and into *Thunderbus*' fuel tank. The petrol sloshed heavily downward, some slopping over the sides of the car and spilling onto the ground. At the same time, Amy swung open the bonnet to check the engine while Christopher scampered around the entire vehicle as he checked the suspension. All bellowed questions at Mr Orpington on how the car was handling, if anything was causing concern, and what the dials in the cockpit were showing.

Poppy watched her father cough dirt from his mouth and shout back the answers. 'The oil pressure has dropped just a little, and the coolant level is showing a minimal loss of fluid. Steering has held up so far, and so has the suspension.'

'Front tyres almost shredded!' shouted William in alarm. 'Clive, take the off side, I'll do the near side!' They heaved on the special levers that quickly released each wheel from the car.

156

'Damn it, what has caused that much damage so quickly?' exclaimed Simeon, frowning at the ragged tyres.

'It's the heavy steering and ridiculous body weight,' snorted Talbot. 'Just as I warned you back on day one!'

'The car is fine,' growled Mr Orpington, wiping a gloved hand over his face. He removed his racing goggles and his exposed skin peeked out, pink and clean, against the grimy mouth, jaw and forehead. 'But I've had to hurl it into the corners to make up the ground on the leaders. That is why the tyres are failing.'

'Then take it easy, Robert, for the Lord's sake,' said Simeon. 'You've practically caught up with those in front. Don't throw yourself into the bends; take them easily and smoothly, distribute your weight evenly, and let *Thunderbus* do its work on the straights.'

'That is where the race will be won,' agreed Talbot. 'On the straights. You'll lose it in the corners if you keep taking them so hard. Remember, we only have one spare set of tyres for the entire race.'

Mr Orpington nodded grudgingly. Poppy, who had to stand to one side as her missing arm made her too slow to act as part of the team, had the role of driver refreshment. She poured a glass of water and took it over to her father, who swallowed it down in one go. 'Are you going to be able to finish, Dad?' she shouted over the noise of the race and the sounds of the pit crew. 'You look exhausted.'

'I'm fine.'

'Are you sure?'

'Damn it, Poppy, you heard what I said,' he snapped.

Poppy stepped back in shock; she had often been on the receiving end of her father's temper, but to have it happen when she was trying to show her concern for him marked a new deterioration in their relationship. At that moment, William and Clive both leapt aside, dragging the front-end jack with them, and shouted, 'Clear!' The new wheels were on and fastened.

'Suspension checked and cleared!' yelled Christopher, releasing the handle on the jack and letting *Thunderbus*' rear end sink back to ground level.

'Refuelling complete and cleared!' called Michael, locking the fuel cap down and hurrying to one side.

'All clear, go, go, go!' shouted Simeon. The crew leapt out of the way as *Thunderbus* growled out of the paddock and nosed back into the race, leaving behind huge splashes of petrol, oil, two wheels with frayed tyres and Poppy's frozen face.

Helena put a comforting hand on Poppy's arm as they walked back to the stands. 'Your father is under a lot of stress.'

'I know,' muttered Poppy, her eyes glistening, 'but it's not just that. Every day he seems to get worse. Everything now is about that car. He's become obsessed by it.'

'I'm afraid that is often how people become successful,' said Helena, sympathetically. 'By obsession, by working themselves relentlessly and by neglecting everything else in life. Success can be a cruel mistress, sometimes.'

'I hope I never see anything like it again,' muttered Poppy.

'I'll have a word with your father after the race,' promised Helena.

Poppy turned her attention back to the track. At first, she couldn't see *Thunderbus* anywhere, though she could still hear the growl of the engine. It wasn't at the back, or the middle, so where?

'He's at the front!' exclaimed Simeon. 'Now, if he can just stay there.'

Poppy looked towards the front of the cars and saw Simeon was right. The leaders of the race, having also come in for their pit stop, had lost their advantage as *Thunderbus* moved with astonishing speed to capture first place. With no cars in his way, her father had settled down and let the huge engine do the work for him.

'It's still going to be difficult,' observed Talbot. 'His racing skills are awful and he's getting worse. It must be the exhaustion of keeping *Thunderbus* on the road. Only the power of that engine is keeping him in the race.'

The crowd cheered in delight as the huge black car thundered along the next straight length of road, but as Talbot had observed, Mr Orpington's exhaustion and flagging driving skills were allowing the best of the competitors to stay in with a chance. On each straight *Thunderbus* would simply leave the other cars behind, but the gap was chased down at the corners where the lighter, nimbler vehicles could manoeuvre with a grace *Thunderbus* clearly lacked. Only sheer power was keeping *Thunderbus* in the lead.

Poppy gasped; one of the other cars, a dark red touring vehicle, was overtaking *Thunderbus* on the inside of a corner, despite the road ahead narrowing considerably. The driver took the corner well, showing his greater experience, but *Thunderbus* snarled and surged forward, its acceleration far more powerful than the red car, and its driver was helpless to get to the tapered road first and was forced to slam on his brakes as *Thunderbus* roared through.

As they emerged onto the wider road, the driver of the red car again demonstrated his skill and the superior steering of his vehicle and it seemed certain he would finally overtake, but as he approached the next bend the nose of his vehicle suddenly juddered from left to right.

'He's locked!' exclaimed Talbot in excitement. 'The brakes or the steering have gone – they can't take that sort of punishment!'

'He's going!' shouted a voice in the crowd. Whoops and cheers erupted, and some parts of the crowd even started chanting, 'Crash! Crash! Crash!' Bloodlust was in the air and Poppy saw the sport was far more brutal than she had realised. There was something elemental in the crowd that craved carnage and destruction – especially if it could be witnessed from a point of safety.

Poppy glanced back at the red car as it skidded off the road, the driver unable to hold the shuddering vehicle. It slammed into the blocks of straw that lined the road, partly for safety and partly to mark out of the track. With a seemingly slow, lazy flip, the car rotated up on end and slammed back down onto its roof. The force of the impact caused the car to bounce back up and incredibly it flipped a full length

161

again before crashing down for one final impact, this time on its side, where it came to rest.

Poppy stared at the car, fearing she would see the crushed remains of the driver, but then she saw the race stewards and some of the spectators running to a figure lying on the ground far behind the wreckage. She guessed the driver had been thrown out of the car on the first flip. He was gathered up, dazed and clutching his arm, but with the help of the stewards he was able to stagger off to a medical tent.

Poppy breathed out as she looked around for her father. The crash had worked in his favour as the rest of the racers had been forced to slow down considerably to avoid the crumpled red car, meaning *Thunderbus* was now half a lap ahead and was still increasing the distance. Even given her father's poor driving, he couldn't be caught; the petrol engine could run consistently at high speeds and he didn't need to come in for another pit stop, unlike the steam cars behind him. As long as *Thunderbus* didn't break down, or crash, it was certain to win.

After this, it was almost an anti-climax to watch *Thunderbus* take the number one spot, though the crowd loved the excitement of seeing the huge, strange-looking car hurtle past them at shockingly high speeds while the roar of the engine shook the ground and animated the crowd in a way the gentler steam engines couldn't match.

Poppy's thoughts focussed on her father and the way he had snapped at her during the pit stop. She wistfully imagined how happy he would be when he got back, how he would hug her and say he was sorry for his harsh reaction, but she suspected she was fooling herself with such hopes as she watched *Thunderbus* streak past the finishing flag, drawing even wilder cheers from the crowd.

Mr Orpington took the car for one final lap, waving at the crowd, before pulling into the paddock. The crowd surged forward, eager to see the team behind the car and to catch a glimpse of the driver. The race stewards, used to holding back the eager crowd from the winner, formed an impassive line around the paddock.

'Well done, Robert, well done!' exclaimed Simeon, pumping Mr Orpington's hand gleefully. 'That was the most incredible thing I have ever seen! I seriously believe we can win at Purley after that display.'

'Amazing run, amazing car,' echoed Talbot, patting Mr Orpington on the shoulder. Although he was stunned by the speed and power of *Thunderbus*, he was still uncertain that Mr Orpington would win anywhere else.

'Needs more work,' replied Mr Orpington after coughing out dust and dirt from his mouth. 'The steering is too much, the gear change is rough, and the engine is beginning to misfire. It will need to be stripped down and cleaned thoroughly.'

'Yes, yes, but that can wait, my dear chap,' waved Simeon, impatiently, 'I swear I've never seen a driver less interested in his win. Enjoy the moment, man!'

'No, we need to repair, to improve,' coughed Mr Orpington, swaying on his feet. Poppy looked at his strained, white face and saw how much *Thunderbus* had taken from him.

'You need to get to the podium and accept the winner's cup,' said Simeon, pointing in the direction of a small portable stage that had been set up in a wide clearing. The drivers who came second and third were already there, ready to take their consolation prizes. Neither looked very happy as they glared towards the Pallister paddock.

Poppy silently watched as Simeon and Talbot hustled their protesting driver to the podium, where he was forced to shake hands with the race officials. They at least seemed to be impressed and happy with *Thunderbus*, and they asked many eager questions about the car. Poppy supposed they were well aware of the reaction of the crowd, and they would be keen to get the car back again for another race.

She observed her father mounting the podium, being presented with the cup after a short speech by the leader of the race officials, and holding the cup aloft to the cheering crowds. Throughout the entire ceremony, he seemed distanced from the proceedings, as though his mind were on other things. Only when he was given a piece of paper did his face change as he registered complete shock.

'What's that?' asked Poppy of Helena.

'His winnings.' Helena smiled. 'Probably more money than he has ever seen in his life. You remember the new rule, that each driver wins a sum of money for being the lap leader? Your father led the way for a dozen laps. At twenty pounds for each lap, that makes two hundred and forty pounds. Plus four hundred for taking first place.'

'Is it enough to pay Simeon back?' asked Poppy while Amy gaped at the huge sum of money.

'No, though it is an excellent start,' replied Helena. 'To pay off everything will require the far greater rewards that will only be found with success at Purley. In any case, it was agreed that any initial winnings from today's event should stay in your father's pocket, regardless of the debt, to provide for both of you.'

'Does Purley also pay for each lap that you lead?'

'I have a feeling they may be forced to do so, after today.'

'Lady Helena, Lady Helena!' bellowed several voices. Poppy turned and saw a dozen men, all holding various recording devices, hurtling towards them. Brass cameras flashed as the photographers snapped everything and everyone at random. 'Any quotes on your husband's new car and driver?' A huge steel microphone was thrust under Helena's nose, connected by a brass cable to the phonogramme recording box held in the journalist's other hand.

'Ah, the press,' murmured Helena over her shoulder. 'This is something you will have to get used to, girls. The best way of dealing with them is to say "no comment" and refer it all to Simeon. They'll just make something up anyway. No comment, please see my husband for a full statement,' she said to the group. Placing her arms around Poppy and Amy, she swept them back into the paddock, away from the frenzy developing outside.

Inside the paddock, the scenes were just as chaotic. Custom demanded that the other drivers congratulate the winner, and while this was being observed in the corner where Poppy's father was now seated, it was clear some of the drivers were not happy about

Thunderbus' participation, or indeed the presence of a working-class driver.

'Shouldn't be allowed,' one driver was muttering in disgust to a friend. 'Totally against the character of the sport.'

'Speak for yourself,' said another. 'Racing is racing. If someone offered me a car like that to drive, I'd take his arm off for it. Right up to the bally elbow!'

'Decorum should have been observed,' snapped a third driver. 'The car should have been made available to one of us for testing and approval.' He gazed hungrily at *Thunderbus,* completely ignoring its driver and creator.

Helena shepherded the girls through the crowd, aware that Poppy was tensing in anger at the comments around her. She reached up to Poppy's broad shoulder and gave her a friendly, supporting squeeze. 'Try to maintain control, my dear,' she whispered.

'Why?' demanded Poppy, her voice low with anger.

'A lady should always be in control in public, no matter how much she gives way in private,' replied Helena.

'Yes, you've told me that often enough, but *why* do we have to maintain control? I expect what people actually mean is "don't make a scene, let the men sort it out." Wouldn't you agree?'

Helena opened her mouth to refute this before realising in slight horror that Poppy was correct; Helena was indeed trying to avoid a scene, despite the fact that the remarks from some of the drivers were undoubtedly unfair, selfish and petulant. 'I expect you'll tell me it is social conditioning at work, again,' she said, finally.

'It is,' said Poppy, emphatically. 'After all, there is no biological reason we can't answer back. We have equal intelligence and wit to do so, so why are we told not to? Especially when faced with complete arses like that?' Poppy glanced at Helena's troubled face and felt a pang of guilt at disturbing her. 'I do appreciate you looking after me, though, and in trying to polish my awful manners and personality, I really do,' she whispered, taking Helena's hand and giving it a quick squeeze.

'There is nothing wrong with your personality,' countered Helena with unexpected spirit. 'Except your temper and habit of rushing headlong into situations instead of thinking about them first,' she added, for clarification. 'Besides, do you not agree that some of these men might have a point? They have trained hard for this day, spending countless hours on their machines. To turn up here and be

168

unexpectedly faced with a car they could not beat, to be faced with an obstacle they couldn't hope to overcome, no matter how much talent or skill or personal merit they might possess – well, I think you understand how that feels, Poppy.'

Helena smiled as Poppy grudgingly nodded. 'Mind you,' she continued in a conspiratorial manner. 'I do agree that their belligerence today is simply part of who they are, although being thrashed by your father has certainly amplified their "charms" somewhat. You need to remember, Poppy, that sometimes diplomacy and hiding your feelings can be a good thing, and a gentle word will turn away wrath.'

'That's exactly what I thought in the garage when Dad was arguing with the truck driver,' exclaimed Poppy in surprise.

'Did you think your father was in the wrong?'

'I think he was, yes,' said Poppy, reluctantly, after a pause.

Helena hid the triumph from appearing on her face; she was worried Poppy resembled her father in too many respects, and she had been subtly working at bringing out the best of Poppy's character. 'If you can only remember that when next you are in an awkward social situation, it may help temper your response into something constructive,' she murmured.

'Yes, I know you think I'm too much like him,' replied Poppy, bringing a hot flush to Helena's cheeks. 'But I will try to think first.'

'That's another area I wish you would improve upon,' mumbled Helena. 'Your habit of reading people so accurately is rather disconcerting.'

'I'll try to do it a little more discreetly, then, but only if you agree that sometimes you need to face a situation directly and not just fade into the background.'

'Agreed,' laughed Helena. 'You can practise on the next group we speak to. Ah, there's Simeon, let's go and – oh!' Helena stopped short as they reached Simeon and she recognised the men with him.

'I take it these are not the best people to practise my manners on?' murmured Poppy, raising her eyebrow.

'The very best,' replied Helena, in hushed tones, 'though perhaps not for novices.' She broke into a broad, false grin as they stepped forward.

'Hello, my dear,' smiled Simeon. 'Let me introduce Poppy, Robert's daughter, and her friend, Amy, both of who work in the pit crew. Girls, this is Lord Oswald Hepplewhite, who unfortunately couldn't race today owing to an injured foot, and his usual retinue of Josh, Slacker and Tindal.'[30]

Poppy looked at Hepplewhite, who was about Simeon's age and build, though the resemblance ended there. Simeon was carefree and charming in his manner, while Hepplewhite glowered around the paddock in disdain.

'Oh dear, nothing too bad, I hope, Oswald?' asked Helena, demonstrating to Poppy how to be disguise her true feelings under cover of graciousness. She looked at the walking stick Hepplewhite was leaning on. 'A touch of gout, I fear?'

'Nothing serious. I will be racing at Purley,' said Hepplewhite stiffly, before glancing at Poppy and Amy.

'So will I,' said Tindal, eagerly leaning forward. Everyone ignored him and he leaned back out again.

Poppy, as she had promised Helena, refused to show that she could follow Hepplewhite's thoughts exactly as he gazed at her lasciviously before a grimace spread over his face on seeing her missing arm; she was all too familiar with the reaction. She was also familiar with the leer that appeared on his face as he gazed at Amy.

---

[30] The name Hepplewhite is familiar with us today as his descendants are still heavily involved in the world of motor racing, while Oswald himself is notorious in British history for his fascist politics.

'How do you do?' purred Hepplewhite before noticing the oil on Amy's hands. 'What, are you *really* working with the pit crew?' he asked, his lip rolling up in disdain. 'I thought Simeon was making a poor joke.'[31]

'Why?' demanded Amy as Poppy gave Helena an openly satirical look. 'We're as capable as any man of working on the engine.'

'Capable?' I'm sure you are, dear. And when you're done, does your husband fetch your pipe and a hot, cooked meal?' mocked Hepplewhite, gesturing at Poppy. Behind him, his three cronies hooted and laughed, nodding vigorously in sycophantic excess.

'I suppose you think women are just fit for the home?' snapped Amy, her colour rising.

'Where they shine in their true domain as the carer and nurturer,' replied Hepplewhite, looking as though he had won a major debate with incisive acumen and irrefutable evidence.

'Then I shall allow my full nurturing side to come out and care for you,' replied Poppy sweetly, never taking her gaze from Helena as she savagely stamped

---

[31] For working on the crew, Poppy and Amy both wore long, somewhat impractical skirts topped off by long-sleeved blouses and light jackets. Anything else, such as a comfortable and practical set of overalls, would have been unthinkable for women at that time.

172

down on Hepplewhite's bad foot.

Hepplewhite howled in agony. Helena gasped in horror and laughter, resulting in a most extraordinary series of rapid-fire hiccupping snorts that she had to quickly stifle behind her delicate lace handkerchief. Her reaction was shared by most of the paddock, divided as it was into silent horror or roars of amusement. Hepplewhite glared at those laughing at him, mentally noting their names, before turning on Simeon who was grinning widely. 'I'll remember this, Pallister,' he snarled. 'You won't be laughing when I trounce you and your unwashed lackeys at Purley!'

'Not much chance of that, my dear little boy,' replied Simeon, neatly deflecting Hepplewhite's anger from Poppy before any further violence could break out. 'You'll find that *Thunderbus*' engine is superior to anything else on the road.'

'I doubt that very much! Our engineering firm is at the forefront of the motoring industry.'

'Then why is British manufacturing falling so far behind the rest of Europe?' asked Simeon.

'We've just had back luck,' snapped Hepplewhite. 'British manufacturing is the best in the world and always will be. A British car has won at Purley for years past.'

'That is because your father does his utmost to

keep foreign manufacturers out of all racing events within the United Kingdom. How many are with us today? None!'

'He's protecting home interests. He is a patriot!'

'More likely he fears anything that may upset his monopoly. He is one of the reasons I drifted away from the sport. Luckily for him, though, I'm happy to say that a British car *will* still win at Purley.' Simeon grinned as he patted the enormous bulk of *Thunderbus*.

'Come on,' snarled Hepplewhite to his three companions. 'I'm not staying at this tin-pot racetrack to listen to my father being insulted.' He hobbled out of the paddock, closely followed by his three friends and a few other drivers, but most were glad to see him go.

'That was a jolly good win, very well done,' drawled another voice. Poppy turned and saw an incredibly tall man beaming at them in a vague manner. He was even taller than her father, but while her father was broad with it, this man was so thin he looked as though he would disappear from view if he turned sideways. With his lanky frame and high top hat, he looked like a badly rolled cigarette.

The man's nose was delicately curved, his mouth sensitive despite hanging slightly open, and his grey eyes set close together, though this was difficult to notice as one was hidden behind a huge, shiny monocle. The combined features suggested some form of good-natured fish floundering in the open air, too diffident to ask the way back to the ocean.

'Good afternoon, Cuthbert, how are you?' asked Helena, having regained her self-control.

'I'm well, thank you, Helena, I'm very well. At least, I believe I am well. My doctor says I am, anyway, and he should know. Clever chap and all that.' The figure nodded and made a long humming noise, as though thinking over a tricky problem. 'Er, are you well?'

'Yes, Cuthbert, we are very well, thank you for asking,' answered Helena.

'Oh, good, that is good, for you were unwell last winter, I recall, with flu. No ill effects, I hope?'

'None at all, dear Cuthbert.'

'Good, good. Now, what am I doing here?'

'You probably came in to congratulate the driver of *Thunderbus* on winning the race.'

'Indeed, that was it. Where is he?'

'Just over there. His name is Robert Orpington.'

'Orpington, Orpington; do we know an Orpington?'

'No, Cuthbert, we don't.'

'Thought I didn't know the name. Fresh blood coming in, eh? Probably what we need, fresh blood.

Hmm. I must see my doctor about fresh blood. Just there, you say? Thank you, Helena, good day. And good day to you also, Poppy.' The tall figure ambled off, his long limbs unwinding in lengthy, lopsided movements like a scarecrow being blown apart by a strong wind.

'The Honourable Cuthbert Gilmore; I've known him since I was a girl,' explained Helena, deciding there was nothing else to be said about the scene with Hepplewhite. 'Lovely man, but totally helpless. Though I sometimes suspect he is not as woolly-minded as he pretends to be.'

'I'm sure he isn't,' replied Poppy.

'What makes you say that?'

'I didn't tell him my name.'

Several hours later, Poppy and Amy were sitting at the back of the paddock, worn out by the day. Poppy still hadn't managed to talk to her father in all that time; he had walked past her on numerous occasions but had never spoken a word. He had, however, spoken to the press at great length about his perfected petrol engine. In between each swirl of reporters, he would pull the cheque from his pocket and read it again, a strange expression on his face.

Eventually, the crowds began to disperse and go home. By that stage everyone was hungry and tired, though Simeon was still elated after the win and was complimenting everyone on their efforts. 'Ah, girls,' he said, pausing by Amy and Poppy. 'It's been a remarkable day, one that will be remembered for a long time. No matter what happens at Purley, I doubt anything can beat this moment – the debut of a brand new type of racing car.' The triumph on his face faded slightly. 'I should admit; I did not think you would be able to cope with being in the pit crew, but I can see I was wrong. Very wrong. You have my sincere apologies for doubting you.'

Poppy and Amy shrugged. They both felt flat after the race. They had been pushed to the back of the crowd as no one – from the press to the spectators to the race marshals – thought two girls worth talking to or even thinking about. Helena had garnered some attention but only as the beautiful wife of an aristocrat, not for any qualities of her own character. Poppy had noted that while Simeon was asked his opinion on how *Thunderbus* would change racing and motoring, Helena was mostly asked about how she balanced the household budget and where she bought her dresses.

'How's Dad taking it all?' asked Poppy, hoping he had been asking for her.

'He's already asked me five times to get a new batch of fuel filters manufactured,' laughed Simeon, as though favouring a small boy with a treat.

'Any idea where he is?' asked Poppy in disappointment.

Simeon looked round and frowned. 'Funny, I thought he was over there. Perhaps he went out the back for some fresh air? Or maybe he's with *Thunderbus*?'

Poppy jumped up, still worried but now also growing annoyed at her father's behaviour and priorities. 'I don't think he's with *Thunderbus*; there are too many people gathered around it. I'll look out the back and see if he's there.'

'I'll check the front for you,' said Amy. 'Just in case.'

Poppy nodded and slipped away into the darkness behind the paddock, to where a small space had been created for the crew to relax when they weren't needed. She immediately saw the huge frame of her father sitting on one of the chairs. She slid quietly onto another seat and waited for him to look up, hoping he would say something about snapping at her during the race.

Slowly, Mr Orpington raised his head and focussed on Poppy, frowning before he nodded in greeting. 'Hello, girl. How long have you been there?'

'I just sat down.' Poppy looked at him, wondering

why he didn't use her name.

'Good. Good.' His huge grizzled head moved back to his former position, staring at something white in his hands.

Poppy squinted in the darkness and saw it was the prize-winning cheque. 'Lot of money, Dad,' she said, trying to prompt him into talking.

'Yes. My money, by rights!'

'What do you mean?'

'If I had entered *Thunderbus* alone, I would still be independent and have all this money. I wouldn't have to share the designs with anyone.'

'We didn't have the money to enter,' exclaimed Poppy, surprised at the heated look on her father's face. 'We would never have gotten here if it weren't for Simeon.'

'He tricked me!'

'How can you say such a thing?' gasped Poppy in shock. 'You know it isn't true.'

Mr Orpington muttered under his breath and frantically ran his hands through his greying hair, refusing to look Poppy in the face. The smell of his sweat was overpowering; he didn't seem to be washing properly recently, and now this sudden anger against his benefactor was further evidence of his disturbed nature.

'What is it, Dad, what's wrong?' demanded Poppy

in exasperation. 'Everyone is talking about *Thunderbus*. People want to know how it runs, how it works. It's what you wanted.'

'I didn't want to share! This money is mine. It's for us, not for them.'

A polite cough made them both look up; Helena was standing in the shadows. 'Poppy, I've been able to get some sandwiches delivered in the paddock. Would you like to go get something to eat? You must be starving. We have been rather remiss in looking after you. I'll keep your father company and have a little chat with him, as promised.'

Poppy reluctantly got up, looking at her father's hunched figure. She didn't like leaving but she had no idea how to talk to him anymore; he had changed so much in recent weeks that she felt as though he were a stranger. Besides which, she suspected Helena had overheard much of the conversation, and so she simply nodded and walked away.

'Now, Robert, why don't you tell me what the matter is?' asked Helena.

'Nothing is the matter, Lady Helena.'

'Then why are you so upset at finally achieving what you have dreamed of for so long? This is your dream, is it not? To create a perfect petrol engine, so you can sell the designs and become rich?'

Mr Orpington looked away, knowing his outburst

had been overheard. 'It is,' he said eventually, turning events over in his mind. 'But at first I was also intrigued by the engineering issues. It was a challenge, something I enjoyed working on, but then …

'But then?' asked Helena gently. She speculated it was her rank rather than the actual questions that compelled Mr Orpington to answer her. As Poppy had once mentioned, deference was difficult to remove once it was bred into a person, but at least Helena could use that to try and close the gulf between Poppy and her father. She jumped in alarm as Mr Orpington suddenly shouted in anger.

'Then it started taking over everything! I sacrificed so much time to the damn engine – time I could have spent with the girl, or earning more money in the workshop so we could have had a better life.'

'You were following your dream and trying to give Poppy a better life in the process,' soothed Helena.

'Yes, and *Thunderbus* must give her a better life; it must work, or everything I've done has been for nothing. I will have been wrong about everything.' He got up and strode around the tiny space in agitation, his voice rising again. 'I must have been right to spend so long on the project. I must have been! It's got to be justified, in the end. Otherwise, I've wasted my life. Wasted it!'

'Robert, please, calm yourself,' said Helena, nervous at the big man's anger. 'Look in your hand! You have the start of your new life there. You have more money now than most will ever earn in their entire lives.'

'Not enough to pay your husband back,' whined Mr Orpington, shaking his head from side to side like a puzzled, angry bull. 'As soon as I get money, I lose it. It all goes out to other people. People leeching it from me! What will be left?'

'The final reckoning will be made after you have completed at Purley,' replied Helena, her tone becoming slightly more acidic. 'I assure you that Simeon has been, and will continue to be, fair in his dealings with you. If, in the meantime, you truly wish to use your new wealth for Poppy's sake, why not do something for the girl? A new arm, perhaps? You once spoke of buying Poppy a permanent prosthesis, yet I have not heard you mention any such thing recently. Other concerns seem to have taken precedence in your mind.'

'Yes, yes, Poppy can have her arm,' said Mr Orpington with an almost savage intensity as he continued to stride up and down. 'She should have a permanent arm, one that can't be taken away. Yes,

182

and money for Amy, for her hard work on the crew.'

'I'm glad you are finally thinking of others instead of yourself; it is refreshing,' said Helena, still upset at the insinuation against Simeon. 'Why don't you tell Poppy now of her new arm, and then we can book the appointment at the Wiltshire Cybernetic Hospital?'

'Yes, yes I will,' muttered Mr Orpington, leaping up and stomping away. He saw Poppy at the far end of the paddock but his attention was diverted by *Thunderbus* and he immediately veered away to run his hands over the frame and dashboard, leaning low over the car as though whispering to it.

Helena looked at the scene and caught her breath; in the dark evening air the huge bulk of *Thunderbus* appeared to her as an ancient idol, one demanding worship, blood and even life itself. As she watched, it seemed as though Mr Orpington was melting into the black mass of the car, blurring the boundary between man and machine.

Helena shivered in dread, knowing it was just her imagination, but she was unable to shake the conviction that soon the car would demand its next sacrifice and her eye was drawn against her will to Poppy, standing alone in what seemed to be a halo of darkness. Stifling a cry of alarm, Helena quickly crossed the paddock and took the young girl's hand

183

in her own, wanting to protect her but not knowing how.

And yet, as Poppy's green eyes look at her in fond puzzlement, Helena realised that all that was bad in the father could be inverted by his daughter; she was surrounded by darkness but she had a warmth and intelligence far beyond any other, And unlike her father, who had surrendered himself to his obsession, Poppy was a fighter with a heart big enough to engulf them all.

'What's the matter?' whispered Poppy in concern. 'You're trembling.'

'Come along, my dear,' replied Helena, suppressing what she assured herself was nothing more than wild imagination brought on by excitement and fatigue. 'The night is drawing in. Let's collect Simeon and Amy and the others and return home.'

CHAPTER EIGHT

Thunderbus' victory at the Sussex racetrack caused an explosion of interest in the press and public alike, as Poppy witnessed when she drove her father into town to do simple things like shopping or cashing a cheque. She was keenly aware that he did not deal well with the scrutiny; he viewed every approach by the public with mounting paranoia, believing those offering their congratulations or asking for an autograph were trying to steal his engine designs.

Poppy assumed they would be isolated from the media interest while inside Pallister Hall, but packs of journalists began squatting outside the gates almost immediately, making the simple task of leaving and returning to the hall a major trial of patience and skill. Unfortunately, a different source of pressure was also manifesting around the pit crew – the natural euphoria at winning was being ruined by her father's behaviour.

'We need to strip the car right back,' he was insisting for the tenth time that morning. 'Back to basics and rebuilt to my specifications.' He waved several sheets of paper in the air, covered in his writing, diagrams and calculations.

'Jack, what's your opinion?' asked Simeon,

shifting the decision.

Talbot shrugged. 'We may need to adjust a few things here and there, but we can't do much to the rest of the car because of the … existing design.'

Poppy looked suspiciously at Talbot; she had the feeling he had only just stopped himself from saying "bad design."

'Small but vital adjustments will improve the car immeasurably,' answered Mr Orpington, violently shaking his papers in the air. 'I have worked it all out to the last detail.'

'Robert, do we need to squeeze anything extra from the car? Really?' asked Simeon. He attempted a smile. 'There is nothing out there to beat *Thunderbus*, surely? We just proved that in quite spectacular fashion at the Sussex.'

'We need to improve! We must improve,' snapped Mr Orpington, seemingly determined to crush any sense of victory or achievement.

Further talk was cut short as a shadow fell over the open door of the garage. Those wearing caps hastily pulled them from their heads while looking nervously down at the ground. Poppy looked round, already knowing who would be standing there – the only person who could provoke such meek submissiveness and unease in the crew: Simeon's father, the Duke of Shalford.

'Father,' said Simeon, his face going carefully blank. 'I would not expect to find you visiting the workshop.'

The duke was an old man, requiring a stick to keep himself upright. His malevolent grey eyes peered out from bushy eyebrows, while his thin lips drew back from his yellowed teeth in a perpetual semi-formed snarl. His gaze swept over the mechanics, who continued to scrutinise the ground in obedient respect. Finally, his arrogant stare came to rest on Poppy, who gazed levelly back, meeting his hostile look with one of her own. His lip curled back to an even greater height, revealing a hint of pink gum.

'Father?' repeated Simeon, his tone slightly sharper.

'So,' said the old man, his voice brittle. 'This is what my son spends his time and resources on. Racing cars.'

'You know perfectly well I have been racing various cars for years now,' replied Simeon, his face showing a hint of exasperation. 'This is nothing new.'

'No, but this is,' snapped the old man, waving his stick in contempt in the general direction of *Thunderbus*. He turned slightly and the tip of his stick jabbed out towards Poppy and Amy before dropping to the ground to support his weight once more. 'It was bad enough when you were racing steam cars, but petrol? Faugh! It's no fuel for gentlemen.'

'It is quite possibly the fuel of the future, Father.'

'It's not a future I want to see,' exclaimed the old man. 'Only the lowest of the low has anything to do with petrol.'

'My pit crew have worked hard to earn their success,' replied Simeon with controlled irritation. 'I will not have anyone insult them without reason.'

'You're on my property,' snarled the duke, but he was cut short by his son.

'No, they are on my property because you signed the Hall over to me to avoid death duties. You live here on a legal technicality, as a courtesy only. Do you want to try my patience? Do you want me to get a court order stating you are unable to look after yourself and have you placed in a secure nursing home?' Simeon's carefully measured voice broke for a moment and Poppy saw a flash of pure anger and guilt flash over his face before the mask was back in place.

'How dare you talk to your own father like that?' demanded the duke, his voice wheezing in anger. 'You would threaten your own blood with legal action?'

'I wonder where I could have learned such things from?' replied Simeon, the sarcasm breaking free despite his best attempts at control. He glanced at the frozen faces of the pit crew. 'If you wish to continue this conversation, Father, perhaps you should retire to the cottage, sit down with Grandmother, and I will join you both shortly.'

The duke's face twisted at the mention of his mother. 'She has nothing to do with this – with anything,' he muttered. 'I came here to see exactly what you are doing, and now I know. Consorting with petrol workers; damn bolshie agitators! And women! Unnatural women doing the work of men. Base women!' He spat the last words out in blazing hatred.

Amy's face turned milk-white. For all her love of working with engines, she was not immune to the reactions her job provoked in others, or from the snide letters she received weekly from her disapproving mother.

Poppy opened her mouth to tell the duke what she thought of him, but to her great surprise the words died in her throat. She realised she was torn between the desire to speak her mind and the habit of blindly obeying the ingrained, unwritten law that workers did not answer back to their superiors. In the time it took her to break through the unexpected yoke of social conditioning, Simeon had stepped up to his father to confront the old man face to face.

'You will leave, now,' he hissed, keeping his voice quiet, 'or I swear to God I will have you turned out of Pallister Hall by nightfall. Do I make myself clear?'

The old man's snarl twitched itself into a vindictive smile at seeing how upset his son was. 'No need for such violent threats to a harmless old gentleman,' he said, emphasising his wheeze as he spoke.

'You are far from harmless, and you are no gentleman, either,' snapped Simeon, goaded once more by the duke's taunts. 'I still remember the day I discovered that. What a disappointment it was to a small boy.'

The duke glared, his triumphant smirk evaporating as Simeon's shot landed. With a snort of contempt, he turned and strode with surprising vigour from the garage.

'I apologise for my father,' said Simeon after breathing deeply for several seconds, though he didn't turn to face the crew as he spoke. 'I will make sure he does not come here again. Now, if you would continue the work on the car, I have some paperwork that must be attended to before the end of the week.' He left without saying more, without even looking at anyone in the garage.

Behind him, Amy gave out a large sob. The rest of the crew stared at her. 'Come on, girl, snivelling won't help,' snapped Talbot, impatiently.

'For God's sake,' hissed Poppy in anger. She grabbed Amy's hand and pulled her friend towards the garage door.

'Poppy, where do you think you two are going?' demanded her father. 'We need to start work on the engine!'

'We are going to get some fresh air,' barked Poppy in suppressed fury.

'What? You're needed here!'

'Then you'll have to wait until we are back,' snarled Poppy without turning around.

Poppy almost dragged Amy through the servant's quarters of Pallister Hall. She had intended to stop there and get some tea and sympathy from Mrs Bloomer, the large, placid, comfortable cook, but once Poppy was walking at full speed she found her temper would not allow her to stop. Amy meekly followed on behind, pulled bodily by Poppy's hand, focusing on the ground to make sure she didn't trip as she was towed by the human juggernaut ahead of her.

Amy only spoke as their pace finally slowed and

she saw in horror that they had passed straight through the servant's quarters and were now in Pallister Hall itself. 'Poppy, we can't possibly be in here!'

'Interesting philosophical point, as we are clearly in here,' replied Poppy, her angry voice loud in the long, quiet corridor.

'But we're not allowed!'

'Says who?'

Amy paused, trying to think who had actually told them they could not enter the hall itself. 'Well it's, you know, just not allowed,' she mumbled.

'Do you know who has explicitly told us we are not allowed in? Nobody, that's who. It's just convention and deference, and I am fed up to the back teeth with it! So, the old man thinks he's better than us just because of his pedigree, does he? In that case, let's go see how much better he is than us by visiting his private apartment.'

'What?' screeched Amy before dropping her voice in fear. Fortunately, this part of the hall seemed to be virtually deserted. 'You can't mean that?'

'I do mean it. I've heard the staff talk about the set of rooms he used to live in. I want to take a look.'

'But I thought he lived out in the cottage now, not the main house?' whispered Amy, glancing around as if expecting a policeman to be hiding behind the next potted plant.

'He still occasionally uses his old rooms as an office,' replied Poppy. 'And where do they get off calling that thing a 'cottage'? It's bigger than an entire row of terraced houses. The rich really do live in another world to us.' They rounded a corner into a short, wood-panelled corridor, rather different from the lighter, airier part of the house Simeon and Helena used.

'Ah, I think this is it. Stevens, the head footman, said the entry was in old wood, and with no modern technology anywhere. See? There's no thermal-control sensors. There's not even an electric light bulb here; it's all still on gas.'

'Poppy,' mumbled Amy, who was still cringing in fear, terrified of the old man's wrath if they were discovered. 'You can't go in there. It's not right.'

'I'll be damned if I'm going to be dictated to by a parasitic capitalist, particularly one as unpleasant as Simeon's father,' snapped Poppy in reply as she tried the door. The handle turned easily and she peered into the chambers. 'Are you coming?' Poppy walked through, leaving Amy dancing from one foot to the other in anxiety before she fled inside and slammed the door shut.

'We shouldn't be in here; there'll be trouble,' she hissed, though she took the opportunity of having a good look round the rooms they were in. 'Blimey,' she mumbled in awe.

To call the duke's private chambers "rich" would be like calling a journalist "untruthful"; neither term did full justice to the reality. The rooms were a sumptuous spread of gilt, marble, velvet, silk, statuettes, superfluous columns, portraiture and frenzied rococo design which pressed in on Amy's senses, telling her she did not belong, that she should withdraw immediately and return to her common province and never again dare to breach the sanctum of breeding which she dirtied by her mere presence.

'What's the matter with you?' asked Poppy as she strode around the rooms, examining every surface with lively interest.

'Don't you feel it?' whispered Amy in an agony of inferiority. 'We don't belong in here; it's not our place. We shouldn't even have seen this, never mind walked in.'

'Balls!' exclaimed Poppy fiercely, shattering the genteel atmosphere. She strode towards Amy and grabbed her friend so she could look her directly in the face. 'That's society talking through you. That's the worm of obedience that is inculcated into everyone born into the lower classes. No one is better than anyone else except through their character and their actions, so don't let this room affect you like

194

that.'

Poppy's smouldering green eyes stared into Amy's frightened expression. Taking a deep breath, she drew Amy into a reassuring hug. 'I'm sorry; I didn't mean to be so emphatic. I'm just angry at the way things are. Just look at the wealth in this place and compare it with a working-class family who are never given the chance to improve themselves.' She kissed Amy's cheek and held her for several minutes until she felt some of the tension leave her friend's body.

'What does "inculcated" mean?' asked Amy finally, in a quiet voice as she snuggled into Poppy's embrace.

'To be indoctrinated into a belief. Are you feeling better now?'

'It's just too much. I feel that I'm trapped in a set of rooms which despises me. And then you shout at me as well.'

'I didn't shout,' objected Poppy. 'I'll admit I may have harangued, but I've said sorry for that.'

'"Harangued"?'

'Berated, lectured, ranted,' explained Poppy as she brushed Amy's blonde hair, the thought flickering through her mind that she never had to explain any words she used when talking to Simeon or Helena. Ruthlessly crushing the observation down,

195

Poppy gently pulled Amy over towards the bookcases which covered one wall.

'At least the duke is a reader; that's the only positive thing I can say about him,' whispered Poppy, immediately enamoured with the leather-bound books practically begging her to pick them up, to brush her hand over the soft rustling pages, to open each one wide and plunge with wild abandon into the hidden treasures inside. 'I think I'll need a cold shower later,' she murmured, feeling slightly faint.

'Why? You're not that grubby, really,' said Amy, missing Poppy's joke entirely.

Poppy decided not to explain; her hand was already reaching out towards one of the books. The faded gold lettering announced she was about to clasp Plato's *Republic* and she trembled as she reverently pulled the book free and placed it on a convenient side table. She ran her finger down the soft spine, brushing the edge of the pages to release the smell of paper and ink before opening the book to reveal the wisdom within. The words 'That's it, love, get it down yer!' leapt from the page and into her astonished eyes.

Poppy blinked and the perspective resolved itself. She was actually looking at a postcard sitting in the middle of the book. The picture underneath the lurid headline was of a naked man being pleasured by a half-dressed woman. Poppy lifted the card and revealed another underneath; in fact, there were several slipped in between the pages of the book. Unlike the elderly but pristine pages, the postcards all looked to be rather well-thumbed.

'Bloody hell!' exclaimed Amy, her eyes popping from her head. 'What are all those doing in there? Ugh, I don't like the look of that at all!' she added as another card came to light, this one focussing solely on a naked man posing like an Ancient Greek statue, his gaze directed towards the mid-distance, his well-defined torso resting against a column.

'You mean the nudity, or his third leg?' asked Poppy, looking with increasing interest through the rest of the graphic collection. She had seen line drawings of men and women in an old biological textbook, but the postcards throbbed with colour, depth and the sort of gynaecological gymnastics she had only ever thought about in the privacy of her own mind.

'Naked men,' exclaimed Amy, her face wrinkling in distaste.

Poppy didn't reply – she was enjoying seeing all the entwined bodies on display, male and female alike; white and brown, tall and short, slender and thickset. Life was a whole smorgasbord of different experiences that Poppy hadn't tasted, and as she looked through the cards she was beginning to feel pretty damn peckish.

'Hey, she looks familiar,' exclaimed Amy suddenly.

Poppy closed down her imaginative orgy and focussed on the face of the naked woman she had been gazing at. Amy was right; they were looking at Anna, the duke's private secretary. Poppy was holding a photograph, not a postcard. 'The dirty, hypocritical old goat! And he called us base women! Mind you, this does explain Anna's continued employment. I didn't think she seemed very efficient as a secretary. No wonder, if she was hired for other reasons.'

'When have you ever spoken to Anna?' demanded Amy in sudden jealousy.

'I've spoken to most people on the estate as I do my exercises,' explained Poppy, too absorbed by the picture to notice Amy's tone. Poppy still chopped wood and did calisthenics to keep fit, even though her father had now abandoned the practice to focus purely on *Thunderbus*. 'I sometimes see people in the orchard, guests or servants collecting fruit, and some of them stop for a chat. I thought then that Anna didn't seem to be particularly bright. I asked her about her job and she didn't know anything about filing, taking down letters, nothing. Now I know why. She's here to take something else down!'

'So, Anna is his mistress?'

'Or a paid escort,' said Poppy, bluntly. 'She's not the right class to be a mistress. I suspect she is paid for her services.'

'That's horrible.'

'As I said, I don't think she's that bright, so maybe this is something she can do which gets her a reasonable standard of living. Shame it has to be with that rancid old swine.'

'I would never have thought you would approve of prostitution,' gasped Amy. 'What about the rights of women that you talk about?'

Poppy gave Amy a sidelong glance. 'Shouldn't she have the right to have full control over her body and its uses?

'Er, um, yes, of course,' stuttered Amy. 'But it's still wrong!'

'Wrong to use her natural – and possibly only – advantage to obtain a better life for herself?'

'She could find a husband,' muttered Amy, looking trapped. She hated debating with Poppy; she had never yet won an argument with her.

'And what is the difference between selling yourself for money and selling yourself into marriage? You're still exchanging your goods – so to speak – in return for profit; either cash or else a house, food and respectability.'

'But, but, marriage *is* respectable,' exclaimed Amy, latching onto Poppy's last word.

'Why is it?'

'Well, because, well, everyone says so,' fluttered Amy, feebly.

'Oh, if everyone says so, it must be right?' demanded Poppy with a sardonic grin. 'Is that your point? If everyone says you shouldn't be let near an engine because you're female, should you simply give it all up?'

'We're not talking about that, we're talking about … you know … bedroom behaviour,' hissed Amy, blushing furiously. She was rather prudish on such matters, as Poppy had discovered several times when trying to coax their relationship beyond discreet kisses and hugs.

'It's the same issue and the same problem – those in power tell everyone else what is acceptable and everyone else is therefore conditioned to think that way. But what if they are wrong? What if sex is a basic need of the species; shouldn't it then also be a right? And if so, shouldn't people be allowed to provide a service free of censure and hypocrisy? A service by men and women for men and women, all equal?'

'What are the chances we'd find a book with these postcards in it?' exclaimed Amy, changing the subject. She was once again helplessly out of her depth when arguing with Poppy.

Poppy dragged herself away from the interesting conversation and focussed on the world around her; Amy had actually made a good point about the postcards. She gazed suspiciously at the rest of the books on the shelves; all looked to be expensive, old and practically untouched. She had heard of people buying an entire library for the sole reason of showing it off to visitors rather than reading the books, which struck Poppy as rather perverse; was this one such example?

She drew down a copy of *Beowulf*, opened it and another shower of illicit postcards fell to the floor. She tried a few more books at random and in every case the result was the same. Soon, she and Amy were standing ankle-deep in the best continental smut money could buy.

'This isn't a library,' laughed Poppy. 'This is a gallery of erotica! You can get two years for importing this stuff into the country. How do you feel about the sanctity of the upper classes now, Amy?'

CHAPTER NINE

Poppy's appointment for the surgery arrived a few days later. Her father offered to take her to the hospital but in such a vague manner that Poppy refused. She watched him rush around the workshop, a stranger in her eyes, trying to work on several components at once while also supervising what everyone else was doing. Having been told by Helena of the conversation in the rear paddock, Poppy knew her father was fixated on winning to validate the years spent working on *Thunderbus*. If he lost, he would be exposed in his own mind as a bad parent and engineer.

Poppy, feeling distraught and isolated, left him to his obsession and gladly accepted Helena's offer to accompany her to the hospital. They made the journey in good time and were immediately shown to the office of the hospice administrator, George Evans, who rose up sycophantically as they walked in. 'Lady Helena,' he smiled, ignoring Poppy completely as he gestured towards a comfortable chair in front of his desk. 'How are you? I believe we have a few mutual acquaintances in common.'

Poppy let the mumble of words flow over her as Evans eagerly brought up the mutual acquaintances, thereby signifying that he was a known man in society. She instead looked around the office with interest; it was like any gentlemen's study, full of dark wood panelling and leather-bound chairs, but against one wall was evidence of the technological nature of the hospital – a huge Duple Ciphering Machine, housed in several wooden cabinets, stood humming quietly to itself. Inside, analogue and digital components were united as intricately inscribed disks and cylinders of brass and steel worked in conjunction with electrical coding blocks and Liquidised Display Screens.

Poppy gazed at the machine. She had never seen a DCM before. They were the exclusive preserve of wealthy professionals. Very wealthy professionals. To even own such a machine took a substantial four figure income. This DCM model was known colloquially as a 'Medi-Brain'. Cables hidden in the walls and floors connected the main unit to auxiliary machines in every operating theatre in the hospital, as well as every patient's room. Its job was to monitor all operations and all patients, ensuring their new limbs were functioning correctly and were not being rejected by the host.[32]

---

[32] This archaic processing system lasted until the late 1930s, some ten years before Duple itself finally went out of business.

'Now, what can I do for you, Lady Helena?' asked Evans, reluctantly acknowledging Poppy's existence with a brief glance in her direction. He wondered why Helena had brought such a base creature anywhere near his pristine hospital. The difference between them was acute. Helena moved gracefully and carefully, testament to years spent at finishing school, and she was now sitting upright on the edge of her chair for it was unseemly for a woman to relax in mixed company. In contrast, Poppy strode into the office as though she owned it and then sprawled in a chair as though using it for comfort.

'My young friend, Poppy, is in need of a new arm,' replied Helena.

Evans' eyes flickered in dislike as he glanced dismissively at Poppy. He had already noticed her deformity but he failed to see what he was expected to do about it. 'A-ha. You are of course aware that our procedures are very expensive, Lady Helena?' he murmured. 'The cost of a fully integrated prosthetic can run into hundreds of pounds.'

'Poppy has hundreds of pounds,' replied Helena.

Poppy watched the disbelief pass over Evans' face before he smothered it in another false smile. 'Of course, I accept your word on that absolutely, Lady Helena,' he replied; those of a certain class knew they could unquestionably believe those of a higher

204

class, no matter how peculiar the occasion. 'However, there are ongoing costs over the years in terms of maintenance, replacement parts and so on.'

'I'll worry about the future costs when they arise,' interrupted Poppy. 'For now, I'm here to have a new arm fitted.'

'The surgery was confirmed by your secretary,' said Helena.

'The entry is in your desk diary,' added Poppy, nodding at the book.

Evans flushed as he realised Poppy had read the book upside down. She truly was no lady, to read someone else's private entries. But why was Lady Helena supporting the wretched girl? If he had realised what type of person the appointment was for, he would never have agreed to it. Even now, he could politely turn her away, a murmured excuse about a clerical error, beyond his control …

'There's the money,' said Poppy, plonking down a large envelope stuffed with high-denomination bank notes.

Evans' middle-class jaw fell open; if there was one thing that enraptured him more than the upper classes, it was the rare and beautiful sight of several hundred pounds within his reach. Most clients of the hospice had to be billed repeatedly for the fees – as was only right, of course, as the gentry disdained such things – but even so, they had been chasing Lord Hooper for the full cost of his Zeus Mark II lower leg (left) for six years now, while Lady Beryl Steeping's last cheque for her Indepit Customised Hand (right) had bounced like a tennis ball. Yet here was the full amount, *in cash*, on his desk, waving at him and almost smiling …

'I think we can stretch a point, in exceptional circumstances,' he replied, his tone hoarse with emotion. The money had already disappeared into his coat pocket. 'If you would like to go through that door there, Miss …' He glanced at his diary. 'Miss Orpington, and go straight through to the Pre-Operative Analysis Ward, the staff will be with you as soon as possible.'

Poppy grinned sardonically as she rose, letting Evans know she could see exactly what he thought of her. She smiled warmly at Helena, pausing momentarily at the strange glint in her friend's eye. Suspecting that Helena was less than happy with Evans, Poppy strolled through the door, closed it and immediately pressed her ear against the keyhole.

For his part, Evans watched in muted resentment as the opinionated girl walked through the door with the same insolent step as she had entered the office. She ought to be grateful he had decided – out of sheer altruism – to allow her into his clinic for the social elite, money notwithstanding. He turned in puzzlement to Lady Helena, expecting some sort of apology and explanation for bringing such a girl into his hospital, though he could not imagine any explanation being at all adequate for such outrageous behaviour.

'Mr Evans, your professionalism is a credit to you,' said Helena, her smile beautiful yet also deadly. 'Do you know, for a moment there, I thought you were going to refuse Poppy a place!' She laughed gaily, but with an edge of fang showing through. 'How foolish of me; after all, the medical profession is founded on the ideal of helping all in need.'

'Er, oh, urmh, yes, quite,' mumbled Evans, who had founded the clinic more on the premise of wealth and social advancement than medical grounds.

'It's such a delightful thing, for a mere woman such as myself, to see the wonderful way in which you welcome everyone, regardless of background,' she continued, her honeyed words dripping with venom.

Evans gaped in confusion; he could sense the underlying menace in Helena's words but, while she continued to speak so conventionally and properly, he could not see the danger ahead. Finally, aware that Helena was waiting politely for a reply, he muttered out an answer that encapsulated – to him – all that was wrong with the situation. 'I must admit, we do not usually deal with ... such people here.'

'But surely you must deal with anyone who can pay,' replied Helena, looking confused and dainty. 'Poppy's father can pay; ergo, you will deal with her.'

'Yes, yes, of course, but there are other considerations to be, um, considered,' mumbled Evans.

'Gosh, really?' exclaimed Helena. 'Do please explain more, Mr Evans, I am agog.' She leaned forward, resting her chin on her hand, a studious pose of academic learning.

Evans coloured slightly, slowly becoming aware that he was being mocked. 'Well, we normally deal with ... private people, with the necessary income to pay, or workers from industry who have suffered an injury.[33] Those who will *benefit* from a new limb,' he finished, pleased with his wording.

'Benefit? But surely Poppy will benefit?' queried

---

[33] As mentioned in footnote #9, such workers would not, in fact, be given a replacement limb; it was always presented as a *loan* from the company they worked for, and the loan had to be paid off, with interest, over several years. And even then, the limb would be taken back upon retirement.

Helena. 'After all, she will have two arms rather than one.'

'Yes, indeed, but I mean to say, when all is said and done, at the end of the day, not to beat about the bush ...' Evans paused, aware that Helena's innocent expression held a definite edge of contempt. He took a breath and plunged forward. 'Why bother giving a girl like that an expensive arm?' he whispered, dropping his voice to involve Helena in a conspiracy of class outrage. 'Or indeed, any sort of arm? She's not going to use it as a miner or a soldier would. She'll just marry some lout and start breeding – I mean, start a family,' he amended hurriedly.

'Ah!' exclaimed Helena, the fury in her voice smothered by years of social convention and rigid self-control, impressing Poppy who could hear the anger even through the wooden door. 'I see; so, she'll simply use the limb to have a normal life?'

'Yes, well, a normal life by their standards.'

'*Their* standards?'

'Yes; the standards of the working class. I know that sort well – and their promiscuous lifestyle!'

'I understand fully.' Helena's smile was now a rictus that would have made a more sensitive man than Evans saunter away quickly in the opposite direction. 'Indeed, the working classes are known for their promiscuity; the better type of newspaper frequently remarks upon it.'

'Exactly,' beamed Evans, feeling he was suddenly on firm ground, which probably explained his next crass remark. 'It is a known fact that the lower orders breed irresponsibly, having children they cannot afford.'

'Yes, working-class women do have children, do they not? Just like any other woman from any other class, really,' replied Helena, her tone almost etching the words into Evans' shining leather desk. 'It's as though pregnancy is a universal issue shared by women everywhere.'

'Indeed! Er, I mean, well, yes, but other classes are not so irresponsible in having children,' coughed Evans, squirming in his chair. The very word 'pregnancy' was never said outside the medical profession, and it should certainly never be said by a lady. Such things were indecorous.

'Yes, it is a shocking fact that working-class women have more children than the upper and middle classes. Of course, the working class can't afford the many forms of birth control that are available to the wealthier elements of society, but they could always practise self-control, could they not, Mr Evans?'

'Er, yes?' whimpered Evans, who felt he was blundering on the edge of a huge pit of social catastrophe.

'Yes indeed; if only they practised the same self-control as the upper classes, who quite coincidently have full access to the contraceptive pill, there would not be so many unwanted children around. It is odd how the upper classes practise their self-control; I often see men and women discreetly staying over at each other's houses when wives and husbands are away, and I rejoice in the self-control that is clearly going on inside each home. The fact there are very few unwanted births amongst my peers shows how much self-control there is. About one birth for every one hundred occasions someone stays over, practising their self-control. Which, by an astonishing coincidence, is about the effectiveness of the contraceptive pill, is it not? I believe that is known to be effective ninety-nine times in every hundred?'

'Please, Lady Helena, your language,' gaped Evans.

'Of course,' continued Helena, her tone still light but only by a supreme effort of self-control, 'if the pill were available to everyone, women would be truly free from the tyranny of childbirth.' The room swam briefly in front of her eyes as she realised the importance of her words. 'But what would all those working-class women do if they were not looking after children all the time? Why, they would probably congregate in public libraries and lecture halls and attend night classes and obtain a better education, so it is just as well that they lack the many forms of contraception available.'

Evans went pale as he realised he was looking at a highly-disturbed woman. 'Are you unwell, Lady Helena? Perhaps some unknown stress has affected you.'

'Unwell? I have never been better! Indeed, I see the world so very clearly now, thanks to your wonderful insights, Mr Evans. Do you not agree it is better that lower class women should be bound to the tyranny of childbirth, to prevent them from learning things that would only disturb them?'

'Ah, yes, indeed,' babbled Evans. 'Women do not understand the world as men do; that is an established scientific fact. Every medical study has confirmed the gulf between men and women.' He nodded vigorously, looking superior as he retreated into medical literature.

'And would those medical studies be run by men, for men, by any chance?' enquired Helena, her voice snapping the air in two.

'Lady Helena, you are clearly out of sorts,' replied Evans, almost sagging with relief as he diagnosed the problem – that Helena was ungovernable with female emotion – which in turn allowed him to control the situation and thus the hysterical woman also. For her own good. 'Come, I will get one of our top surgeons to prescribe a gentle sedative to restore your good temper.'

'You will do no such thing, Mr Evans,' replied Helena, finally abandoning polite irony and letting loose with a straightforward blast of measured anger. 'And furthermore, you will see to it that the best surgeon in the hospital fits the best arm available to that child, or I will see to it that you are indicted for medical negligence and you will face a lawsuit that will bring this hospice down about your ears. Do I make myself clear?'

Evans rocked back and forth in his seat, seemingly unable to process being told what to do by a woman. 'You are unwell,' he bleated, retreating to the only explanation he could believe in. 'Your emotions are making you unreasonable.'

'I am perfectly well, and it is thanks to that girl out there – the one you consider to be a working-class breeder – that my judgement is so clear, possibly for the first time in my life. Now, are you going to complete the operation or do I need to find another hospice that does not discriminate against its patients?'[34]

'Good for you, Helena,' whispered Poppy on the other side of the door, wiping her eyes with her handkerchief. She was delighted that her friend had not only stood up to the ghastly Evans, but had firmly trounced him also. Helena clearly still had much to teach Poppy about dealing diplomatically with people and the world in general.

The stunned Evans, having strengthened his nerves with a quick gulp of brandy, made his way to the Pre-Operative Analysis Ward, where Poppy was being examined by Doctor Pender and a nurse whose name Evans did not know. Evans saw with displeasure that both Pender and the nurse seemed to be chatting quite amiably with Poppy as they recorded her biochemistry with the Throxmorton Scanner. He would have to have a word with Pender about

---

[34] In presenting this scene, I have had to choose between two contrasting records of the events. In his personal diary, Evans merely notes that he was 'confronted by a disturbed woman in the throes of sexual perversity, quite beyond treatment.' He mentions Poppy not at all. Helena's journal, supported by Poppy's diary, paints a very different picture. I believe that their testimony is the more likely to be accurate, and if I have occasionally had to speculate on the feelings and reactions of any participant, it has been done with a genuine regard for authenticity based on the diaries, letters and reports of each individual.

decorum, and put the nurse on a charge.[35]

'Good, good,' Pender was saying as Evans drew nearer. 'Your general health is superb. I've seldom seen a fitter patient. Wouldn't you agree, Clara?'

'Yes, Doctor Pender,' replied the nurse, busy with a read-out. 'Apart from the right arm and left knee, you're as healthy as anyone I've ever seen. All your scores are in the top ten per cent of the range.'

'I wish I had your vitality,' agreed Pender as he turned off the body scanner by pulling on a large, ornate lever. 'I feel quite weak in comparison.'

'We're just outside the Black Country,' explained Poppy, 'so we don't get the filth from all that industry dropping down onto us, and we've always been able to eat properly by bartering chicken eggs and doing odd jobs for neighbours in return for better food.'

'Odd jobs?' asked Pender.

'Yes. I used to earn a few pence raking over Mrs Lowman's manky allotment, and a few more tending Mr Clarke's flower beds. That was always a battle between me and the ginger tomcat that used to come

---

[35] A formal reprimand exists in the Wiltshire archives against one C. Nagle, nurse, and signed by Evans himself. The reprimand was for 'inappropriate medical behaviour.' The date fits in with Poppy's stay at the hospice.

round and scratch up all the seedlings.'

'I'm not sure odd jobs can explain your remarkable muscle tone,' replied Pender, holding Poppy's scan up to the light and peering at it through the small lens fixed neatly over his spectacles.

'I've also been accompanying my father on his training sessions; he needed to be fit enough to handle the car during the race.'

'Oh, is he a racing driver?' asked Pender. 'I misunderstood what you said earlier. I thought he was one of the engineers as you said he designed the car.'

'Designed and drives.'

'Ohh, be careful around Clara, then,' teased Pender. 'The nurses can't hear enough about that breed of man. Quite a bout of hero-worship going on with them, isn't that right, Clara?'

Clara blushed prettily. 'They are very popular,' she explained. 'They seem so bold and brave, racing everywhere at such dangerous speeds. All the girls think they're very romantic.'

'Yes, I believe one of the nurses even has a signed photograph of Sir Horatio Windslip, twice winner of the Alp Cup,' laughed Pender, gently. 'No doubt it's her most treasured possession. We had him in here after his big crash, you know; we got him walking again but his racing career was over after that.'

216

'Dad has only just started,' replied Poppy. 'He won the Sussex last week.'

'Was he driving that huge black car?' exclaimed Clara. 'I read all about it in the papers and heard it on the radio. A whole new type of car, the reporter said!'

'Not exactly new,' said Poppy, trying to be accurate. 'It runs off petrol, but it's the first reliable, fast and smooth petrol engine ever made.'

'It certainly left the steam cars standing,' said Pender, showing the same enthusiasm as Clara before coughing in embarrassment. 'Well, so my wife and children informed me. They were very impressed.'

'If I might have a word, Doctor Pender,' interrupted Evans, appalled that the sport of gentlemen should have seen fit to allow workers anywhere near it.

'Certainly,' replied Pender, looking in surprise at Evans' stony face. 'I think we are about done here. Poppy, your existing nerve endings are all in perfect working order, so there is no reason why they shouldn't connect to the prosthetic. We'll have to remove most of your upper arm, but you'll retain the shoulder, at least. I'll leave you with Clara; she can show you to your room, and the rest of the hospice if you want to see it.'

Poppy nodded, looking rather pale as the full

extent of the surgery was explained. Clara smiled, took Poppy's hand in a friendly gesture and gently drew the young girl out of the assessment room, chatting quietly to put Poppy at her ease.

'What's the problem, George?' asked Doctor Pender once they were alone.

'You know that girl is working-class!'

'Well, yes. She has been telling us about her father's work and from the context I gathered he is one of the many independent designers that cover the land.'

'Designer?' snorted Evans in contempt. 'He's just a mechanic, by the sound of it.'

'Backbone of the country,' replied Pender, his eyes narrowing slightly. 'If it weren't for the hundreds of dreamers in their private workshops, the empire would never have had so much technological enterprise to draw on. You know it was one such man who designed the first functioning airship? He was able to approach a wealthy manufacturer with his designs and get funding and support for them. Back then, there was far more movement between the classes. And there was respect on both sides.'

Evans waved away the truth of this with a disdainful gesture. 'Yes, yes, salt of the earth, always said so, but the workers are not like us. They may excel at the practical hands-on work but they have no refinement. No appreciation of higher truths. It's a waste of time giving her an arm. What will she do with it?'

'Do with it?' echoed Pender. 'I suppose she will use it to have an ordinary life, just as you or I do. Now, if there is nothing else, Mr Evans, I wish to open the cold store and see which arm will best suit Miss Orpington's size, strength and neural brain patterns.'

'All right, but I am the director of this clinic and I say she is to have titanium alloy only, do you hear? And that is too good for her.'

'A perfect choice,' said Pender in contempt. 'Given that she works on her father's pit crew, a titanium arm will be strong yet delicate enough for the job. The Turner-Casbach should be just what she needs, I would guess.'

'The Turner-Casbach range is for men only! Men who have lost limbs in battle, or in specialised industry.'

'And now it is for young women working in a man's world. The world changes, Mr Evans, and we must adapt or die out. If you will excuse me, I have work to do.'

Poppy was kept unconscious for a week after the operation, to allow her nerve endings to heal and link to the electric filaments of her new arm. She was turned several times a day by the nurses to ensure she didn't develop bed sores, and her legs and arm were massaged lightly to prevent muscle wastage. The Medi-Brain scrutinised her bio-signs minutely as her body adapted to having a new limb.

Finally, Poppy was brought out of the induced coma and left to sleep naturally, though she was still kept torpid by the power of the tranquilisers flowing through her system. She awoke once or twice, muzzy and frightened, unable to remember where or even who she was before drifting back into unconsciousness.

She also experienced nightmares about something large, black and terrifying approaching her, drawing closer and closer until the creature was close enough to smother and devour her before it faded away, grumbling in the darkness. The Medi-Brain recorded the agitation but couldn't register the terror she felt before the medication once again pulled her back into an uneasy slumber.

Doctor Pender noted the brainwave patterns and guessed that Poppy was suffering nightmares, a common side effect of technology being grafted into the human body. He ordered a mild increase in sedatives to give her peaceful rest. Evans, still smarting from the hysterical attack on him by Lady

Helena, secretly countermanded the order. He wasn't going to waste expensive drugs on a working-class girl, though the medication did find its way onto the final invoice.

After several more days, Poppy's strength triumphed and she awoke properly, conscious of her surroundings and of herself. She looked up at the ceiling of her private room and listened to the clatter of a trolley being pushed along the corridor outside, as well as the low murmur of doctors and nurses speaking to each other about their patients.

She was aware of a strange heaviness in her right side. Her new mechanical arm was far denser than her organic left arm, and it felt as though she were completely unbalanced. Doctor Pender had explained before the operation that she would soon get used to it, and she hoped he was right; it felt as though a lead weight had been grafted onto her. She was also aware of a series of strange sensations in her right shoulder, rather like pins and needles, and she guessed it was the mechanical nerve endings receiving and transmitting to her organic nerve endings. Which was presumably good.

Poppy knew she was putting off the moment of looking at – and moving – her new mechanical limb, but she didn't yet feel ready. Instead she lay back and gazed determinedly at the ceiling, feeling the press of the bedclothes on her body, an itch developing on her right leg, the sudden sensation as she wriggled her toes.

She eased her left arm down and gently scratched the itch, moving in a slow, deliberate manner, feeling her soft skin respond under her light touch. She lifted her hand and moved it slowly over her body, inching it towards her right arm even though she did not feel brave enough to touch it. She wanted to creep up on it, to ready herself before making contact, but suddenly her probing fingertips brushed against the unfeeling cold metal.

The surprise made her jump and her new arm jumped with her, responding to the sensations firing along her nervous system. She stared at the bed sheet which was now being lifted up by her hidden arm which had been tucked under the sheet by the nurses, and Poppy wondered in slight hysteria why they had bothered; it wasn't as though the metal could feel the cold.

With a sudden movement that hardly required any thought, Poppy flung the sheet back and stared at her new metal limb. The shock of seeing the robotic arm, somehow separate yet undoubtedly also part of her, made her heave and she found herself leaning over the bed and retching uncontrollably. She would have fallen from the bed but she automatically reached out and grabbed the bedside table to steady herself. Reached out with her false arm. Without thinking.

She slowly looked up from the floor and gazed both at the arm and the hand clasping the side table, the fingers splayed out exactly as an organic hand would have done. She lifted herself back upright, keeping her arm raised high above her, the limb reacting perfectly to her impulses. She didn't have to consciously will any movement; the arm reacted to the needs of her unconscious commands. Just like her other arm. Her natural arm. She had two arms.

Poppy laughed out loud, still slightly hysterical and woozy, but with acceptance now firmly in her mind. She gazed at her new limb, noting the highly-polished surface and the craftsmanship in the joints of the elbow, wrist, hands and fingers. Two dials were embedded just above the wrist, one a pressure warning for when doing heavy work, the other showing the battery reserve. As she moved the arm around the first dial barely twitched, showing the limb was working well within tolerances. She rotated the arm vigorously in different directions, feeling the weight of it pulling at her body, but even this unusual sensation was beginning to feel normal.

She rolled the sleeve of her gown up; it was disturbing to see the severe join where the skin finished and the polished steel began underneath her shoulder. It was also odd to see the smooth outline of the detachable plate on the back of the upper arm which gave access to the batteries and inner workings, and to hear the faint whine of the machinery as she moved, but she now knew she would get used to it.

Poppy settled back and linked her fingers together, wary in case her mechanical hand should twitch and crush her organic fingers, but it responded no differently than her natural hand. She looked up at the ceiling again and grinned.

During her long convalescence in the hospital, Poppy was increasingly disturbed by the lack of visitors. She had suspected her father wouldn't bother, for he was now obsessed solely with *Thunderbus*. She also realised Amy would have trouble getting away as she wasn't a confident driver in their borrowed runabout, but Poppy was surprised when Helena didn't visit for several days. She found out the reason when Helena finally appeared at the end of the week.

At first, after an impulsive hug and smile, Helena tried to distract Poppy by asking about her new arm and how she was coping. Poppy happily showed off her prosthesis but quickly turned the conversation to her father and the upcoming race. Helena parried and dodged the questions as well as she was able, but

Poppy was relentless and the older woman knew she had no choice but to tell Poppy what was going on.

'Your father has been getting ever more demanding, of himself as well as the others,' she admitted. 'He works constantly on *Thunderbus*, from first thing in the morning until last thing at night. It's as much as anyone can do to make him eat and sleep.'

'How is everyone else reacting?'

'They are tired and I fear tempers are beginning to fray, though Amy has been acting as a peacemaker between everyone. She is very upset, incidentally, that she cannot get away to visit, but your father is working everyone as hard as possible.'

'What is Simeon doing? Surely he has the authority to step in?'

'*Thunderbus* is your father's project, so there is little Simeon can do. He does insist that the pit crew goes home at a reasonable time but that does not stop your father from working late into the night by himself, or continually taking *Thunderbus* out for practice runs. The strain is telling on him. I fear either his body or his mind will give in.'

'What?' exclaimed Poppy. 'I can't stay here any longer. Where are my clothes? How do I discharge myself?'

'I think the doctors need to complete the discharge

papers,' began Helena before seeing the look on Poppy's face. 'I'm sure they'll agree, though. Will you be sad to leave here?'

'I'll be sorry to leave Doctor Pender and Clara, but I certainly won't miss that idiot in charge, what's his name? Oh yes, Evans.' Poppy laid her mechanical hand on Helena's. 'And thank you for everything you've done for me.'

Helena smiled, noting the girl had developed a fresh level of confidence. Not that she had needed it, as such, for Poppy had never been lacking in self-belief, knowing – without arrogance – that she was far more intelligent than most other people. That belief, however, had been balanced by the inescapable knowledge that she was 'guilty' of being female, working-class and a cripple – all crimes in the eyes of society.

But now, with her new mechanical arm, she could truly compete against the social order – and given her anger and intelligence, she would have a real chance of winning her battles. Poppy was about to be unleashed onto the world and Helena suddenly felt both apprehensive and oddly thrilled at what lay ahead.

CHAPTER TEN

Poppy accompanied Helena back to Pallister Hall that afternoon. They travelled in one of Simeon's limousines driven by a chauffeur, Langley, who was unknown to Poppy, and she realised anew just how many people Simeon had working for him. The costs of running the hall had to be immense; the further costs of funding *Thunderbus* could explain Simeon's reluctance to interfere too much with the project and thus risk its premature end.

'Langley, please drop me at the front of the hall, and then continue with Miss Orpington to the garage,' said Helena through the car's speaking grill.

'Yes, my lady,' murmured the chauffeur, glancing back in respect. His expression shifted as his eyes skipped over Poppy before he focussed on the road again, though it wasn't long before his gaze once more slid back in the driver's mirror to the young, flame-haired girl on the back seat.

Despite her concerns, Poppy found herself distracted by Langley's covert glances in the driver's mirror; although she was familiar with sexually-charged interest from men, that interest usually disappeared as soon as her missing arm was noted, yet Langley's gaze was almost continuous. It took

Poppy several seconds to realise that her new prosthetic had changed not only what she could do with her life, but the way in which others viewed her. Presumably, having two arms 'balanced' her in the eyes of the outside world and made her more appealing to those given to superficial judgements.

Helena gave Poppy a quick hug before getting out in front of the hall, leaving the driver to take Poppy to the workshop. Mindful of her new discovery, Poppy coldly told him to wait outside in case there was no one around, which proved wise as she found the garage empty. She walked back out into the bright sunshine, wondering where to start looking, and heard quick footsteps pattering around the side of the building. She smiled. She could recognise Amy's light movements anywhere.

Amy appeared, looking flushed, upset and hot, but her face changed swiftly to delight when she saw Poppy standing in the yard. 'You're back!' she squealed as she hurtled forward and hugged Poppy tightly, uncaring if anyone was around to see them.

'Hello, Amy,' whispered Poppy, burying her face in Amy's blonde hair, happy to be in her arms.

'Oy!' exclaimed Amy a minute later as her bottom was unexpectedly squeezed. She looked in pleasurable surprise at Poppy, who smiled innocently and held up her left hand.

'It wasn't me; my hand is up here.'

Amy reached behind her, her face changing as she felt the cool metal hand cupping her bottom. She gently pulled it away and saw Poppy's new arm for the first time – or at least as much as she could see under Poppy's jacket.

'That is amazing,' she breathed, holding Poppy's mechanical hand in her own, inspecting the craftsmanship of the prosthetic.

Poppy flexed her fingers slightly, making Amy jump, before lifting the hand so that the metal palm was lying flat against Amy's palm. They gently linked their fingers together, entwining around each other. Poppy couldn't feel anything, at least physically, but the moment of quiet, with Amy close to her, their bodies almost touching, gazing into each other's eyes, was exquisite, and they stood for some time without speaking.

Amy came out of her trance with a jolt. 'Oh, I need to get back. I forgot the wrench for the sparking plugs and your dad – well, I ran back to get it. I said I'd only be a minute!' She disappeared into the workshop and reappeared again with the wrench.

'You mean Dad actually ...' Poppy hesitated, uncertain of what she meant. 'He shouted at you?'

Amy shrugged. 'He's under a lot of pressure and he's very easy to anger at the moment. It's not just me; he's been like that with everyone. Even Simeon.'

'He still shouldn't be acting like that,' said Poppy, quietly.

'Oh, Poppy, it doesn't matter,' said Amy, looking at her friend's face. 'We just have to accept it. Come on, I need to get back. We're at the track in the lower field.' She set off but stopped at seeing Poppy's face. 'Poppy, please don't.'

'Don't what?'

'Don't say anything. I know that look. It's the same one your father wears a lot these days. It won't do any good and we can't afford to get distracted. It doesn't matter,' she added again.

Poppy looked at her friend and saw the anxiety on her face and the nervousness in her eyes. She moved forward and cupped Amy's face in her hands so she could examine her closely. She was appalled at how tired and fragile Amy looked. 'Amy, you look on the verge of collapse. Have you been eating and sleeping properly? Have you been getting regular breaks?'

'We don't have time for that; we have to get *Thunderbus* ready …' began Amy, before being cut off.

'*Thunderbus* is as ready as it ever will be,' said Poppy firmly, her anger rising at the way her father was treating the crew, and Amy especially. 'The past few weeks should have been nothing but tactics and maintenance. There wasn't any real reason to do any major work on the car when I went into hospital, so what have you been doing to wear yourselves out so much?'

'Your father thinks we can get more out of it, so we have been stripping down and rebuilding to new standards every day.' Amy suddenly sobbed as tears poured down her face. 'I'm sorry, Poppy, I shouldn't be so disloyal. Your father gave me this job, but since you went away he's become an ogre! You know how big the car is, and how heavy. The strain of rebuilding it every few days has exhausted everyone. And as soon as it's back together, we check the performance and it's always worse and then we get cursed and we have to start all over again!'

'Amy, it's not your fault. It's not you, it's him,' said Poppy, quietly. She felt tears stinging her own eyes at how unhappy her friend was, as well as the changes in her father. Was this the same man who had raised her, taught her mechanics, walked with her to the public park and the swings when she was little? What had happened? What had gone wrong?

'Come on,' said Poppy, giving Amy a hug. 'Let's get over to the track and sort this out, once and for all. We can get Langley to drive us over. That will save time.'

They found the team on the road next to one of the many orchards that abutted the home-built racetrack. There seemed to be some sort of argument going on, judging by the finger-pointing and other hand gestures. Poppy found herself hoping it was all a terrible mistake as she leapt from the limousine, that her father hadn't become an unrecognisable tyrant, but as she drew nearer she could no longer deny reality as she heard her father yelling at Christopher about the suspension.

'It's still suffering from too much body roll – what the hell do you think I told you to adjust it for? Now we have to strip it all down and start again! You hear me?'

'For Heaven's sake, we cannot keep stripping down and rebuilding,' interrupted Talbot. 'There is nothing more we can do.'

'We'd have better cornering if he'd done what I told him to do!' raged Orpington.

'I did exactly what you told me and that is why the suspension is labouring,' snarled Christopher in reply. 'It's your bad design and planning that's to blame, not me.'

'What do you know about anything?' screamed Orpington, his face purple with rage. 'You're just on the pit crew! I'm the one who designed the world's first perfect engine. You hear me?'

'You just built on what others had done before you,' sneered Christopher. 'All you ever did was tinker with the designs. Designs no one else could be bothered with!'

'Have you rebuilt the steering like I told you to?' bellowed Orpington, suddenly swinging round to William, the youngest member of the pit crew, who looked ready to burst into tears.

'Yes, Mr Orpington,' he stuttered, 'but it won't make any difference to the understeer problem. You've got too many issues with the steering rack.'

'There aren't any issues, not if you followed my exact designs,' interrupted Orpington in fury. 'I'm testing this car right now and if the steering hasn't been fixed, you'll be for it, boy. You hear me?'

'Robert, will you calm down?' pleaded Simeon, desperately. 'We are all doing our best to help.'

'Your best?' exploded Orpington, clutching his head in pain. Although no one was aware of it, as his mental health disintegrated he was being overloaded with stimuli from the outside world. Sights, smells and sounds were pounding his head, sending waves of disorientation through him. 'Your best is nowhere near good enough. No crew should be this incompetent.' He swayed and his face went rigid. 'That's it, isn't it?' he hissed. 'It's not incompetence;

233

you're out to ruin me! You're deliberately sabotaging my project. You want me to fail, don't you?'

'Robert, for God's sake, man, just listen to yourself,' exclaimed Simeon. 'You're becoming paranoid. Of course, we want you to succeed, all of us. We've all worked hard. I have sunk money into improving *Thunderbus* …'

'Yes, you're the ringleader, you're the one against me, you're trying to ruin me,' snarled Orpington. 'You want my designs. You want *Thunderbus* to fail so you can exercise your release clauses in the contract and claim it all! Well, it won't happen, see. I know what you're doing. I can run *Thunderbus* by myself. You won't have a chance to ruin me! It's all mine. Mine, do you hear? Mine!'

With a final, inarticulate scream of rage, Orpington ran to *Thunderbus* and leapt into the car. Foam flecked his lips and beard while his face contorted grotesquely, darting suspicious glances left and right as he started the car. 'None of you will get me!' he screamed as *Thunderbus* roared to life. 'None of you! I'm free, you hear me? Free!'

Thunderbus leapt forward, almost crushing several of the pit crew who darted desperately out of the way, and the last Poppy saw of her father was his furious face, locked in a grimace of hatred and triumph, as he sped away. He didn't even glance at his daughter as he passed.

'What do we do now?' exclaimed Talbot in frustration.

'I ... I just don't know,' muttered Simeon in shock. 'I just don't understand.'

'Ah, let him go,' said Christopher in disgust. 'His mind's gone. It's all over. We'll never compete at Purley now.'

'Simeon!' shouted Poppy, running up to the group. 'We have to go after him.'

'Poppy! How long have you been there?'

'Long enough to see my father is unwell and a danger to himself. We have to stop him.'

'Yes, but ... but ...' spluttered Simeon, unable to deal with the situation.

'Langley is still over there; we can follow Dad in the limousine. Come on, Simeon,' urged Poppy. She found herself pulling Amy along with her. She had a terrible feeling she had just lost her father, and she didn't want to lose her best friend as well.

'I'll drive,' commanded Simeon, gathering his dazed wits as he followed Poppy to the car. 'Langley, take the crew back to the house so they can explain to Lady Helena what has happened. Tell her we need a doctor there for when we bring Poppy's father back.'

'Yes, my lord,' murmured Langley, wondering

how he was supposed to take the crew back to the house without a vehicle.

Poppy and Amy had to sit in the back of the car as there was no space for them in the front. They leaned up against the glass, peering out around them, hoping for a glimpse of *Thunderbus*, but they saw nothing all the way around the estate until they reached the gates of the hall.

'Surely he hasn't gone off the grounds completely?' Simeon asked through the partition that divided the driver from the passengers.

'He may have done,' said Poppy in reply. 'I didn't see any dust being kicked up anywhere on your home-made track.'

'But where would he go?' asked Simeon.

'Home, and his own workshop,' said Poppy. 'It's all I can think of.'

Simeon nodded and turned the car towards Stourbridge, accelerating as quickly as he could, but unfortunately the limousine was designed for comfort rather than speed. They had no chance of overtaking *Thunderbus*; their only hope was to catch up with it when it stopped. Surprisingly, they did not have far to travel before doing so.

As they passed through Ombersley village, they saw a cart at the side of the road. The driver of the cart was lying on the ground, being tended to by some of the villagers while his horse was soothed by a farmer. Simeon slowed down carefully so as not to scare the horse, which was sweating and tossing its head in agitation. 'What happened?' he asked a small boy at the edge of the crowd.

'Some huge loud car went racing through the village and scared the horse; made it bolt, it did,' gabbled the child, his eyes wide. 'Threw the cart driver right off!'

'Is he injured?' called out Simeon anxiously.

'No, sir, just frightened and shook up,' said one of the women. 'He should be fine soon.'

'More than that maniac will be if he comes back up this way,' rumbled the landlord of the local pub, to the muttered agreement of the crowd. 'He came tearing through here like the Devil himself was after him. Sounded like it an' all, the noise that car was making. We're lucky no one was killed.'

'Where did the car go afterward?' asked Simeon, torn between comforting the villagers, many of whom were tenants of the Pallister family, and denying any liability.

'He swung off the road to avoid the horse and shot down the old farm track, towards the ruin of Fowler's place,' said another man, striding towards them. The crowd fell silent at the information; all knew of the

Fowler farm by repute. Decades earlier, working under the stress of trying to make the farm profitable for Simeon's grandfather, Fowler had gone insane and killed his wife, his children and then himself. The farm had decayed over the years and was now the source of many superstitious tales across the area. As such, the villagers all looked relieved at Simeon's next decision.

'We'll go down and get him,' he announced. 'Everyone else, please stay here.' He guided the large, cumbersome limousine down the old, cracked, mile-long concrete track, stopping just short of the main courtyard and thus blocking *Thunderbus'* only way out.

The steam turbine whistled to a stop and utter silence surrounded Poppy, Amy and Simeon as they climbed from the car. Trees and bushes stood thickly around the courtyard, blocking out much of the light, yet there were no birds singing anywhere. Amy wondered if the car had scared them away, or if the birds simply never nested near the old farm.

The ground around the farm itself, like the road in and out, was old broken concrete, so they had no tyre marks to follow; they would have to trust to luck in finding Poppy's father. They walked towards the numerous dilapidated buildings ahead. The first was a barn, the roof falling in, the huge double doors hanging lopsidedly in the frame. Amy peered into the darkness, illuminated by the filtered sunlight coming through the many gaping holes in the roof. It was empty.

They passed a cattle shed, a grain store and a workshop, all abandoned, all empty, all smelling of damp and neglect, and still they could see no trace of *Thunderbus* or Poppy's father. They cautiously peered around the edge of the workshop and saw a range of other buildings dotted around. The farm was so large, it was almost like a tiny village in its own right. No wonder Fowler had gone mad trying to work the place single-handedly. The strain would have killed anyone, sooner or later, especially as he was threatened daily by Simeon's grandfather to increase his yields and profitability.

Without saying anything, they found themselves splitting up and walking in different directions between the numerous buildings. Amy found herself in front of the huge farmhouse itself, which at one time would have housed at least a dozen labourers. Then it would have been bright and cheerful, a place of perpetual movement, of cooking, laughing and hard work. Now, it was stained by the weather, time and neglect. The large front windows looked like baleful eyes staring down in resentment at Amy as she passed by, making her shiver.

Simeon's route took him to the edge of the pastureland, all overgrown. Ahead of him was the old dairy, ancient and decrepit, like the rest of the place. He knew the stories as well as Amy and Poppy. New tenants had been found after the killings, but none stayed. Tales of strange noises in the night, of unearthly shrieks, of unseen children sobbing, became the main talking points of the village. The place was spoken of as being cursed. One farmer lost his hand in a threshing machine. His replacement died within a month of taking on the lease. Another lost his family, who refused to stay at the farm after being frightened by the unexplained noises. The farmer left soon after but misfortune followed and he lost his savings and died a pauper in the workhouse.

Poppy walked deeper into the farm, getting lost in the labyrinth of roads between the various buildings. More workshops, an old-fashioned forge, a lambing shed, a second barn, even an abattoir and butchery, most of wooden construction, all decrepit with age and neglect. Her attention slowly moved back to the second barn; this was even more ramshackle than the first. Many of the planks that made up the walls had fallen away, but the dark shadows from the dilapidated roof and surrounding buildings made it impossible to see inside clearly. Nevertheless, Poppy thought there was a gleam in the darkness.

She walked towards the doors, both of which hung permanently open on broken, sagging hinges, wedged against the ground by time and their own weight. The opening was just big enough to drive a car through. Poppy sniffed. The smell of petrol was in the air. Her father had come this way. Was he still there? 'Dad?' she called out. 'Are you there, Dad?'

'You see the way it is?' shouted a voice hoarsely from the dark, making Poppy jump. 'You see the way the rich use and abuse us? Look around you, girl; this is what it's like the world over! They work us, control us, even own us, and eventually they break us. Old Man Fowler was a good man, driven to the edge by Lord Pallister. Pallister demanded more money, more produce, more profit, while all the time he scaled back the workers, sacked them one by one, said Fowler could do it all himself. Said he could do it with his wife and children. Said what else were the kids for, if not to work? He threatened Fowler with debtor's jail and deportation for his children if he didn't work. He broke him! That's the way of it, girl. That's the way the world works. But they won't break me! I've broken them! I've escaped them!'

'Dad? Simeon isn't like that,' replied Poppy, trying to keep him talking as she edged closer to the open doors.

'They're all like it,' snarled the voice. 'Nothing

ever changes! We work, they live off us! But they won't get *Thunderbus*! *Thunderbus* is mine. All mine!'

'Dad, please, listen,' said Poppy, but her words were lost as *Thunderbus*' engine roared back into life and the car erupted from the dark, bearing down on her. Poppy hurled herself to one side, feeling the mighty wind of the huge car as her father shot past, the gears screaming as he crunched the gearbox.

Simeon and Amy came running around the corner of the building, drawn by the sound of the engine. Mr Orpington didn't think as the two people suddenly appeared in his way; he just reacted, flinging the wheel around. The car skidded and collided with the lambing shed which immediately erupted in a plume of dust and falling wooden beams. Simeon and Amy ran for cover, blind to the events behind them as they tried to avoid the terrific roar of destruction, while Poppy could only watch in horror as *Thunderbus* disappeared under the falling timber.

As the noise settled, Poppy leapt up and ran towards her father, peering into the great cloud of swirling dirt and filth for any sign that he was still alive. She could dimly see *Thunderbus* and realised that most of the wooden beams had somehow missed the car, but a few were lying across the vehicle and her father

242

was slumped, unmoving, over the wheel. Coughing and gasping, Poppy strained to reach her father but the beams lying across the top of *Thunderbus* were in the way. She could now see that the windscreen had been crushed by one of the beams and she feared the worst.

She placed her mechanical hand under one of the planks and lifted upward. The dial registering the stresses acting on the arm flickered briefly. Poppy pushed harder and the length of timber flipped to one side with a sudden movement. She grabbed the next beam and hurled it aside with ease. In seconds, she had cleared the heavy planks and reached her father. As her hand brushed him, he jerked and mumbled, pushing back at some unseen menace that existed only in his mind. Despite the blood on his face, caused by the broken glass from the windshield, he was alive.

'Poppy, is he …? Are you …?' cried Amy incoherently as she and Simeon ran forward.

'I think the planks all missed him,' coughed Poppy in reply, dust and tears stinging her eyes.

'Let's get the car clear; then we can drive your father straight to the nearest hospital,' said Simeon. There was little point in returning to Pallister Hall; Poppy's father clearly needed more care than a country doctor could give. The three of them gently pushed Mr Orpington into the passenger seat so that Simeon could take his place. He nervously started the car and clumsily drove it forward, grunting as he heaved on the large steering wheel to angle *Thunderbus'* nose away from the shed and back towards the track. He just managed it, though it tore at his shoulders and arms to do so, while his leg screamed as it barely managed to operate the heavy clutch.

Poppy and Amy ran to the limousine that was still blocking the way out. Poppy manoeuvred the car into the farmyard without thinking, her mind on her father, before following *Thunderbus'* rear lights through the darkening sky, impatient with Simeon's slow speed. He was clearly having enormous trouble driving the heavy, unforgiving car. Poppy heard the gearbox grind on more than one occasion, while corners were taken at a walking pace as Simeon heaved on the steering wheel, frequently having to stop and reverse as he didn't have the strength to turn the car fully.

Eventually, they turned off the road and onto a lengthy drive which led to a large eighteenth century house that had been converted to a hospice. Simeon made no attempt to park but simply left *Thunderbus* as close to the front door as he could before hobbling up the steps and pressing the doorbell, all the while holding his neck in pain. A small plaque next to the door announced they were at St Patrick's Private Rest Home.

Poppy pulled up behind and ran to her father, who was now stirring and mumbling incoherently in the passenger seat. She threw her arms around him and whispered soothingly in his ear. She was aware of the doors of the hospice being opened, of hurried explanations, and then two men, orderlies in white clothes, were by her side examining her father briskly and professionally.

'No obvious sign of any injury,' said one of them. 'I think we can move him inside.' He looked at Mr Orpington's face which was locked in a grimace of mental anguish, tears rolling freely down his cheeks. 'Can you hear me, sir?' he called loudly. 'We need you to get out of the car, sir. Please step this way. Please leave the car, sir,' he said again for emphasis, trying to gently pull his patient out.

This was a mistake. Whatever was passing through Mr Orpington's mind was now focussed exclusively on *Thunderbus*. Aware that someone was trying to part him from the car he loved and hated in equal measure, he shouted and swore, randomly swinging his arms and trying to bite anyone who came too close.

'Dad!' shouted Poppy in alarm. 'Calm down, Dad, we're here to help you!'

'Robert, control yourself,' said Simeon in alarm. 'These people are medical orderlies.' Unfortunately, he got too close and was shoved violently backward, causing him to yelp as fresh waves of pain engulfed his neck and arms.

'Out you come,' grunted one of the orderlies, grabbing Mr Orpington by the arm and heaving him from the car. His companion grabbed the other arm but both were immediately flung to the ground, unable to deal with Mr Orpington's strength and rage. Two more attendants rushed forward to help. All four smothered Mr Orpington, trying to pin down his flailing limbs and drag him to the entrance. With a single effort, he straightened and hurled the men from him, scattering them over a wide area.

'Get the restraints and the batons!' yelled one of the men as he got back up again.

'You are not going to use batons on my father,' snapped Poppy in reply.

'There's no other way of getting him inside, girl,' replied the man with contempt, staying well away from his patient.

Poppy looked at her father as he swayed from side to side, his hands balled into fists, looking ferocious yet also lost. 'You can get a restraint but nothing more,' she ordered.

'And how do you think you'll get him into it?' sneered the man.

'Just get the restraint,' said Poppy as she moved towards her father.

'Be careful!' shouted Amy in concern.

'Come on, Dad, it's me, Poppy. You know me, don't you, Dad?' said Poppy, moving closer.

'Poppy, I don't think he does,' said Simeon in warning. 'One of those wooden beams must have struck his head. I don't think he recognises anyone or anything!' He looked at the striking silhouette of Poppy and her father against the setting sun, Poppy's wild hair flaming, Mr Orpington's huge beard bristling, two titans in a world of smaller mortals.

'You wouldn't hurt me, would you, Dad?' continued Poppy, who was now almost in reach of the panting man. Behind her, she heard the orderlies returning, presumably with the restraints. 'Dad? Come with me inside, Dad. It's nice and warm in there. Come inside, Dad.'

Silence fell as she reached forward until her father unexpectedly swung his arms around while screaming incoherently. Poppy had been ready, however, and she caught one of her father's wrists in her mechanical hand, stopping his movement dead. For a moment, he stood immobilised before he

247

roared anew, thrashing his free hand in wild circles and kicking out with both legs.

Poppy evaded the blows without releasing her hold on him and then gave a single, savage twist of her hand that brought tears to her eyes as she unwillingly hurt her father, who screamed and fell to one knee as his arm was rotated up behind him, making escape impossible.

'Move, you men!' bellowed Simeon to the shocked orderlies, who finally strapped the restraints around Mr Orpington's body. A wooden wheelchair was brought out and he was secured to it so he could be moved, struggling, swearing and crying, into the hospice and an examination room.

Poppy tried to follow but a kindly nurse stopped her in the entrance hall and gently explained that all Poppy could do now was wait for the night doctor to examine his new patient and report back to them. Poppy turned and blundered past Amy and Simeon, running back outside until she found herself next to *Thunderbus*. Alone except for the car which had cost her father so much, she cried helplessly to herself.

CHAPTER ELEVEN

An hour later, Poppy was standing at her father's side as he lay unconscious in a hospital bed.

'I'm sorry, Miss Orpington,' said Doctor Jameson. 'I just can't give you a full diagnosis. Physically, it's easy enough; it's clear that your father's body has been under immense pressure for some time. His muscles and ligaments are strained well beyond endurance, and I'm worried about the state of his heart.'

'I'm sorry, Poppy, I'm so sorry,' said Simeon. 'I knew he was under pressure but I never thought he couldn't cope. He was just so strong. Now that I've driven *Thunderbus* a few miles, I can appreciate what sort of physical stress he was under. I think I've pulled several muscles,' he added, wincing in pain. 'How your father managed to keep driving it for so long, especially throughout the Sussex race, I do not know.'

'All this is simple enough to deduce, but it isn't the physical side of things that worries me,' continued Doctor Jameson. 'The body can usually be fixed. It's your father's mental condition that is of concern. Has he been under mental strain? Considerable mental strain?'

Poppy nodded in despair and quickly explained about the upcoming race. 'He's become obsessed with it, to the exclusion of all else,' she finished.

Jameson nodded. 'Yes, I feared as much from the way your father was raving when you brought him in. His mind has snapped under the pressure.'

'Surely not, Doctor?' gasped Simeon. 'Why, the man is built like an ox!'

'There is no correlation between mental and physical strength, Lord Simeon,' replied Jameson sadly. 'The mind is a delicate instrument. If it is injured, it can be forever damaged.'

'What can be done about it?' asked Amy, her voice small in the dark, cheerless room. 'Can you help him? Can you cure him?'

Jameson shook his head. 'I know it sounds silly to say this, given the revolution in medical care that has occurred over the past few decades, but while our understanding of the body has leapt forward, our understanding of the mind is still in its infancy.'[36]

---

[36] What Jameson was glossing over here was the social stigma attached to mental illness, a stigma that hampered any serious research and understanding of the mind. Society assumed that only the feeble would experience such issues, and that if sufferers just made an effort they could pull themselves together. In reality, of course, nothing could be further from the truth. It is incredible to think that our Edwardian ancestors could attach a false limb to the body and integrate it perfectly

'But surely it's a physical problem,' interrupted Simeon, not wanting to believe that a man's man like Mr Orpington could ever suffer from such a feminine weakness as a brainstorm. 'He must have been hit on the head by one of the falling wooden beams we told you about.'

'No, there is no sign of any head trauma. He was struck across the one shoulder but nothing more.'

'Is there anything we can do?' asked Poppy.

'I would advise keeping your father sedated for a while, purely so his body can have a chance to recover. Then the real issue of repairing his mind can be looked at, but I fear I am not the man for that. I do however know a few doctors who work in that particular field, and I will gladly call them in.'

Poppy closed her eyes, her mind awash with misery at the thought that her father's physical strength counted for nothing. It was his mind that had snapped, not his body. 'How could I have been so blind, so insensitive to his suffering?' she whispered. 'I saw he was pushing himself to the limit but I never once thought he would collapse like this.'

'We had no way of knowing,' said Simeon firmly, leaving Poppy wondering if he was reassuring himself rather than her. 'Your father was totally

---

with bone, muscle and nerve impulses, yet their understanding of what lay behind those impulses was so shockingly limited.

committed. All the best drivers have to be, in order to win. I saw nothing that gave me any concern for his mental wellbeing. We have nothing to reproach ourselves with. We could not have known.'

Doctor Jameson diplomatically left the group alone to discuss matters, telling them he would be in his office if they needed him. Poppy thanked him, her face white and strained, her eyes never leaving her father.

'He can get better, I know he can,' said Simeon, patting Poppy awkwardly on the shoulder. 'He's so strong. He can get through this.'

'Yes, but he needs help that doesn't seem to exist,' replied Poppy. 'What can be done for him, really? What, except bedrest? And how will that help his mind?'

'And where can he get treatment?' asked Amy quietly. 'This isn't a charity hospice, is it?'

'Er, no, it is a private hospice. I sit on the board of directors,' answered Simeon. 'You're right, of course, the costs here would be ...' He paused, choosing his word carefully. 'They would be far more than your father can afford, Poppy. Though I'm sure what's left of the prize money from the Sussex race will keep him here for at least a few weeks, which gives you time to, er, well, to decide what to do.'

'You mean what to do once the money runs out?' said Poppy, sharply. 'Take him to Pallister Hall for bedrest? Or would that not be suitable? If not, I can take him back home and look after him there.'

'Yes, but for how long?' asked Simeon. 'Your father could be unwell for weeks to come, maybe even months, based on what the doctor just told us. Whatever the outcome, he will not be able to race at Purley.'

'Is that all you are thinking of?' demanded Poppy.

'I'm as concerned for him as you are, Poppy, but I'm afraid that isn't quite the end of the matter,' said Simeon, apologetically. 'You see, my lawyer drew up many clauses to provide for any eventuality that could arise. He did this to protect both your father and myself. Unfortunately, one of those clauses …'

'What about it?' demanded Poppy, her voice harsh.

Simeon fidgeted, looking uncomfortable. 'One clause states quite clearly that if *Thunderbus* does not participate in the race, then all the patents and designs, and the car itself, become my property.'

'What?' exclaimed Poppy. 'How could you do such a thing?'

'It was for my protection that Mr Pippin inserted those clauses. I didn't like them but I appreciated that I needed them in case something unexpected happened. I have invested a considerable amount into *Thunderbus* and I needed security for the project.'

'I quite understand,' retorted Poppy. 'I can see that Simeon the capitalist approves, while Simeon the man is unhappy with the clauses.'

'Poppy, that is unfair,' replied Simeon. 'I didn't know you or your father when we started on all this. I had no idea if he was trustworthy or reliable. I took an enormous chance on him. Indeed, Mr Pippin didn't want me to invest in the project and tried to talk me out of it, not out of spite but simply because he is paid to protect my interests. When I made it clear I was going ahead, he therefore protected my interests by inserting those clauses.'

'So, that's it, is it? After all our hard work, we go back to having nothing? To *being* nothing?'

'You retain one quarter of a per cent on all patents, so if the petrol engine can be manufactured, you will at least get something. I asked for that to be the case no matter what.'

Poppy turned on her heel and strode out of the small room and down the corridor, her knee brace supporting her long, angry strides. She was fuming at the situation and felt even more livid that she could see things from Simeon's perspective; many other investors would have simply taken all the patents, so at least he was leaving them a percentage, but would the engine now be put into production? And what would the shock do to her father when he learnt he had lost *Thunderbus* without even racing it?

Poppy realised her new mechanical hand was clenching itself into a fist, responding to the angry impulses flowing through her. She could have yelled at the bitter irony of the situation. She had a new arm, the chance to participate fully in life for the first time, and the joy had been wiped away by her father's collapse. She wanted to rage and punch the wall but she knew it was pointless. In fact, given the enormous strength of her new arm, it would have been rather unwise; she could easily splinter the plaster and brickwork.

She looked at her prosthesis as she continued along the corridor, aware also of the sounds from her knee brace as the tiny pistons ran back and forth while the cogs turned smoothly, supporting her and allowing her to walk properly. More than that; the brace gave her strength enough to kick over a huge oil drum ... her arm could damage a solid wall. . . if *Thunderbus* didn't participate ...if *Thunderbus*? 'Simeon!' shouted Poppy, whirling around and facing back down the corridor.

Simeon walked out of her father's room, followed by Amy. Both looked pale and upset. 'Yes?'

'This clause, the one that gives you everything. It

states quite clearly that it is activated only if *Thunderbus* does not take part in the race? That is what it says? *Thunderbus*?'

'I'm not sure I understand,' replied Simeon in confusion.

'The clause does not state that my father must participate in the race? It states in black and white that it is *Thunderbus* itself that must race?'

'I think so,' said Simeon, bemused at Poppy's resolute tone.

'So, if *Thunderbus* does race, the clause is invalid?'

Simeon opened his mouth and then closed it again. 'I don't know,' he said eventually. 'I suppose, legally, the letter of the law and all that, then yes, that would be right.'

'And all the paperwork for the race has been done in the name of P. Orpington? I know my father. He hates his first name and he only ever uses his initial. That's why everyone calls him by his middle name, Robert.'

'Well, yes, I believe so, but I still don't quite understand …'

'It's very simple,' replied Poppy, her expression allowing no argument. 'P. Orpington is expected at Purley, and P. Orpington will be at Purley. I will drive *Thunderbus*.'

'Poppy, do you think this is a good idea?' asked Amy as she followed her friend out of the hospital some twenty minutes later.

'Possibly not, but it is the only thing we can do,' replied Poppy, her voice firm. 'Otherwise, we lose everything.'

'Yes, but driving *Thunderbus*? Actually driving it? You saw the pain Simeon was in just from wrestling it the short distance to the hospice. How will you cope on the racetrack?'

'I have this,' said Poppy, flexing her artificial arm. 'And my knee brace. And I'm in better condition than Simeon, having followed Dad for so long on his training exercises.'

'But do you really think you can do it? Really?'

'I don't know, Amy, but what else can I do?' asked Poppy, her voice tired and carrying a hint of desperation. 'Can you see any other solution except to walk away, beaten before we start?'

Amy fell silent. That was the problem; there wasn't any other way. She nodded and took Poppy's hand. 'You're right. If we give in now, we'll have achieved nothing. I suppose we have to at least try.'

'Thanks for saying "we",' said Poppy with half a smile.

'Even so, I'm still scared,' continued Amy. 'You

saw what *Thunderbus* did to your father.'

'Dad didn't have any mechanical help when driving the car. I have. I'm stronger than he is.' Poppy stopped in shock. It was true, of course, but it was still an alarming moment to realise she suddenly surpassed her father in certain ways.

'She's still an absolute beast,' said Amy, looking at the huge black car in the moonlight. Simeon had left it awkwardly in the hospice driveway, having made no attempt to slot it into a parking bay.

Poppy looked at the long black shape and nodded before squeezing Amy's hand. 'Now it's our beast and our problem. All or nothing.'

'I'm actually scared,' mumbled Amy. 'Not just of *Thunderbus* but the whole situation. We're doing it all now. Us. Two girls. You saw the hate we got just for being in the pit crew. How bad will it be when they see you driving?'

Poppy nodded, her brow furrowed as new thoughts moved through her mind. 'I think there are going to be a great many changes, some of which we'll be able to control, some of which we can't. But you know what the most important changes will be? Those on the inside.' She tapped Amy's chest gently as she spoke. 'This is where everything starts. On the inside.'

'Yes, but we've been dropped into the situation by

accident.'

'It still all begins from the inside. We may have been dropped into this, but we can adapt and we can participate. Not just on the track, but against the world that hates us for doing what the world says we shouldn't.'

'It's too daunting to think about,' whispered Amy.

'Then let's break everything down into smaller problems and deal with them one by one. We'll start with the simple problem staring us in the face.'

'You mean getting *Thunderbus* back to Pallister Hall?'

'Exactly. And there is one mental change we can make right now. It's something that has always annoyed me slightly.'

'What's that?'

'Why does everyone refer to a car as a "she"?'

'I don't know,' said Amy, not sure what Poppy meant. 'Everything mechanical is always female. Ships, boats, motorbikes.'

'Do you see *Thunderbus* as a female? As being in any way feminine?'

Amy looked at the huge, snarling radiator grill and menacing headlights. 'I suppose not. It does snort and grumble and bellow enough for any man!'

'Then that is our first change; from now on, *Thunderbus* is definitely a male. Now, I've checked the costs of the weekly care. With the money left over from the Sussex race, Dad can afford to stay here for about a month. Less, if Doctor Jameson calls in a specialist in mental health. They will take care of him while we get *Thunderbus* back to the workshop and prepare him for the race. We have one week to strip him back and rebuild to the best specifications.'

Amy looked at her friend and shivered. There was a determination in Poppy's face that said anyone getting in her way would be crushed. Underneath, Amy could see that Poppy was like a seething volcano, ready to explode, yet she was under full control – and it was the control that was truly frightening. 'Are you sure?' she asked timidly. 'Your father has spent weeks trying to make the car faster and better, but he just made it worse.'

'That was a manifestation of his illness. He lost sight of reality. You know better than I do when the car was at its best because you've been there all the time during each rebuild.'

Amy nodded. '*Thunderbus* was at his best when your father first raced him at the Sussex track. But what about you learning how to race? How to change gears, even?'

'I know the theory of it – we both do – and I watched Dad often enough on the practice laps. He always explained out loud what he was doing and why. Hopefully, I can practise in one of Simeon's cars with a gearbox while you put *Thunderbus* back to the way it should be.'

'All right, let's concentrate on getting back to the Hall.' Amy looked at *Thunderbus* and shivered in apprehension. 'Where's Simeon?' she asked, suddenly remembering her employer.

'Having a lie down,' said Poppy, her voice flat. 'I think it's all been a bit too much for him. I've got the ignition key for *Thunderbus* and given him back his limousine key.' She settled herself behind the steering wheel and carefully adjusted the mirrors and seat, ensuring she was centrally placed to operate all the controls. She turned the ignition key in the dashboard and flipped the switches to start the petrol feed and warm the ignition coils, keenly aware of *Thunderbus'* usual impatient hum filling the air. Unconsciously holding her breath, Poppy pressed the starter button and the engine roared into life.

'Are you getting in?' asked Poppy, breathing out as she looked at Amy.

Amy nervously slid into *Thunderbus'* passenger seat, wishing Mr Orpington had found time to fit some seat belts. She watched as Poppy slowly pressed the enormous clutch pedal down towards the metal floor. Poppy knew how to steer a car after many journeys in the little yellow roadster loaned to them by Simeon, but this was something else entirely. Would Poppy be strong enough?

At first, it didn't seem so. Poppy released the clutch with a curse. She hitched up her dress and adjusted some of the settings on her leg brace, rotating the outer toggle to reduce the length the linking rods had to move, thus increasing their power. Then she pressed back down on the clutch, which dipped down far more smoothly than on the first attempt.

Poppy held the clutch in place for a few moments before taking hold of the gear stick and pushing it forward and up, trying to find first gear. The gearbox, salvaged from an old charabanc, was awkward and slipping slightly. The stick bobbled back and forth until it suddenly popped into place.

She revved the accelerator a few times, which was much lighter than the clutch in order to be more responsive to the driver's need for speed and power. Then she gently eased up on the clutch while pressing on the accelerator, balancing the two. *Thunderbus* snarled in a low tone and tried to jerk forward. Poppy eased the clutch down a little and the engine note changed. The car tried to move again but less aggressively. Poppy released the handbrake and *Thunderbus* moved forward.

Poppy drove along the front of the hospice,

pressing down on the accelerator and causing a shower of pebbles to spit up from under the rear wheels. They reached the corner of the building before Poppy needed to change gear, so she slowed and concentrated on the steering. This was her biggest fear. Would she be strong enough to cope? *Thunderbus* had taken its toll on two grown men, so how would it react to a young girl?

Poppy grimaced; damn that sort of thinking. With a grunt, she wrenched the steering wheel around with her false hand and *Thunderbus* slewed violently to the left, almost crashing into the building. Poppy spun the wheel back and *Thunderbus* responded perfectly. She laughed. With her mechanical arm, it was not just possible; it was easy, though the pressure gauge on her prosthetic flickered towards the red zone as she hauled the wheel left and right. She accelerated again, flying past the illuminated windows of the hospice which shone down on the driveway at equal intervals, moving continually from light to dark and back again.

The car picked up speed and Poppy changed gear, smoothly hitting second. She pressed down on the accelerator as she released the clutch pedal and *Thunderbus* surged forward with a fresh growl of pleasure, a growl that was shared deep in Poppy's throat as she felt the power that lay under her control.

They lapped around the hospice and approached the driveway; Poppy swung the steering wheel and the huge nose turned obediently to the right, away from the hospice and towards the main road. The wide snout of the car seemed to gobble up the ground as the car moved forward at increasing – and alarming – speed.

'Lights!' shouted Amy. 'We haven't got our lights on!'

'Whoops!' shouted Poppy in return. She had forgotten the headlamps as the hospice had been illuminating enough of the driveway for her to see. She flipped the two great switches for the front and rear lamps and, with *Thunderbus* illuminating the way ahead, the two girls drove on into the darkness.

CHAPTER TWELVE

The following day, after barely a few hours' nervous sleep, Poppy and Amy walked towards the garage to explain the previous night's events to the pit crew. 'Are you worried?' whispered Amy as they approached the door.

'Very,' replied Poppy, 'but I'll try not to show it.' They slowed down outside the garage door as voices drifted out to them.

'I'm telling you, it must be over,' said one. 'It looks like Orpington has gone off his head. Why else would he take off like that?'

'Aye, and where is Lord Simeon?' asked another. 'I heard from the butler he didn't come home at all last night.'

'Annie the maid told me that Lady Helena had a call to her private room in the early hours,' said Clive, the voices now recognisable as Poppy and Amy drew closer. 'Annie reckons it was probably Lord Simeon. She says her ladyship looked worried this morning, but not *that* worried.'

'But look,' said Christopher in a reasonable tone, 'if Mr Orpington has gone off his head, then who brought *Thunderbus* back? No one else can drive it. You remember Jack could only just about manage a straight line, and how much experience has he got of driving?'

Poppy and Amy walked in to grunts of agreement from the rest of the crew, who were all standing around *Thunderbus*. Clive was rubbing his hand absentmindedly along the top of the car, while everyone else was simply looking lost and worried.

'Morning, everyone,' said Poppy, while Amy smiled uncertainly in the background. The crew looked surprised but pleased to see them and launched into various questions, all overlapping each other. 'One at a time, please,' said Poppy, flapping her hands to quieten them, and noticing the same reaction from the crew that she had received from the chauffeur the day previously; her new arm meant changes in more ways than one. 'To sum up for everyone: Simeon is fine, he just spent the night at a hospice with my father. I'm afraid my father is too ill to drive.' Her face clouded but she shook off the mood as best as she was able. She had to concentrate on her new role, to the exclusion – if need be – of all personal feelings.

'Then I was right, it is all over,' said William sadly.

'It is not over,' replied Poppy firmly. 'We are going to race as planned, but to do that we need to strip *Thunderbus* down one more time and put him back the way he should be, the way he was before my father's illness made him lose his edge. You all know your jobs, your own areas of expertise. You all know the best configuration for *Thunderbus*. We need to work quickly, as one unit, to be ready for the race.'

'Er, but Poppy, who is going to drive?' asked William, putting up his hand.

'The same person who drove *Thunderbus* back here in the early hours of the morning.'

'Er, and who was that?'

'Me.'

The crew went quiet. Most of them had grudgingly come to respect Poppy's ability and character, but what she was suggesting just didn't fit into their world view. Women did not participate in racing. Such things weren't done, otherwise they would be done, and everyone would be doing them, but they weren't, proving that they didn't.

'*You* drove it back?' asked Christopher finally, latching onto one aspect he could deal with. 'How?'

'Well, I sat behind the wheel, started the ignition, engaged first gear,' said Poppy, giving him a look.

'It's your arm, isn't it?' said Clive, a look of illumination spreading over his face. 'You can control it because of your arm!'

'Exactly,' said Poppy, putting her mechanical

hand onto her hip so that the smooth metal gleamed in the early morning sunlight.

'All right, you can drive it physically, but you'll never be able to drive it at Purley. You won't be allowed in.'

'Why? Is there a rule saying women are not allowed to enter?'

The crew hesitated, looking at each other in confusion. 'Not that I'm aware of,' admitted Clive eventually, 'but then, it's never come up before.'

'The lads are right, though,' said Talbot, harshly, refusing to look at Poppy at he spoke. 'The other drivers won't be happy. They won't allow it.'

'They have no legal way of stopping it,' said a voice from the door. They looked round and saw Simeon lounging against the wall. He was holding a stout walking stick and his neck was encased in a leather brace.

'Are you hurt, my lord?' asked Talbot, hoping to distract attention from his lofty comment. While Poppy was a subordinate, he could tolerate her on the crew, but as the owner/driver, as she now appeared to be, her influence would be the greater – something Talbot did not like the feel of at all.

Simeon grimaced as he nodded towards *Thunderbus*. 'Not really; I just strained myself trying to drive that monster yesterday. I was in pain all night and it was worse this morning, so I asked a doctor to check me over and he discovered I've damaged the muscles in my neck, shoulders and arms. I have to wear this thing for a few days until I heal. So, I know from first-hand experience that only Poppy can drive *Thunderbus*, and by Jove, she is going to! Poppy has taken Robert's place, so we dance to her tune now.'

'Right you are, my lord,' muttered Talbot, less than pleased.

'If you say so, but I still reckon the other drivers won't take to it,' said Clive, who liked to be the prophet of doom.

'We'll sort that later,' said Simeon. 'Why are you rubbing *Thunderbus* like that?'

'Oh, there are some odd dents along the top that weren't here yesterday,' explained Clive. 'Some of them have gone right down to the metal. I assume whatever smashed the windscreen did the damage here as well?'

'Yes, an accident with some wooden planks,' said Simeon. 'Just replace the windscreen and ignore the dents, unless they interfere with the aerodynamics of the car.'

'The entire shape of the car interferes with aerodynamics,' grunted Talbot.

'Yes, but *Thunderbus* just rips right through

269

physics and out onto the other side,' replied William with a shy smile.

'Agreed. Make a start on the repairs, please,' said Simeon, 'while Poppy and I go to London.'

'London?' asked Poppy, who was feeling slightly guilty at her dismissive reaction to Simeon's injuries the night before.

'Yes. You probably didn't know because of your stay in the hospice, but today is registration day for all the drivers who are going to take part in Purley's main racing event, and it must be done in person at the Gordon Club.'

Poppy nodded. 'Right. Then let's get started.'

Some hours later, Simeon's chauffeur turned onto Berkeley Road and drove towards the Gordon Club, the unofficial headquarters of British racing. Poppy, drained after the emotional trauma of the previous day, had slept for most of the journey.

'I hope you can stay awake during this,' said Simeon as they neared the club. 'I need you alert and firing on all cylinders. I fear the pit crew is right; the other drivers – and especially the organisers – will not be happy about you entering.'

Poppy shrugged. 'I shall be fine. I'm more worried about the race and my dad than offending the sensibilities of a group of privileged upper-class wastrels. Oh, no offence,' she added, hastily. 'I do appreciate what you're doing for me, truly. Not many would support me like this. They'd just invoke the release clause of the contract and take everything. Let's face it, that's how the rich get rich in the first place, and it's a large part of how they stay rich. Oh, no offence again.' She put her hand on Simeon's arm and squeezed him affectionately.

'None taken,' answered Simeon. 'There is a core of truth in what you say, but we're not all tarred with the same brush. And please be careful with your mechanical hand; I wouldn't want you to twitch and pull my arm off. I had no idea there was such strength in those things.'

'There isn't in the cosmetic, pretty arms made for the wealthy,' replied Poppy. 'This is the functional version, made for working men and soldiers in the field, so it's designed to be robust and strong. Mind you, it's still rather beautiful, isn't it?' She held the arm up, her face and mane of red hair unconsciously framing the polished steel.

'Er, beautiful, yes,' replied Simeon in a high tone, gazing at the view before blinking rapidly and coughing. 'Form and content in one package,' he added in a more normal voice as he tore his eyes away.[37]

'I opened it up and adjusted the cylindrical muscle a little to increase the power,' said Poppy, oblivious to Simeon's hot flush. 'You never know when you may need a little extra strength.'

'We may need it just to get in,' said Simeon in surprise, looking at the scrum of people outside the club's front doors as the chauffeur pulled up alongside the pavement. 'This place is usually rather refined.'

'Are those reporters?' asked Poppy, noting the heavy brass cameras and recorders.

'Yes. Damn and blast it – I'm not being pictured with this ridiculous brace on.' Simeon hastily undid the clasp at the back of the support and peeled it off, gently rubbing his neck as the air made his skin tingle.

'Is that a good idea? It's there to help you heal.'

'I'm on so many painkillers I should be able to cope for an hour or two, more than enough to get in,

---

[37] Many have accused Poppy and Simeon of having an affair, with some even going as far as saying Poppy became pregnant by him. Personally, I discount this entirely; although a mutual attraction did develop between the two of them, I do not believe they ever acted on it. After all, the betrayal of Helena, whom they both loved, would have been immense. And she, high-spirited as she was, would scarcely have sat quietly by while her husband cheated on her with a young girl.

get registered and get out. If anyone tries to speak to you, it may be best to keep quiet and let me do the talking.'

'Why? Do you think I'm too stupid to deal with them?' demanded Poppy.

'No, no, certainly not,' exclaimed Simeon in horrified surprise. 'No, the problem is – not that it's a problem – the issue is … well, it's your accent.'

'What's wrong with my accent?'

'Nothing, nothing,' said Simeon, hurriedly. 'It's just that it's pure Black Country, and if you don't have the right accent you won't be taken seriously.'[38]

'God, this country,' spat Poppy. 'Good people are kept down by the system that exists only to perpetuate itself. The whole thing stinks!'

'This will do, Langley,' said Simeon to the driver. 'You go and wait in Turner Street and we'll see you there as soon as possible. Get yourself something to eat while we're gone.'

'Yes, my lord, thank you,' said Langley, smiling as he parked and leapt out to open the door for his

---

[38] A state of affairs that still continues today. Anyone outside the Home Counties is judged, at best, as being a stereotypical northerner. I have not attempted to write Poppy's speech as it would have been, as in *I cor do tha'* and *'ow bin ya?* Too much confusion would arise. Besides, she did lose her accent after moving out of the Black Country, as one of the few surviving audio-recorded interviews with her demonstrates.

master.

'Come on, Poppy; you're right but we can't do anything about it now, so let's concentrate on getting registered,' said Simeon gently. 'Besides, perhaps your appearance here today could be the start of a better system.'

Poppy snorted but followed without saying anything else. Despite her anger, she suddenly felt rather self-conscious about her appearance in front of the press. She was wearing her best dress, yet it was still old, faded and frayed around the edges. Society would judge her by her cheap clothes and dismiss her as being poor and therefore of low character, the two things being synonymous in the minds of the ruling classes and their media supporters. She stomped after Simeon, her mood getting worse as they pressed through the reporters and loiterers shouting questions, bribes and threats at the club's doorman, who ignored them all with stoic indifference. He only spoke as Simeon and Poppy walked up the steps towards the doors.

'Good morning, Lord Simeon, and how are you today?'

'Very well, thank you, Thomas,' replied Simeon, ignoring the sudden explosion of voices behind him at his name being spoken out loud. 'Yourself?'

'Very well, thank you, sir.'

'Lord Simeon, Lord Simeon!' shouted the reporters. 'Can we get an interview about your entry to Purley? Interest has been running high since your man won at the Sussex racetrack!'

'Is it?' whispered Poppy in surprise. 'I thought it would have died down by now.'

Simeon shrugged. 'I've been too busy with *Thunderbus* and worrying about your father's behaviour the past few weeks to keep up with the media reports. Besides, my father hates the free press and refuses to have any newspaper in the house, or even to have the news on the telecasting receiver, so I have been rather neglecting the media side of things, I'm afraid.'

'Where is your driver, Orpington? Will he be driving the car again?' shouted another reporter.

'And what is your long-term plan for the car?' shouted another. 'Will you be making the engine available commercially?'

'Gentlemen, all your questions will be answered in due course. Now, if you will excuse us, we must attend the drivers' registration.'

'If you're here to register, where is your driver?' demanded another reporter. He looked blankly at Poppy, but seeing only a female, he ignored her.

'Excuse me, Thomas, coming through,' said Simeon, heading for the doors.

Thomas looked in confusion at Poppy. 'Sorry, my lord, but you know women are not allowed in the Gordon Club.'

'I do indeed,' replied Simeon loudly, 'and I am bringing her in anyway, for this is Poppy Orpington, the driver of car number six, known as *Thunderbus*. So, if you will excuse me, we are going in.' He pushed past the stunned doorman, leaving the journalists squawking in outrage on the street behind them.

'Are women really not allowed in here?' asked Poppy as they entered the large reception hall.

'No, they are not,' said Simeon, casting his eyes over the club's interior of breeding, wealth and exclusion. 'And until I met you, I never questioned that. I just accepted it as part of the natural order of things.'

'Won't you get into trouble?'

'Probably,' replied Simeon, cheerfully. 'And won't that be fun?' He nodded at a sign announcing that the driver registration was being held in the Clarendon Suite. He guided Poppy through the reception, up a very wide set of stairs and along a corridor. She had never seen such luxury before, except in glimpses of Pallister Hall. The place gave off blatant overtones of upper-class exclusivity. Even more blatant was the reaction of the staff on seeing a female walking the premises. One footman blanched, another dropped his tray, while a third stood gibbering incoherently at the strange phenomenon in front of him, further fuelling Poppy's anger.

They reached the Clarendon Suite and walked in. The suite was a large room with plenty of tables, chairs and food for everyone present. The place was packed with drivers and their sponsors, mostly representatives of various British motor manufacturers. The noise level was intense as drivers laughed, joked and jostled each other, but silence exploded around the room in a shockwave as Poppy strode through the crowd.

'Ah, there's the registration table, at the back,' murmured Simeon, suddenly wondering if this was a good idea after all. He hesitated and then had to hurry to catch up with Poppy as she marched through the horde of astonished men, the room deathly quiet. Simeon could even hear Poppy's knee brace clanking as she walked.

'Good morning. We are here to register. I believe you should already have the application form?' said Simeon as they reached the table, covering his nerves with light charm.

The three men at the table stared in disgust and anger at what they were seeing. 'What is the meaning of this, Simeon?' demanded Lord Geoffrey

Hepplewhite, the supremo of British Motor Racing.

'I would have thought my application, which I can see in the small pile of unprocessed forms on the desk, and of course the fact that I just said we are here to register, would have removed all ambiguity to the matter.'

'You know perfectly well I am referring to the presence of this, this …' Hepplewhite came to a halt, unable to articulate his words. He couldn't have been more overwhelmed if a fish had ridden through the room on a bicycle. Women were not allowed in the club; therefore, women did not enter the club. He found his voice in the articulation of this hallowed rule. 'No women are allowed!'

Poppy leaned forward, placing her mechanical hand on the polished mahogany table as she glared at the three men. She could feel her disgust rising as she looked at their arrogant faces and well-fed bodies, all clothed in suits that cost more than a worker could earn in a year. 'Then we shall register and take our leave,' she replied. 'Believe me, I have no desire to remain in a room with so many ungallant men in it.' A gasp went around the room and a few protests were muttered, though one strange snort could have been a laugh of amusement.

'This is absurd,' gasped Hepplewhite. 'Mathews! Mathews, I say! Escort this, this, this *woman* off the premises at once!'

'This young woman is here as my guest, so you shall not molest her in any way,' snapped Simeon, his nerves disappearing in anger at Hepplewhite's offensive reaction.

'Besides, I wouldn't advise you to try,' said Poppy, slowly clenching her metal fist on the table. The fingers dragged over the wooden surface and left four substantial grooves in the hard wood. 'I'm here to get the race registration sorted, nothing more, nothing less.'

'Race? You? Race?' echoed Hepplewhite in anger. 'You can't enter the race!'

'Why not?'

'Because women do not race! It is unheard of.'

'Show me the clause in the rule book that specifically bans women from racing,' said Simeon, raising his voice so the room could hear.

'Women do not race,' repeated Hepplewhite, obstinately.

'Show me the rule,' repeated Simeon. The two men stared at each other, neither backing down.

'Perhaps someone else can show me this rule?' demanded Poppy, turning to the other two officials. 'As you are so certain I cannot race, then you must be able to show the regulation in the rulebook?' She watched the two men squirming in angry silence, thus demonstrating there was no such written prohibition.

'You cannot race because you have not registered,' interrupted a sneering voice from the side. Poppy glanced round and saw the familiar – but unwelcome – face of Oswald Hepplewhite.

'Indeed, Oswald is quite correct,' snapped Hepplewhite Senior with relief, feeling a rare spurt of gratitude towards his son. 'If you did not get your registration in by the fourth of the month, you are not permitted to enter.'

'The application form is directly under your hand, Geoffrey, old boy,' said Simeon. 'You will find it correct to the last detail.'

'It is not correct, for it is made out to your racing driver from the Sussex race,' pointed out Hepplewhite Senior, grabbing the form and waving it in triumph.

'I suggest you look again,' said Simeon. 'Look at the name and read it out loud. After all, everyone wants to know what is going on, don't they?'

'The name on the form,' said Hepplewhite with a superior smile as he brought the paperwork close to his face, for he was short sighted but refused to wear glasses, 'is P. Orpington. Eh, P. Orpington?'

'Indeed, and you sent the receipt and acknowledgement for P. Orpington on the seventh of the month. I have it here,' replied Simeon, taking the form from his jacket pocket and holding it up for the room to see. 'And we have here P. Orpington herself. Poppy to her friends and well-wishers.'

'So that will be Miss Orpington to you,' said Poppy to the three organisers.

'You know full well this form was made out to your driver of the Sussex race,' raged Hepplewhite. 'It was not made out to a girl!'

'The driver at the Sussex is, in any case, an irrelevance,' replied Simeon. 'This form is for Purley, a separate racetrack and event. It clearly states P. Orpington as the driver, and this is P. Orpington here, in front of you. Now, you will kindly validate this or you will be facing an action in the courts for breach of contract, and I am sure the media will love that. Lord Hepplewhite, who so often claims his word is his bond, reneging on the rules he himself helped draft when motor racing took off in this country. Whatever happened to him, by the way? I'm told he used to be full of fire and passion for the new sport. How did you end up like this? A fossil so frightened of change?'

'I ... I ...' stuttered Hepplewhite before relief showed on his face. Mathews, the porter, had finally arrived with two other large, solid footmen. 'Mathews, please escort this woman out. She has no right to be here.'

'Yes, my lord,' rumbled Mathews. 'You come with us, miss, and all will be well.'

'I'm going nowhere until I have my racing permit,' replied Poppy.

'This way, miss,' said Mathews, his face getting redder as his authority was ignored.

'No,' said Poppy, standing square and looking him in the eye. Mathews took a step back, completely unable to deal with a woman refusing to obey her betters, both social and sexual.

'This way, miss,' he growled, clamping his fingers on Poppy's arm.

'Take your filthy hand off me,' snarled Poppy.

'Move!' bellowed the porter, losing his temper completely and dragging Poppy violently forward, taking her by surprise and making her stagger sideways. Some of the drivers muttered in protest, though others grinned in delight at what they were seeing.

Poppy looked round, her face distorted with rage, and shoved Mathews with her mechanical arm, hurling the large man several feet through the air until he collided with the rear wall, the impact making him scream in agony. He collapsed in a heap and lay curled up on the floor, coughing and groaning in pain.

'Oh, I say, steady on, that is too much,' said a voice from the crowd.

'Yes, do we really need such behaviour?' asked another, though Poppy had no idea if they were protesting against Mathews' actions or her response to them.

'Are you ashamed of your committee, using three men to attack a sixteen-year-old girl, or do you agree with such actions?' demanded Simeon, angrier than Poppy had ever heard him before. The room divided into those outraged by Poppy's presence and those outraged by the response towards her.

'You still have two footmen standing,' snarled Poppy to Hepplewhite. 'Do you want to try violence again?'

'Get out of here, girl!' growled one of the other footmen, rushing forward but taking care to stay away from Poppy's mechanical arm. This proved a mistake as he walked straight into a firm punch from Poppy's flesh and blood fist, which dumped him forcefully and painfully on his backside.

'Two assaults in less than two minutes, ordered by you, Hepplewhite,' hissed Poppy, swinging back round to face the table. 'Do you want to make it three? Perhaps you'd like me to lay charges for assault against you? I like the idea of that headline. *Gordon Club thugs attack young woman on Lord*

Hepplewhite's orders.'

'Very well,' snapped Hepplewhite, hurling the form on the table and stamping it with extreme violence. 'There is your registration and don't think you have heard the last of this, Simeon! You're turning us into a laughing stock.'

'You're doing that very ably by yourself, old boy.'

'Now leave! This is private property and I would be in my rights to see you arrested for trespass.'

'You wouldn't, for that is a committee decision and the club committee is not here,' replied Simeon, before raising his voice. 'And I will add, in the presence of all you drivers and manufacturers, that I am disgusted at what I have seen here today. Disgusted with the racing committee, and disgusted with all of you who stood there and accepted such behaviour!'

Hepplewhite Senior opened and shut his mouth several times but could think of nothing to say in reply. Simeon and Poppy turned and walked back through the quiet room. Some of the men looked away, some scowled, while one or two seemed uncomfortable, but no one said anything as Poppy and Simeon walked out.

News of Poppy's registration generated huge waves

of publicity, so much so that Poppy began to feel under siege from reporters at Pallister Hall. Although the hall had been similarly inundated after *Thunderbus'* win at the Sussex track, Poppy had been largely ignored by the assembled press as she was female, crippled and lacking social standing.

Now, however, the attention was very firmly on her, and wherever she went in the grounds she saw journalists swarming on the walls, in trees outside the property and, of course, outside the main gates, where they would lie, beg, plead and threaten her in order to get an interview. She made a mistake one day by responding to a reporter who provoked a reaction by demanding to know why her father had been sacked.

'My father has not been sacked,' snapped Poppy in anger. 'He is unwell and cannot compete. I am taking his place.'

'Unwell? Has he been poisoned by petrol fumes? I'm told the car is highly dangerous and will explode at speeds greater than eighty miles an hour! Can you confirm that, Miss Orpington?'

'What? Whoever claimed such a thing?' asked Poppy in disbelief.

'I have my sources,' smirked the journalist, who had in fact made up the claim at that moment in order to bait Poppy.

'Leave them, Poppy, come away,' said Helena, running out to rescue Poppy. 'Don't say a word to them, my dear,' she added. 'They will make up anything to get a reaction, and they will create further fictions thereafter. Just say "No comment" and leave. And don't forget to smile and be gracious while you do so, otherwise they will attack you for being unwomanly, also.'

Helena's words were confirmed the following day when she and Simeon took Poppy out on a mysterious errand into town. On the way, they were able to show her a national newspaper as Simeon was now having all the papers secretly delivered to the hall, despite his father's objections to the free press. On reading the spurious item, Poppy found herself in rare agreement with the old man.

"Daily Post exclusive," ran the headline. *"We alone have the exclusive inside scoop on the mysterious POPPY ORPINGTON!*

Our intrepid investigative reporter, Mr STEPHEN DINWOODY, beat all our rivals to the scoop here, in Worcestershire, yesterday, when he stumbled upon Poppy Orpington, as she walked alone and grief-stricken in the grounds of Pallister Hall.

'My father is near death,' she explained, in

response to the sympathy shown to her by our correspondent. 'It was always his dream to see his car enter the famous Purley *race, and I intend to honour his wishes, and drive it myself.'*

At this point, the young girl gave a terrified gulp, and gave many nervous glances at the workshop, where Lord Simeon Pallister was standing. Then, as though afraid of being overheard, she quickly cried out, 'I won't let the chance of death stop me from honouring my father, even though there is a chance that the car will explode and I will be killed! It is a risk I must take. I have no choice!' She was then ushered away, by the grim-faced wife of Lord Simeon, Lady Helena, who appeared to be scolding the girl as she was dragged indoors.

What fears must this young girl be feeling as she is pushed out of her natural, God-given, sphere of domestic tranquillity, to compete with men? This reporter fears greatly for her moral character, if she is allowed to race, for the stress will be too much for her tiny frame to bear. Let us hope that reason and feeling, both of which seem to be sorely absent from Pallister Hall, and the world in general, soon return to our once great land, as enjoyed in our grandfathers' time."

'Where do they get this rubbish?' demanded Poppy. 'I never said anything like that! And as for the lousy standard of the writing …'

'I know; it's just the way the press is,' explained Simeon. 'I suppose the price of a free press is that we have a press free of any truth. That will never change. By the way, my dear,' he asked, turning to Helena. 'Why have I received a letter from a Mr John Evans, Director of the Wiltshire Cybernetic Hospital, informing me that my wife is close to a complete mental breakdown and advising me to have her restrained for her own good?'

'Because Mr John Evans of the Wiltshire Cybernetic Hospital is a small-minded arrogant bully,' replied Helena, tartly.

'Fair enough,' said Simeon, sliding discreetly along the seat to give his wife some extra space. 'Ah, here we are, Poppy,' he added as they drew up outside a dress shop. 'Helena has made an appointment for you with her dressmaker, to get you sorted with some racing clothes.'

'Racing clothes?' asked Poppy, who had never considered what she was to wear during the race.

'Indeed,' said Helena. 'A dress is not suitable for racing an open-top car. Marie is expecting you.

Please take whatever you need. This is my gift to you.'

'Helena, I couldn't, really, you and Simeon have already done so much for me,' stuttered Poppy.

'But not nearly as much as you have done for us,' interrupted Helena. 'You have made us look at things in a new way, to see the world in a different light. For that we may never be able to repay you.'

'Or forgive you,' remarked Simeon. 'Well,' he protested as Poppy and Helena stared at him. 'No one likes having their unknown prejudices brought up and confronted.'

'See you in an hour,' cried Helena as Poppy grinned and jumped out of the limousine. The car hissed away, leaving Poppy to gaze at the shop front. She had never been inside such a place before. Many of her clothes had been hand-me-downs from her father, whose shirts and knitted tops were at least large enough for Poppy to wear, while her skirts and dresses came from jumble sales and the needle of Mrs Grieg, a local seamstress who was adept at letting out clothes to suit Poppy's large frame. She walked in and found a small Frenchwoman waiting patiently at the counter, surrounded by dresses, skirts, jackets, various fabrics and what looked like literally miles' worth of lace and frills.

'*Ah, bonjour*!' cried the small woman, flinging her

hands up in the air. 'You are Poppy, *oui*?'

'Er, *oui*, I mean yes,' replied Poppy, somewhat taken aback at the enthusiastic greeting.

'Come in, come in, I am Marie and I have been waiting for you.' Scarcely pausing for breath, Marie exploded onto the next sentence. 'You are here for some clothes for the racing, yes? Good, good, come through, come through, this section here is where we keep the sporting wear for ladies. Jodhpurs, riding boots, shooting jackets, everything for the active lady in the great outdoors.

'Now, let me get your size, off with your coat, please, yes, just on the chair there. My word, you are a big girl,' goggled the seamstress as she took in Poppy's height, curves and chest. 'And still a little growing to do, I should think, but just a little. Hum! What do I have in your size that suits your character, for the clothes must match the person, you agree, *non*?'

'Er, you know I'm driving in a race,' said Poppy, overwhelmed by the tornado that was Marie. 'A motor race. In a motor car?' she added, in case there was any doubt.

'*Oui, oui*,' cried the little Frenchwoman as she zipped around the shop, pulling clothes seemingly at random from rails, boxes and shelves. 'You need clothes that are tough, hard-wearing, but flexible enough to allow free movement. And something warm, of course, as those racing cars, they are cold, but cold! Here, try these to begin with.'

Poppy retired to the changing room. There followed a dizzying forty minutes in which she tried on and discarded various items, some on Marie's insistence, some on her own. 'I just need something practical,' said Poppy finally, utterly confused by the vast range of styles and colours passing through her hands.

'No, no, no,' scalded Marie, wagging a finger. 'Be guided by me, little one, you need more than practical clothing, you need something beautiful also. Remember, we women are judged on our looks rather than our abilities. You are trespassing into the world of the men and so you, my dear, will be judged twice, and harshly, on your ability *and* your appearance. It is unfair, but that is the way of the world. It is not enough that you compete as an equal; you must also look feminine and lovely while doing so, otherwise the English society, it will mock and shun you.'[39]

Poppy considered Marie's comment as she firmly discarded a frilly jacket. 'Fair enough,' she said eventually. 'But it has to be practical. The riding

---

[39] Sadly, this has not changed at all. Just open any magazine or newspaper for proof of that.

boots are good, they're strong and tough, and so are the jodhpurs as they'll allow easy movement with the gear change, and make getting in and out of the car easy.' Poppy glanced at her leg; she had been forced by the tight material to remove her knee brace and put it back on over the jodhpurs, meaning it was no longer hidden under her skirt.

'You are worried about having the brace on display, yes?' asked Marie with an understanding smile.

'I am, yes. People don't like seeing cripples or people with deformities. I see it in their faces every day.'

'It is the prerogative of people, I'm afraid, to be stupid and uncaring,' said Marie, giving Poppy a quick, comforting hug. 'Do not be ashamed of the way you are. You have lived with your afflictions and dealt with them, conquered them, and anyone of worth will see that.'

Poppy smiled in gratitude. 'I know it's stupid to feel apprehensive about having the brace so openly displayed; after all, my arm attracts attention wherever it goes. Not that I have much choice there, of course.' She looked down once more and decided the hell with it – and to hell with anyone who made judgements about her. 'The brace stays where it is, on the outside. But the jackets are still too restrictive.

I need something with more freedom. Can't I just wear a blouse like the one I'm wearing and be done?'

'*Non*!' exclaimed Marie. 'With your twin blessings heaving away underneath the thin material? There will be a riot!'

Poppy blushed. 'Agreed, I need to cover the top half, but I need full movement in my arms at all times.'

'This way, this way,' said Marie, pulling Poppy towards a door hidden by a heavy curtain. She pressed a buzzer and grinned at Poppy.

Poppy smiled back before asking something she had been wondering about. 'Why do you sometimes speak English brokenly, with lots of French thrown in, yet other times you speak English perfectly?'

Marie's grin became even wider. 'Ah, the Lady Helena, she said you were sharp. The English, they are a little bit insular, alas, and they expect foreigners to behave in certain ways. Being French and a fashion designer, I have to be a little flamboyant and exaggerated now and then, just for effect. People expect temperament from designers, especially foreign ones.'

'You're just giving people what they want? It's all just a performance?'

'Isn't everything?' asked Marie as the door opened, revealing a short man with a round face and slicked-down hair. 'Can we come in, Henri? We need to find something for Poppy that is practical and hard-wearing, but there is nothing on my side that will do.'

'Come through, come through,' said Henri, stepping back. 'Ah, Miss Orpington, a pleasure, a pleasure. My sister and I, we admire your spirit in taking on the challenge of the grand race!'

Poppy walked through and found herself in the gentlemen's outfitters next door. The masculine atmosphere permeated every polished wooden surface and chair, unlike the frilly, feminine counterpoint of Marie's shop. 'You're racing fans?' she asked, going slightly red at the compliment.

'Yes, yes, we attended many of the famous town-to-town speed trials in France when we were children, back when the steam cars first started the racing.'

'What have you got, Henri,' asked Marie, 'that Poppy can wear that allows full movement of the arms and will keep her warm as the car speeds around the track?'

'Hmm,' pondered Henri, gazing into the mid distance. Then he snapped his fingers and struck himself on the head; he clearly shared Marie's philosophy of putting on a show for the customers. 'Ah, thirty-six times an imbecile! I have the very thing! It was a special order for the Duke of Devonshire, but he disliked it when he saw it and refused to pay. Now, where is it, where is it?' He hurled himself into various sliding recesses around the shop, disappearing into one and popping out of another as he hunted for the elusive garments until, with a shout of triumph, he emerged once more.

'Try these, they should fit,' he beamed. 'A waistcoat made of the toughest, but supple, leather. It was designed for the Duke to go shooting in, so it has many more pockets than usual, and all these hoops, designed to hold cartridges, you could use to hold your tools. And the overcoat, three-quarter length, snug and warm, but with longer arms and looser shoulders to give the Duke full movement while crawling through the grass after his dangerous pheasants.'

'The goggles, you must have the goggles, it is mandatory,' said Marie, pressing a pair into Poppy's hand. 'Many gentlemen buy them even if they don't race. It gives them the satisfaction to think they could race, if they wished to. You need them to keep the dirt and bugs out of your face.'

'And a driving helmet, for protection, in case the car flips and you land on your head,' added Henri, passing over a thin, rounded piece of leather that looked barely adequate for repelling small insects, never mind deflecting solid concrete at speeds in excess of ninety miles per hour.

'And good, thick gauntlets,' continued Marie. 'I know you don't need the right one, but take them both, your left hand will still need to be kept warm and safe. And have these wide scarves also, they can be lifted to cover the lower part of your face; see how you can knot it at each corner for stability, so they will not blow in the wind? All the colours to choose from are in the box!'

'Finally, the *pièce de résistance*, the crowning moment, just to wear for the photographs, of course, not the race itself,' exclaimed Henri as he approached with a glossy top hat. He handed it over with a bow. Poppy took it, feeling that she shouldn't, that only the upper classes wore such things, that it wasn't right or proper … then the fires gleamed in her green eyes and she clapped the hat down on her head. It was a perfect fit.

'*Magnifique!*' exclaimed Henri as Marie sighed in contentment.

Poppy looked at herself in a full-length mirror, hardly able to believe the transformation. The coat and waistcoat could have been made for her, as could the jodhpurs and boots. Her mane of red hair hung down over the coat, which fell open to reveal the figure-hugging waistcoat which in turn emphasized the curve of her hips and the swell of her breasts. The hat, fitted at a jaunty angle, spoke of rebellion against the existing social order, while the scarf and goggles made her look like some exotic modern-day highwayman. Or highwaywoman.

She looked ready to take on the world. And she felt like it.

'Ouch! Why did you brake so sharply?' complained Simeon. 'I've dropped the stopwatch now! And that gave my elbow a really painful bang on the door. We'll have to go round again for an accurate timing.'

'Oh, let's not; I want to drive on a proper road, and so does *Thunderbus*,' replied Poppy. She and Simeon, on returning to Pallister Hall, had decided to get a few practice laps in so Poppy could get used to her new racing clothes.

'I don't think this monstrosity really wants anything at all,' began Simeon before being cut short.

'Don't listen to the nasty man,' cooed Poppy, patting *Thunderbus*' dashboard. 'You're not a monstrosity; you're mummy's little darling.' She grinned as Simeon sighed. 'Come on, a proper run on a real road and we'll call it a night.' She guided *Thunderbus* out of the grounds of Pallister Hall and onto the road.

Simeon had to admit that Poppy was improving

every day; her gear changes were smooth, or as smooth as possible with *Thunderbus'* truculent gearbox. Her reflexes were good and her control of *Thunderbus'* steering was absolute. 'Fine, we'll have a quick run to Malvern and back,' he said. Malvern was only a few miles away, and the steep hills would be a good test of Poppy's clutch control. 'Turn left at the crossroads up ahead.'

It was only when they reached the outer edge of the small town that Simeon realised he had made a terrible error. A blur of green was approaching from the other end of the road, while the tranquil air was disturbed by the loud hiss of a powerful steam engine. Simeon blanched in horror as he recognised the driver gawping at *Thunderbus,* wild glee stamped firmly on his face. 'Keep going, keep going,' he hissed in rising panic.

'Why, do you know him?' asked Poppy, glancing in the rear-view mirror and noting that the green car was doing a sharp U-turn behind them. 'That's a Pearson 280, isn't it? Fast, but unstable.'

'Yes, and that's "Mad Jack" Thornton driving it, who can be described in exactly the same terms. Get your foot down and get out of here!'

'Why?'

'Because he'll want to race and he's been banned from every race course from here to Ireland, that's why. The man's a maniac and a menace to all other road users!'

'Sounds like he could be useful,' replied Poppy.

'He's a liability and an accident waiting to happen; get us out of here!'

'Too late,' said Poppy as the Pearson pulled up alongside them.

'Simeon, old boy, how are you?' bellowed Thornton, his bulging eyes never looking up from *Thunderbus* as the two vehicles ran parallel to each other.

'I'm fine, thank …' began Simeon before being cut off.

'Is this the famous petrol-fuelled car I've heard so much about?'

'This is …'

'Spiffing! How about a race to town?'

'We're only here …'

'Excellent! First one to the Post Office is the winner!'

'We're not here to race!' shouted Simeon, who had found in the past that volume was the best way to get through to Thornton, but even then, the message was likely to be addled by the time it reached what passed for his brain.

'Of course you are – car like that, got to race,' yelped Thornton. 'Besides, your filly looks up for it!'

He grinned widely, showing a gap between his front teeth and a devilish gleam in his eye.

'I am not Simeon's "filly", you patronising buffoon,' bellowed Poppy, torn between anger and laughter. There was something in Thornton's expression that seemed to ask to be excused for anything that came out of his mouth.

'Now there's true fire and passion,' commented Thornton. 'My apologies, sweet lady. Will you ignore your timid co-driver and indulge in a race to the top of the town?'

Poppy flashed him a smile and gunned the engine, the growl filling the air. 'Are we taking the main road that circles up the hill?'

'I should ruddy well cocoa,' answered Thornton. 'Far too boring! I follow my own route. See you up there!' He slammed his foot down on the accelerator and the green car shot forward, the wheels spinning madly as the car slithered from side to side like a drunken snake dancing on black ice. Smoke poured up from the tyres as the rubber screamed on the road surface before the car hunkered down and sprinted off.

Poppy reacted almost as quickly, bringing the clutch up while balancing the throttle, but in the excitement she misjudged the clutch control and *Thunderbus* lurched forward in a series of short hops before Poppy controlled her exhilaration and engaged the gears properly. By that stage, Thornton was already five car lengths ahead.

'For heaven's sake, Poppy, it's not worth the risk,' yelped Simeon.

'This isn't risk; this is practice,' answered Poppy, slamming up through the gears. 'This is something you just can't teach; actual racing against a real competitor.' Although Poppy had raced Simeon around the hall grounds, the practice runs had lacked any real edge.

'That man is not a competitor,' shrieked Simeon as *Thunderbus* hurtled around a wide bend in the road. The vibrations coming up through the car's body seemed determined to shake him to death, while the acceleration pinned him back like a windswept butterfly on a collector's card. 'He's a maniac,' he squeaked, giving Poppy as pointed a look as he could manage from the corner of his seat.

Watching her rival ahead of her, Poppy did understand Simeon's concern; the concept of keeping to a straight line, of slowing down at bends, or even steering into the bends, seemed to be unfamiliar to Thornton. Instead, he hurled the car forward at the greatest possible velocity, apparently trusting divine intervention to turn the road underneath him. As promised, he had turned off the main highway and was instead using a series of smaller roads that weaved up the beautiful Malvern Hills.

Deciding that any attempt to overtake would be difficult – if not downright suicidal – on the narrow, winding roads, Poppy contented herself with keeping on Thornton's rear end, watching and learning as he thundered along lanes designed for little more than a small pony and trap. It was all she could do to keep up as she had to constantly change gear[40] to suit the gradient of each track, while also hauling the intractable steering wheel left and right to avoid leaving the road altogether at each sharp bend. A small, treacherous thought erupted in her mind that maybe the steering design could have been better, but she quickly crushed the idea and concentrated on not flying off the hill which now resembled a small mountain.

Finally, they reached the end of the tracks and turned back onto the main road. From there it was a clear, open run to the top of town and the Post Office. Thornton was almost out of sight as he rounded a bend, but now they were on *Thunderbus'* terrain and Poppy plunged forward, closing the gap

---

[40] Bear in mind also, this was before synchronised gearboxes were the norm, so changing gear was far more complex than in today's cars.

between them. She rounded the bend and attacked the final gradient, feeling the raw power of the engine haul the heavy chassis upward with increasing speed, chasing down Thornton's lead.

Unfortunately, the lead was just a little too great and the green Pearson passed the Post Office just as *Thunderbus* was drawing level with the rear bumper. Thornton gave a triumphant blast on his horn and waved his cap in the air as he slowed down, grinning over his shoulder in happy triumph. Poppy waved back, acknowledging his victory with a salute.

'Marvellous, simply marvellous!' yelled Thornton in delight. His manner was open and happy, delighted with the race and the competition as much as the win, and Poppy couldn't help but laugh. 'You'll flatten the competition in that beast, my dear, flatten them!'

'I certainly hope so,' replied Poppy. 'Thanks for the experience.'

'We must do it again sometime,' called out Thornton.

'I think once was quite enough for me,' retorted Poppy in a firm but good-natured tone.

Thornton laughed again as he accelerated away with a fresh blast on his horn. Behind him, Poppy grinned and shook her head. 'He's not too bad a man, really, is he Simeon? Simeon?' Poppy looked at the passenger seat as Simeon clawed his way upright, his face almost pure white. He had spent most of the race buffeted by the wind, suffocated by the acceleration and rattled by the car's vibrations like a dry pea in a tin can until he had slithered into the foot well and curled into a defensive ball, waiting for a safe moment to emerge.

'Are you feeling all right, Simeon? You look quite awful. Oh, really; if you have to be sick, at least aim it outside the car – I have to race in this tomorrow!'

Poppy had been continuing Simeon's policy of using his little yellow car for non-essential journeys rather than risk anything happening to *Thunderbus* on the open road, and that evening she borrowed the quiet roadster to visit her father at the hospice. This would be her final visit before the race. She had hoped to find him awake as she quietly walked into the reception area, but the sympathetic nurse on duty shook her head even before Poppy could ask.

'I'm sorry, Miss Orpington, he's still sleeping under the sedation.'

'Is there no change at all?'

'The doctors are happy with his physical reactions, so there is hope there. Other than that, we just have to wait.'

'Can I sit with him again for a while? It will be

the last chance I have for a few days.'

'Of course; just for ten minutes, though. Doctor's orders.'

Poppy smiled her thanks and slipped into her father's darkened room. She sat next to his huge figure and took his hand in her own. 'Well, Dad, this is it,' she whispered. She often spoke to her father when visiting, in the hope that her voice was somehow getting through to him. 'It's here. The race. Purley. We made it this far, Dad. I hope we can make it all the way.

'We're in a better class of hotel, this time,' she added. 'Simeon thought we were joking when we told him about that rat-infested fleapit he booked for us in Sussex. When he realised we weren't exaggerating, he apologised and said he would choose more carefully for Purley.

'Of course,' she added with some acidity, 'the social distinctions must still be observed. We're all in one guesthouse, while he and Helena will be staying at a far superior hotel in a better part of the town. Oh well; some things never change. At least *Thunderbus* is running well, Dad. You'd be proud. I hope you'll be proud of me, too.'

She stood up, kissed her father on the forehead, and turned to go. As she did, her eye caught the bedside cabinet which she knew contained the few personal effects found in her father's pockets when he was admitted. She pulled the drawer open and saw a few coins, a grubby handkerchief and the old, cracked watch her father habitually kept loose in his trouser pocket, the chain long ago having broken. She smiled sadly at it before tucking it away in her waistcoat pocket, so she could have something of his with her as she raced.

She took one last look at his still figure before quietly closing the door and walking away to face the unknown.

CHAPTER THIRTEEN

Race day dawned. Poppy and the pit crew rolled out of their hotel as they had done over two months ago when heading for the Sussex racetrack. On that occasion, however, her father had been the driver. Now, the responsibility was Poppy's alone.

They arrived at Purley in good time and found their pit. Unlike the Sussex racetrack, which had originally been for horses before being adapted for motor cars, here the track was purpose-built. Poppy looked around. The course was a two-and-a-half-mile expanse of unforgiving concrete. It had been built well over two decades ago for manufacturers to test their vehicles, and then expanded as racing became extremely popular with the paying public.

It was so popular, the circuit had recently received an upgrade; electronic information boards over the track could transmit information on the competitors, while the Telecommunication Camera Relay posts dotted around the course fed live images to huge screens set up around the track and even in the fields outside, where spectators were already assembling.

'Poppy, look at that sign,' gasped Amy in shock, pointing at one section of the crowd. Poppy squinted and made out a home-made banner held by two men.

It read: *"Racing is for men! Women cannot drive!"*[41]

'Yes, but look at that one over there,' responded Simeon, pointing to another part of the crowd. There, a smaller sign proclaiming *"Poppy Forever!"* was being waved energetically in the air. 'You've certainly made an impact.'

'For better or for worse?' wondered Poppy.

'For better,' said Simeon firmly. 'You can't buy this sort of publicity. Even if you don't win, if the level of interest continues to get this highly charged, we may yet cover our costs.'

'Is that why you've got me wearing this ridiculous outfit?' asked Poppy, gesturing at the blue frock coat and waistcoat that Simeon had unexpectedly presented her with that morning.

'As I have now explained four times,' replied Simeon with a theatrical groan, 'that coat makes you stand out far more than the brown affair you got from Marie and Henri. And you need to be visible.'

'I'm certainly that,' snorted Poppy in embarrassment. 'I mean, seriously, bright blue cloth with yellow epaulettes? I can probably be seen by the steamers in the lower atmosphere! And why in the name of sanity has the waistcoat got cogs printed all

---

[41] A view still strong in motor sports even today, as well as wider society.

over it?'

'All publicity is good publicity,' remarked Helena, loyal to her husband despite sharing Poppy's horror of the vivid blue clothing. 'Advertisers pay drivers to endorse their products, you know. I believe Dobby Sanderson pulled down almost eight hundred pounds for just six months of endorsements after he won the European Grand Continental, and that was some years ago, so a good race can reap dividends in all sorts of ways.'

'There's a lot of advertising around, isn't there?' observed Amy redundantly, looking at row after row of huge billboards plastered with pictures of washing powder, clothing, medicines and many more products besides. Her attention moved to the various telecommunication crews setting up their cameras and hence she saw one of the engineers glance over, recognise Poppy far away in the pit, and shout in triumph. Cameras swung around to point at her.

'Quick, get your hat on and look mysterious,' hissed Amy in warning.

'Look confident and relaxed,' advised Simeon.

'Look casual and elegant,' added Helena.

'What, all at the same time?' demanded Poppy, hastily putting on her top hat.

'Image is ninety per cent of the battle,' said Simeon.

'Unfortunately, this is true,' agreed Helena. 'What you actually achieve is of less concern to the media than how you appeared as you did it.' She gazed innocently into the far distance. 'I've often wondered if I could murder Simeon and get away with it by wearing a really pretty dress.'

'You'll have a shock if you do,' spluttered her husband. 'I've left all my money to the donkey sanctuary.'

Poppy smiled, appreciating her friends' efforts to distract her, but she was getting increasingly worried about the race. She was torn between wanting the moment to stretch out forever and wanting to have it all over and done with. She turned her attention to *Thunderbus* as it was carefully unloaded from the flatbed truck. 'Come on, Amy,' she said. 'Let's check him over one last time.'

The check had only just been completed when the loudhailers around the track let out an ear-piercing howl, indicating they had been turned on. Poppy glanced up and realised the stands were now full of spectators, while even more were gathering in the far distance outside the track, clustering around the screens set up in the numerous surrounding fields. Presumably, the scenes were the same all the way around the course.

'Look at that, Poppy,' exclaimed Simeon. 'I've never seen a crowd like it, and all because of you! You know various film companies are working together to capture the entire race? They want to record history in the making; the first petrol racing car and the first ever female racing driver. Well, the first in this country, at least.'

'Don't the Telecommunication Relays do that?' asked Poppy as she assimilated the information, her stomach giving her another nervous kick.

'No, they simply transmit live images; that's why so many of the big companies are here. I'm told by a friend who works in the business that they've never tried filming such a large race from start to end. They've had to divide the track into sections for each crew to cover. Then they will splice the film together to make one reel, ready to be shown in cinemas across the land.'

'Oh, my word, I didn't know about that,' said Poppy, faintly. She looked around at the huge crowds. 'I didn't even notice how busy it was getting; I was too absorbed in checking the engine.'

'That's good,' replied Simeon. 'You need to recapture that intensity of focus. That way, all your attention will be on the race, not worrying about other things. It can make the difference between winning and losing.'

'You must focus completely,' agreed Helena, 'if only for your safety. Remember, it is dangerous out there for a standard steam car; you are in the most powerful car ever built.'

Poppy grimaced, suddenly feeling as though she had no right to be there. This wasn't her world. She was only there because her father was ill. She was a stand-in. A makeweight. She couldn't do it.

'Well, well, the working-class girl has been stupid enough to turn up,' sneered a voice. Poppy turned and saw Oswald Hepplewhite, accompanied by a large retinue of his friends. Some of the men, like Hepplewhite himself, were dressed for racing, while the women clearly had little function other than ornamentation. All were smirking in superior disdain at Poppy and Amy.

'I can see the worst excesses of her class written plain in her physiognomy,' exclaimed one of them, staring as much at the bright blue coat as Poppy's face.

'I'm surprised my father has allowed this,' continued Hepplewhite loudly. 'Allowing the riff-raff in!'

'If he *were* to ban the riff-raff,' replied Poppy, her uncertainties evaporating as anger began to build, 'I wouldn't have to look at you. What are you without your inherited money and title? Nothing! A sneering bully sponging off his daddy's connections because he hasn't got the character to achieve anything on his own merits.'

'I'll show you who is better when we get on the racetrack! I doubt you'll finish even a single lap, never mind the entire run of twenty.'

'Care to make a wager on that, Oswald?' asked Simeon. 'I bet one hundred pounds that Poppy completes a lap.'

Hepplewhite opened and closed his mouth, suddenly realising the bet was rather foolish as Poppy probably could make at least one lap. Besides which, his father had made it clear he was not to gamble any more. He had lost a small fortune already through pointless wagers.

'Oh dear, he's suddenly lost his bluster,' said Poppy, laughing.

Hepplewhite flushed. 'You'll not cross the finish line before me, Orpington; that I will make a bet on!'

'Very well, the bet has been accepted in front of witnesses, and the stake is five hundred pounds,' snapped Simeon, upping the figure in irritation at Hepplewhite's boorish manner.

'That piece of scrap will probably blow up before then,' brayed one of the women.

Poppy looked with close interest at the woman. She was standing close to Hepplewhite as though she had a proprietorial interest in him, a suspicion confirmed by the fact that the other women in the group maintained a small but definite distance, as though they had been told in clear terms to keep off the Hepplewhite grass. She was wearing a new, expensive dress, coloured the most hideous green and cut in an old-fashioned manner that made her look much older than her years.

'Quite right, Margaret,' said Hepplewhite in reply.

'Come along, Oswald,' sniffed Margaret, her nose pointing in the air so she didn't have to look at Poppy or her crew. 'Let's go and get your car prepared.'

'Really?' said Amy. 'You're going to prepare his car? How will you adjust the couplings on the inner turbine?'

'We have workers to do that,' snapped Margaret.

'So, you aren't actually going to do anything?' observed Poppy. 'Just stand there and eat and drink while everyone else does all the hard work?'

'Not everyone has to earn a living. Come, Oswald, let us leave this place.' The woman swept away with her nose still in the air, provoking a roar of disdainful laughter from the *Thunderbus* crew. Typically, Hepplewhite had to make one last comment as he turned to go.

'You'll be sorry, Orpington. You wait and see.' He walked hurriedly away, his friends trailing him.

As they departed, the immensely tall, lanky frame of the Honourable Cuthbert Gilmore strolled by, looking as always like a confused fish searching for the sea, albeit an impeccably dressed fish forever mindful of the need for good manners. He turned and peered at Poppy through his monocle.

'Jolly good luck and all that,' he said. 'I hope you do beat him. He can be a complete pill.'

'My word, Cuthbert,' grinned Simeon. 'I've never known you express yourself so forcibly on anything before.'

Cuthbert blushed. 'Well, young Miss Orpington is right about him, you know. Makes me realise I was born lucky. Plenty of money, reasonable mater and pater who don't mind me toddling off and doing my own thing. Place on the family board in a year or two. Never had to think about anything, really. Now I am. And my sister, Fliss, thinks you're the top, Miss Orpington! She is tremendously impressed with your courage and fortitude.'

'Oh, er, well, please thank her very much, that's very kind of her. And of you to tell me so,' mumbled Poppy, going slightly red. Cuthbert beamed in a vague way and wandered off towards the racetrack and certain death.

'Other way, Cuthbert!' bellowed Simeon in alarm. Cuthbert turned, saw the way Simeon was pointing, raised his hat in thanks and walked off in the direction indicated.

'Hmm, seems you have an admirer there, miss,' murmured Christopher as he fussed around *Thunderbus*.

'Ah, young love,' sighed Clive, theatrically.

Poppy blushed harder. She was still surprised at the compliment, never mind the thought that the Honourable Cuthbert Gilmore could be an admirer. She just couldn't see him that way. He seemed to exist in a little world of his own that only occasionally brushed up against reality.

'Attention all drivers, attention all drivers!' shouted the loudspeaker system. 'All drivers make their way to the start line. The race will commence in ten minutes!' A roar went up from the crowd at the announcement. Poppy forgot about Cuthbert, his sister, even Hepplewhite. She had a race to run, and she was going to compete as best she could.

'Miss Orpington, Miss Orpington!' bellowed a voice. Poppy looked round and saw a reporter was trying to scale the fence dividing the spectators from the pit. 'Any chance of a few words?' The man was pulled back by the stewards, hence missing the few words Poppy aimed at him and which shocked Helena deeply.

Poppy quickly hauled off the blue coat and

waistcoat, gratefully swapping them for her racing brown, a simple, unconscious act which scandalised some of the crowd for indecency even though Poppy was wearing three other layers underneath, and despite it being the habit of many male drivers to remove jackets and coats in their paddocks before climbing into their cars.

Poppy pulled her scarf up so it covered her lower face before swapping her top hat for the leather helmet, forcing it over her wild tangle of hair and doing up the strap as firmly as possible. She attached her goggles over the top and finally pulled on her leather driving gauntlets. She didn't need the right glove, as such, but it would help improve the grip of her mechanical hand on the smooth metal steering wheel, while the left glove would protect her from blisters.

She climbed into *Thunderbus* and started the ignition process, her hands trembling slightly, but when she pressed the starter button and the engine roared, flame licking the air and silencing the noisy crowd behind the pit, her nerves vanished. This was her car, even more than it had been her father's. It had almost killed him, but it could not kill her. It accepted her and obeyed her. She looked at the steam-powered vehicles on their way to the starting line and she knew the track belonged not to them, but to her and to *Thunderbus*.

With a smooth movement, she engaged reverse and backed out onto the track with speed, grace and a touch of insolence. She paused for a moment, letting the crowd grow even wilder as the famous car made its appearance, the engine growling, impatient for the fight ahead, before snarling forward to the start line. A steward consulted his clipboard, checked the number painted on the car and waved her towards a vacant spot on the grid. Thanks to her father's victory at Sussex, she was placed halfway up the starting line.

'Car number twenty-two, a Kineton 4404 Racing Special, nicknamed *"Silver Bullet"*, owned and driven by Lord Oswald Hepplewhite takes its place at the front of the grid,' announced the loudhailer. The commentator sat in a tall wooden tower next to the starting line, where he was able to see almost the entire racetrack and thus narrate what was happening to the crowd below, as well as to the nation via radio. A film crew had settled in front of the tower, ready to record the beginning and end of the race for posterity.

'There is Count Lorenzo Sellini, twice the European Road Champion, in car number twelve, a Wyndham coupe 300 Power Tourer, known for its tight turning ability,' continued the track commentator. 'He is followed by Lord Derek Scott in his four-seater De Luxe Massingham Grand Tourer, a relatively new car to the racing world but showing much promise with its innovative turbine electro-boost system.

'And there is Poppy Orpington, wearing a very large brown overcoat and a yellow scarf over her face – well, of course, a lady must be mindful of her complexion! And she is followed by Sir Grenville Hutch in a Wyndham two-seater sports car, a controversial choice as the Wyndham lacks the power of the other vehicles but does have far better cornering ability, which I wager will be at the forefront of Sir Grenville's mind as he races. Following him is Sir Robin Dalton in a two litre Dexter-Speedster, splendid acceleration though slower on the straights compared to other vehicles, and next we have Lord Roxborough …'

'Ignorant, imbecilic, dunderheaded numbskull,' muttered Poppy as the announcer continued to introduce the car specifications, past racing history and individual pedigree of every other driver; she just had her clothing mentioned. Not that she had any pedigree, of course; *she* was working-class. But that would change today. Anger bubbled under the surface, feeding her determination.

At the mention of her name, whistles, cheers and

boos echoed around the area. More home-made banners were held aloft, some supporting Poppy, some criticising her. She squinted at one and read "*Poppy Orpinton is a fat slag*". Her lip curled back. If she had the time after the race, she would find the maker of that sign and force feed it to them. If nothing else, they would remember how to spell her name in the future.

'My word, look at that,' gasped the announcer. The crowd looked up and saw three airships had gathered over the racetrack. They slowly turned, revealing the word "*Go*" printed on the first, "*Poppy*" on the second, and "*Go!*" on the third. 'I have never seen such a reckless display from the steamers. There'll be questions about air safety asked about that!'

Poppy grinned and waved at the three airships, heartened by the support. The airship pilots were a different breed; for them to support her was astonishing. It was annoying that the narrow-minded announcer could only see the negative aspect of such a manoeuvre, but Poppy was quickly learning that most people laboured under a series of prejudices disguised as 'common sense' or 'our values'.

'All the cars are now on their marks,' continued the announcer. 'The stewards are off the track. The flag goes up. When it comes down, the race will be under way!' The flag was, in fact, a huge banner that stretched over the width of the track. It was held between two mechanical poles which, when operated, would drop the flag halfway down their length. It was a system every driver could see clearly.

The tension rose even further as the banner fluttered in the breeze. The race steward responsible for dropping the flag could take as long as he wanted, thus building the pressure and teasing the crowd. Poppy leaned back in her seat, breathing deeply, focussing on the track, the vehicles around her, the flag above, the grumble of *Thunderbus*, the hissing of the car to her right, the grass verge to her left – wide enough for *Thunderbus* to drive over, if need be.

The banner dropped.

Poppy dipped the accelerator while bringing the clutch up in a perfectly synchronised movement. The roar of *Thunderbus* stunned the crowd into brief silence; they had never heard anything like it, though Poppy barely registered it anymore. To her, it was now normal. It flattened the hiss of the steam engines and even managed to quieten the announcer up in his tower, especially as the tremendous vibrations from the car caused the tower legs to wobble as it passed by on the track.

The noise also scared some of the other drivers; a blue car directly ahead of Poppy weaved from side to side as the roar of *Thunderbus* enveloped it before the driver regained control and pressed down on his accelerator, giving the turbines all the power they could handle. The car accelerated away, leaving a widening gap between itself and *Thunderbus*.

Poppy gauged the space to the left of the blue car before changing gear and slamming her foot down on the accelerator. *Thunderbus* sprang forward, dwarfing the steam-driven vehicle in height, length and power before another burst of speed left it behind. Poppy had overtaken her first rival.

In fact, she had overtaken several other vehicles and she was yet to hit fourth gear. She changed up and *Thunderbus* hurtled forward, the snarl of the engine turning to a sweet trilling song as the car did as it was designed to do in its natural habitat, hunting down its prey and devouring all that stood in its way.

Poppy glanced ahead and saw the first corner approaching. This was one of the gentler bends, a long sweeping ribbon of concrete that allowed cars to accelerate even faster without worrying about braking for sharp corners.

Ahead of her, the race leaders were already hurtling around the bend, spreading out on the wide road in order to overtake each other, with Oswald

Hepplewhite just ahead of the pack. Poppy grimaced under her scarf, choosing her route through the widest part of the corner; she was going for the outside lane.

Her speed steadily increased, the needle on the speedometer showing she was already hitting eighty. She passed one car, making it look like a toy when seen side by side against *Thunderbus*' bulk. She continued on the outside edge, the wrong line to take as she had more ground to cover than those on the inside, but the only one open to her as the other competitors were all clustered together, getting in each other's way. Besides, she had the extra power of the petrol engine to call on.

Poppy held her nerve and the line, keeping her foot pressed firmly down on the accelerator, passing one car and then another. Two more were overtaken as the road straightened and *Thunderbus* purred in pure satisfaction as it was allowed to reach its full potential. The valves sang and the flames from the exhaust ports on the side of the bonnet flickered in rotation as the fuel ignited within, feeding the beast.

They pounded over the straight and approached the huge banking bend nicknamed the Widow Maker. Here, the track was almost thirty feet high, meaning the fastest of vehicles could take the outside edge, high up over the cars on the inside, and sweep past them in a dizzying spectacle that the crowd loved. Often, the cars would be too flimsy to hold the road at such speed, or the drivers would be unable to control the vehicle, or they would simply run out of luck. Whatever the reason, the doomed car would veer off the top of the track, smashing through the rails as though they were matchwood before spinning out into the void and plunging down to the unforgiving ground. Very few survived a crash on the Widow Maker. Those who did survive never raced again.

The crush of cars ahead was too tight for Poppy to overtake except by once more going up to the outside edge, the most dangerous part of the bend. Poppy considered the move, her thoughts running smoothly and fluidly; she had far superior speed, weight and strength, all the factors required to use the topmost edge. She had to believe in her abilities or else stay forever in the middle of the pack.

She chose her space and guided *Thunderbus'* nose upward and to the right of the track, her foot constant on the accelerator, refusing to give in to physics, to fear or to doubt. *Thunderbus* roared around the edge of the bank, looking as though it were almost flying over its rivals clustered below. With a snort of flame the mighty black vehicle passed car after car, holding the line perfectly, and then Poppy was ahead of the pack and guiding *Thunderbus* back down to the middle of the track as the road straightened and levelled off. She had two or three rivals right behind her but there was now just one car in front; number twenty-two, Hepplewhite's *Silver Bullet*.

'An astonishing scene here at Purley,' bellowed the announcer, 'as car number six, driven by Poppy Orpington, somehow gets clear of the pack and takes second place. I do believe there is a lot of glare on the track, though, which is most likely dazzling the eyes of the drivers and thus allowing number six to get slightly ahead. No doubt Lord Oswald Hepplewhite is far too experienced to be overcome by the haze, and indeed he is now using all his considerable skill to keep ahead of car number six; what an excellent display of motor driving expertise!'

Poppy snarled under her scarf at Hepplewhite's manoeuvres as he zig-zagged wildly across the track. He had clearly realised there was no way his car could outpace *Thunderbus* and he was therefore doing everything he could to block Poppy from passing, including trying to frighten her off the road by swerving towards her. They continued for a few laps in the same manner, with the less experienced Poppy continually having to brake in order to avoid a collision with Hepplewhite as he cut off any chance to pass him by.

Poppy fell back slightly, giving herself space to move, and saw a long stretch of straight road ahead. She dropped down a gear and went full throttle. *Thunderbus* screamed forward with such force and speed that Hepplewhite couldn't react fast enough to block her and they were suddenly running parallel to each other, the huge form of *Thunderbus* overshadowing the tiny *Silver Bullet*.

Hepplewhite deliberately veered over, again trying to scare Poppy into thinking he was going to ram into her. 'Excellent control from number twenty-two there, marvellous tactics,' boomed the announcer.

Poppy refused to be intimidated and slammed the gearbox back into fourth, giving *Thunderbus* the power to rocket forward. As she did, Poppy twitched the wheel and she swerved across *Silver Bullet*'s front end. Hepplewhite, panicking at seeing the huge, wide juggernaut swing towards his lightweight car, slammed his brakes on, losing ground. Poppy was ahead.

'Very bad sportsmanship there from the woman in car number six, swerving across the track like that.' bleated the commentator. 'Very bad form indeed.'

As hard as he tried after Poppy had passed him, Hepplewhite could do nothing to regain first place.

He managed, at first, to gain a little when they reached a set of sharp corners, but always his slight advantage was utterly wiped out on the straights as *Thunderbus* sprinted away, contemptuously showing its huge twin exhausts. Besides, Poppy was evidently growing into the race and was handling the turns far better with each passing lap. By the time Hepplewhite came in for his first pit stop, Poppy was almost a complete lap ahead.

Hepplewhite jumped out of his car and strode up and down in fury as his crew hastily poured fresh water into the tank while also checking the lubrication of the engine and the condition of the tyres. He shouted at the crew for their supposed mistakes, roaring that they would lose him the race if they didn't hurry up, and promising mass sackings if such an event occurred. As he walked and raged, he couldn't take his eyes from the display board over the pit showing his position against *Thunderbus*.

The Honourable Reginald Tindal pulled up behind *Silver Bullet* for his pit stop. He climbed out, fastidiously leaving the mechanics to do the dirty work, and approached his team mate. 'I say, that blasted petrol car is making a mockery of us! I can't get close to it.'

'It should never have been allowed,' snarled

Hepplewhite. 'My father was grossly deceived by Pallister and that working-class trollop he's got driving for him. Why he has to openly flaunt his thick tart I do not know. Have you actually heard her awful accent?'

'What are we going to do, though?' bleated Tindal, looking worried and taken aback at Hepplewhite's venom.

Hepplewhite stared hard at Tindal's vacuous expression. He had always told Tindal what to do, ever since they were boys together at school, and Tindal had always done as he was told – which was right and proper, in Hepplewhite's view. Some were born to lead, and those with less talent should be grateful to be allowed to follow.

'They cheated to get here,' he said, slowly, 'so we are entitled to use their own tactics back at them.'

'I say, are you sure?' asked Tindal, shifting uneasily from foot to foot.

Hepplewhite realised that the silly little tit actually believed in the old sporting nonsense of fair play. No wonder he was so useless. 'Yes, I am sure. When the other side breaks the rules, it's fair play to fight fire with fire, and we will. You're going to take out that car!'

'What?' gaped Tindal, his mouth flapping.

'You're going to smash it off the road.'

'I ... I ... I don't know, really, isn't that a bit, what, you know, a little bit off?' squirmed Tindal.

'No, it is fair return,' snapped Hepplewhite. He saw Tindal remained unconvinced and started working on his weak points. 'Do you want that working-class tart to win and make us a laughing stock? Do you want to go back to your family and friends as a loser, knowing we could have won and didn't? Do you want to let the old school down?'

'Well, no, of course not. But why don't *you* smash her off, then?' asked Tindal, looking miserable.

Hepplewhite raised his eyebrow at the uncharacteristic questioning of his command. 'I am already ahead of you, so I have the best chance of winning,' he said, coldly.

'You're only half a lap ahead,' muttered Tindal, but already the unfamiliar flame of assertiveness was dying in his eyes. Hepplewhite moved to extinguish it for good.

'A few seconds is the difference between winning and losing; you're too far behind to get on the podium at all. Of course, if you think you know best, if you want to let down your oldest friend, your school, the old network that stands for something, then go right ahead.'

'All right, all right,' muttered Tindal, knowing he was beaten and feeling an unexpected sense of disquiet about his own meek reaction. 'I'll do it.'

'Good. As soon as you get the chance. No hesitation. Get behind her and sweep her back end out so she spins and then make sure you hit her straight in the middle of the bodywork, to break the car's axle and chassis.'

'Won't that be dangerous for her?' squawked Tindal. 'And for me?'

'That car is big enough and strong enough to protect the driver, and your engine will cushion you from harm,' lied Hepplewhite; he had no idea how strong the petrol car was, but he did know that a straight-on collision could push Tindal's engine back into his legs and possibly cripple him. It could even kill him, if the speed were high enough, but at that moment Hepplewhite simply didn't care. All he could see was his family honour at stake, as well as the honour of his entire class, and he would not fail them, no matter what price others had to pay. [42]

As Hepplewhite seethed and plotted in his pit, Poppy

---

[42] For any who query how I could possibly have reconstructed this conversation, I would point out that Tindal admitted in private correspondence what had happened, and eventually he publically admitted the conversation and his actions. Hepplewhite vehemently denied it, of course, but in any case, the cameras at the track do clearly show Tindal deliberately crashing into Poppy.

pulled up into hers. She rolled to a halt and cut the engine, her crew quickly refilling and checking *Thunderbus* while Simeon checked on Poppy's condition.

'Are you tired?' asked Simeon in concern. 'You've run a hell of a race so far, my girl. You must be exhausted.'

'Only a little. My mechanical arm is strong enough to hold *Thunderbus* by itself.'

'Are you sure?' bellowed Amy as she checked the engine, which was running perfectly. She examined the sparking plugs and found they were blackened, albeit functional, and decided to be safe rather than sorry, and began replacing them.

'Yes, I'm fine,' shouted Poppy over the noise, a smile on her face at the concern being shown for her. She pulled her scarf down and gratefully accepted a glass of water from Helena, which she gulped back in one go.

'Just keep eating the track on the straights, take the corners and bends with respect,' muttered Talbot, unable to find any compliment for the young woman. Around him, the pit crew began to shout out as they finished their checks and moved clear.

'Refuelled!'

'Tyres good!'

'Steering good!'

331

'Suspension good!'

'Engine good, go, go, go!' yelled Amy as she leapt backward. Poppy pressed the starter and accelerated almost simultaneously, flames roaring from the vents along the long bonnet as she made her way along the pit.

'We're almost there,' said Helena, her mouth tight with emotion. 'I hope she can do it.'

'She's a natural,' replied Simeon. 'She's far better than her father at driving. She's already adapted to the course and mastered some of the bends on the track, which is more than Robert could; he just used *Thunderbus*' speed to win. Poppy is using genuine skill to keep ahead.'

Poppy's new-found skills were needed even before she got back into the race. As she drove down the slip road leading back onto the track, she glanced sideways and saw in horror that a car was skidding towards her, the back tyre having exploded, completely out of the driver's control. Poppy hit the brakes, bringing *Thunderbus* to a quick, controlled stop.

The other car hurtled past, the number eleven on the side identifying it as Sir Robin Dalton's Dexter-Speedster. The speed and distance the car travelled was astonishing; within seconds it was almost level with the next pit, used by Lord Edward "Tubby" Edward III. Unfortunately, Lord Edward was at that moment roaring out of his slip road and while he, like Poppy, saw the skidding car, his brakes were not good enough to bring him to a quick stop.

The hideous noise of two cars colliding rasped out over the track, metal shrieking and tearing under the forces involved. Lord Edward's car was shunted through ninety degrees, while Sir Robin's smaller vehicle bounced off, spun around in a complete circle, and finally came to rest a few yards further down the track after colliding with the hay barriers. Lord Edward's pit crew dashed out onto the track to help the two men, both of whom immediately signalled they were unhurt.

'Despite his car being in a skid,' shouted the announcer in a fresh frenzy of misogyny, 'Sir Robin was able to steer past the panicked figure of Poppy Orpington, who froze at the wheel. I suspect she actually caused the accident by recklessly pulling out onto the track like that. No doubt Sir Robin's gallantry was the reason for him crashing into Lord Edward, further proof this is not the environment for a woman. She distracts the men, who of course have to be chivalrous at all times, which is not a consideration that hampers Miss Orpington on her way around the track.'[43]

Poppy, oblivious to the announcer over the noise of *Thunderbus* and the crowd, breathed out in relief that both drivers were fine. She carefully drove around the wreckage which moments before had been two functioning cars. It was a dismal reminder of the damage that could be done on the track. Two powerful machines of metal and wood had been contemptuously crumpled by the laws of physics. It focussed the mind on what could happen to the frail human body if caught in a crash. She hoped she would never be involved in anything like it.

Poppy took a calming breath and smoothly changed up through her gears as she re-entered the race. Glancing behind her, she saw Hepplewhite's *Silver Bullet*. She increased the pressure on the accelerator and Hepplewhite all but disappeared. She was ahead and clear, and as long as she stayed sharp, she would win.

Poppy realised that many of the drivers had conceded the superiority of her car and were allowing her free space to overtake as she lapped

---

[43] I'm afraid the announcer, William Pretherick, insisted to his dying day that he had been fair and unbiased in his race commentary. Although today most people can see his obvious sexism, to the contemporary audience he was spouting good, solid sense that many agreed with, male and female alike.

them. She waved in acknowledgement at those who allowed her through, and received acknowledgement back. So, not everyone was as blinkered and unsporting as Hepplewhite and his crew.

With the race almost over, and Hepplewhite nowhere near her, Poppy looked ahead and saw something puzzling; Hepplewhite's driving partner, Tindal, was now ahead of her. He certainly hadn't passed her so she must have lapped him, but he had been in the third or fourth spot throughout the race, so how come he was now so far behind? He must have had mechanical or electrical problems. It was astonishing he hadn't retired to the pits in the hope of a hasty repair.

Ahead of her, Tindal watched in his tiny rear-view mirror as *Thunderbus* growled up behind him. Sweat poured from his face as he considered his instructions and his responsibilities. He was gripping the steering wheel so tightly he could barely direct the car in any direction. He forced himself to move to the one side, his throat making a strange mewling noise while tears welled up in his eyes. He angrily blinked them away; Oswald was counting on him, and Oswald was a friend from school, as well as a well-respected member of society.

Even so, despite Oswald's assurances, Tindal was desperately worried about his own safety, and he didn't really want to hurt the girl, either, regardless of her class and bad character. So, instead of doing as he had been told and trying to sweep Poppy's back end out, he instead allowed her to draw level with him. He glanced over and saw her controlling the huge car with enviable skill, her long red hair escaping out from under her leather helmet and streaming behind her in the wind. Then he stopped thinking and swung his car across the track, aiming to sideswipe Poppy and hence safely shunt her off the track and onto the siding lined with bales of hay.

Poppy swore as Tindal's car rammed into *Thunderbus* and almost knocked her off the track. Possible explanations for the collision ran through her mind as she regained control. Had he gone into a skid? Had his steering system sheared off? She heaved the steering wheel to the left, shunting back against Tindal.

The two cars continued together for several dozen feet, metal scraping on metal, but it was clear that the impact had done far more damage to Tindal's lighter roadster than to the solid, two-ton bulk of *Thunderbus*. The roadster was bobbling up and down and Tindal was unable to hold onto the steering wheel as it spun underneath his hands.

Poppy wrenched her own steering wheel right and left, trying to dislodge Tindal as the two cars slowed down even more. Realising that for whatever reason he wasn't helping, she dropped down a gear. The tone of *Thunderbus*' engine turned into an ominous snarl that vibrated through Tindal's car, telling him of the power and fury he had stupidly become entangled with. Poppy stamped on the accelerator and powered out of the unwanted clinch. There was a thump, the front left quarter of *Thunderbus* lifted momentarily, there was an awful noise of rending, tearing metal, and a wheel rather improbably bounced up and over *Thunderbus*' bonnet and off the track.

Poppy glanced over, knowing the wheel was far too small to have come from *Thunderbus*. Sure enough, she saw the front right corner of Tindal's car was a mass of crumpled metal set around a gaping hole where the wheel had been. His car slewed round, the body and bare axle slamming onto the concrete and sending sparks out in all directions until it came to rest at the side of the course. Stewards came running over and pushed the car off the track while Tindal stumbled out, looking dazed and unwell.

'Oh dear, there was some form of collision there,' boomed the track announcer, mentally grappling with what his eyes were reporting – that a man had purposely crashed into the female driver – before his mind rebelled and he rejected reality. 'Miss Orpington lost control and hit car number twenty-three, driven by the Honourable Reginald Tindal. No bad intent, I am sure, she is just a young girl, after all, though it does prove the foolhardiness of having women on the track.

'We must also remember the terrible driving conditions here today; the sun is very bright and has probably dazzled these brave drivers, all factors in her leading the race and possibly a factor also for the Honourable Tindal in colliding with her.' The voice hurriedly corrected itself. 'That is, in her colliding with him.'

CHAPTER FOURTEEN

Poppy frowned at Tindal's actions but then shook her head; she had no time to speculate on why he had crashed into her. She still had a lap to complete and the collision had allowed her rivals to gain on her, though thankfully the overhead display showed she was still far ahead. She accelerated and changed gear again, *Thunderbus* responding well, but just as she thought she had avoided any serious damage she turned the wheel and the vehicle shook in protest, the car juddering as though something was blocking the steering.

It was lucky that the bend ahead was little more than a gentle curve as it gave Poppy the space and length to manoeuvre into it. She continued to turn as much as possible so that *Thunderbus* was now moving at a slight angle that took it off the track and onto the grass verge. Poppy immediately leapt out and ran to the front left quarter, fearing the worst. If she couldn't fix the damage then her race, and her father's dreams, were finished.

She skidded onto the ground, running her hands over the tyre and wheel. Both were fine. The steel wing and running board had protected them from any damage from Tindal's car, so what was causing the problem? She rested her hand on the wing and the entire front section juddered up and down, rubbing up against the tyre, and Poppy realised the bolts at the front of the wing had been sheared off by the collision.

Recognizing there was no way she could reattach the wing, Poppy crawled underneath the mid-section, hoping to detach and drop the entire thing and continue without it, but she saw in horror that the three remaining bolts holding the panel to the chassis had all been bent by the force of the impact; there wasn't any way of getting a spanner around them. It would require a blowtorch to cut them off. Her race was over. Unless …

Poppy got back to her feet, wondering just how much strength was contained in her mechanical arm. She took a firm grip on the defective panel with her steel fingers, braced herself firmly on the ground, and pulled. Nothing happened except the pressure dial on her arm flickered briefly upward. Poppy took a breath and pulled again, straining her sinews and nervous system. The pressure dial skipped up to the middle of the display as more power flooded through the arm, while the mechanical elbow whined slightly under the increased pressure.

Poppy gritted her teeth and exerted more pressure, willing her nerves to integrate with the mechanical appendage, flesh, bone and muscle fusing with metal and wire to become one. The needle skipped into the red zone and a small red light began flashing, showing that the stresses on the arm were reaching high levels, but then with a rasping croak the metal wing buckled and ripped cleanly away from the bent restraining bolts under the car. *Thunderbus* was free.

Poppy laughed as she hurled the wing away, sending the heavy metal flying through the air for several feet. She jumped back in the driving seat and re-entered the race, glancing behind her to check the way was clear. As she did, she saw a glint of silver and realised in dismay that Hepplewhite had almost caught up with her, before remembering that she was still a lap ahead of him. All she had to do was cross the finish line, barely half a lap ahead, and she had won.

Poppy glanced up at the electric display system and almost swung off the track in shock. The screens were showing that Hepplewhite, like her, was on his final lap, which was impossible. The last time she had checked the display, he had been an entire lap behind. She couldn't possibly have misread the information.

Many in the crowd were roaring in disapproval as they, too, noticed the change in the display system which now falsely showed Hepplewhite to be on his final lap. Those closest to the electronic control tower, where the lap information was fed into relay monitors by the race stewards, watched in bafflement as a young woman wearing a hideous green dress emerged from the tower with a smug look on her face.

'Keep calm, Orpington, keep calm,' muttered Poppy to herself. She had no idea why the lapboard was wrong, but she was still ahead of Hepplewhite and only a catastrophic mechanical failure could stop her now. She breathed out, changed down to third gear to attack the rising slope of the road, and experienced a catastrophic mechanical failure as a great plume of smoke erupted from underneath the car as something in the gearbox ground itself in fury against what felt like an immovable object. The gear stick shuddered and refused to engage until she shifted back up to fourth.

Poppy looked down in alarm. The gearbox, taken from an old charabanc and unused to high speed racing, had given its all but was now falling apart. She couldn't engage third and already the engine was labouring as it tried to drive up the slope in too high a gear. If Poppy couldn't change down the car would stall, and *Thunderbus* was now slowing alarmingly. She stamped down on the clutch again, reassured that the pedal itself was working, and heaved on the gear stick. Even with all her strength, she still could not engage third gear.

'Aha ha ha,' cried the announcer. 'It looks like number six is in trouble. Poppy Orpington has broken her car. Well, it *is* a complicated piece of machinery, it was bound to happen.'

Poppy swore as she tried again to get third, realising as she did that it was impossible. She put the car into neutral, leaving *Thunderbus* to coast forward under its own momentum, and when she had slowed sufficiently she thumped the gear lever across and down into second gear. The stick moved reluctantly into position and she released the clutch; *Thunderbus* jolted but it did continue up the hill.

She now faced the dilemma of either continuing at the slower speed for the entire slope and risk being caught, or speeding up as much as possible and risk fully destroying the gearbox. She glanced behind her and saw the gleam of Hepplewhite's *Silver Bullet* gaining on her. She grimaced and pressed down on the accelerator, building the revs, the engine note getting higher and higher in protest, pleading for a gear change to third, but Poppy had no third to give.

Poppy coaxed as much out of the engine as she could, and as she crested the hill she slammed the gear stick into fourth, bypassing third completely. *Thunderbus* coughed in surprise, shaking and rumbling in protest as Poppy slammed her foot down on the accelerator, slowly building her speed.

The engine complained that the wrong gear was being used but the protests became muted as the revs, power and speed began to synchronise. More smoke poured from the gearbox and there was an almighty whine coming from somewhere under the car, but the finish line was now in sight and it was downhill to the race official standing ready with the finishing flag.

Poppy cautiously eased off the accelerator but the high-pitched moan from the gearbox continued, so she buried her foot into the metal floor, determined to pick up as much speed as she could. If the gearbox did disintegrate, hopefully she could put the car into neutral again and simply roll over the finish line.

She looked behind again and saw *Silver Bullet* was almost upon her. She could even see the grimace on Hepplewhite's face as he stared in manic loathing at her and *Thunderbus*, but it was too late for him. With the gearbox whining all the way down, muffling even the sounds of the snorting engine, *Thunderbus* staggered past the chequered flag, leaving Hepplewhite a car's length behind in second place.

'And the winner is …' The announcer struggled with

the horror of announcing that a woman had won. 'The winner is *Thunderbus*, a three and a half litre petrol-fuelled car, and my word, people will be talking about that engine for a long time to come. And in second place is Lord Oswald Hepplewhite in car number twenty-two, *Silver Bullet*. Oswald Hepplewhite is, of course, the son of Lord Geoffrey Hepplewhite, well known to racing fans for his tireless work in motor racing and his commitment to fair play. *Silver Bullet* ran an excellent race there, showing true skill throughout. In third place is Lord Roxborough in car number twenty-eight ...'

The announcer droned on, listing all the drivers and their titles, past triumphs and car specifications, all the while ignoring the huge black car triumphantly juddering along the track, its driver waving to the whooping, cheering, jeering crowds. Finally, thankfully, Poppy reached her pit and rolled in, slotting neatly into the bay and cutting the engine.

She had barely stepped down and peeled the now filthy scarf and goggles from her grime-encrusted skin before she was surrounded by a vast crowd of spectators who surged forward and broke though the wire link fence to get a closer look at the first woman to race – and win – at Purley. Ahead of them were Simeon, Helena, Amy and the pit crew.

'Poppy!' bellowed Amy in delight, flinging

herself into Poppy's arms and hugging her tightly. 'You did it! I'm so proud of you. You were brilliant and clever and brave and I was so scared when that car hit you and you just got out and ripped the bodywork off with all the other cars belting past you and I thought you'd be killed and …'

'And breathe, Amy,' interrupted Simeon. 'Poppy, you were fantastic. There is no other word for it!'

'You should be very proud, my dear,' agreed Helena. 'You've started something here today. We'll be feeling the repercussions of this for some time yet.'

'I couldn't have done it without you all,' replied Poppy, her eyes growing moist. Amy was still in her arms and she had no desire to ever let her go. 'Without you and Simeon to guide me, and all the pit crew, and Amy to support me and do the engine, I would never have done this. Never!'

'And tonight, Amy,' Poppy added in a low tone, 'we are finally going to celebrate.' Amy blushed but nodded enthusiastically. The past few stressful days had given them no opportunity to move their relationship on, emotionally or any other way, but victory had lifted their spirits and boosted their confidence. They still had the sense to quickly move apart, however, before anyone grew suspicious of their enthusiastic hugging.

'You were amazing!' shouted someone in the crowd.

'What about that dodgy lap recorder?' yelled another, to a chorus of agreement. '*Silver Bullet* was only on lap nineteen, then suddenly it was shown as being on lap twenty!'

'I thought I'd got it wrong!' exclaimed Poppy. 'So, Hepplewhite was still a lap behind me?'

The crowd roared again. 'Yeah! Something dodgy there!' bellowed one, while another bawled out for the need for an inquiry, though some were determined to deny what they had just seen.

'Nah, he did all twenty!'

'Yeah, I counted him, all the way.'

'Probably just a mechanical error, I'm sure.'

'Of course,' grumbled one man, unable to deal with the idea of a successful female racing driver. 'You know why she's wearing that scarf? Because she didn't race at all! You mark my words; this is all a publicity stunt. What happened, right, was they get this girl to walk around at the start of the race, right, then she slips behind a wall or some such and the real driver, wearing the same clothes, he gets in and actually drives the car, then when he gets back the girl pops up again and pretends she was the one who was in the car all the time.'

'Geronn!' said another man in disbelief. 'We just

saw her get out and take the scarf off! Course it was her! And well done, I say.'

'Will you be taking part in the Continental Touring Race next?' demanded another spectator of Poppy.

'No, you'll want to do the Alp racetrack,' responded another member of the throng. 'Bring the Alp Cup back home to England!'

'How about the European Cross-Country?' shouted another. 'You could enter that!'

Poppy and Simeon looked at each other. 'Well, Poppy?' asked Simeon. 'What do you think of that? Another race? A career of racing?'

Poppy hesitated. 'Right now, I just want to take in all of this. And get my winnings and pay off everything we owe. For Dad.' A shadow passed over her face as she thought of her father, lying still and silent in a hospital bed.

'Your father will be thrilled when he finds out,' said Helena with an understanding smile. 'You have achieved what he wanted. *Thunderbus* is going to be the talk of the country, but you've gone way beyond that. You've achieved all this not just for him, but for yourself as well.'

'Come on, everyone,' yelled Simeon to the crowd. 'We have a cup to lift and winnings to collect, and you are all invited to accompany us as guard of honour!' A cheer went up around the multitude. Before she could say anything, Poppy was lifted up on the shoulders of the surging, happy group of friends and strangers and she was carried towards the platform where the winning driver traditionally received the cheque, the huge silver cup and the congratulations of the race marshals.

The crowd deposited Poppy in front of the podium. The other drivers were gathering, and Lord Roxborough was already positioned on the step reserved for third place. He smiled and waved as Poppy stepped forward. The other drivers turned and saw Poppy, and though many grinned and clapped, a substantial few muttered and looked away.

'Splendid race, my dear, simply splendid, you did yourself proud,' said Lord Roxborough through his large silver moustache. 'Wish I had a car like yours. The speed is astonishing!'

'*Si*, an excellent race!' cried out Count Sellini, pulling off his white racing helmet to reveal his handsome stubbled face, while his thick, dark hair sprang free in wild abandon. 'When I saw you in the Gordon Club I did not know what to think, but the way you handled yourself was wonderful. And the way you handled that car was beautiful!'

'Indeed, you fully deserve to be here,' said

Roxborough, nodding.

'Thank you, you're very kind,' said Poppy with an uncertain smile. She was exhausted physically and mentally, and could barely concentrate. She looked round in confusion. 'Er, what happens next, Lord Roxborough?'

'Please, call me Anthony,' replied Roxborough with a cheerful wink. 'In short, the marshals come out, make a speech, award the cups for second and third places and then give the big cup and cheque to the winner.'

'You just have to look modest, say a few words about being very proud and thank everyone who helped,' added the count. 'Be English and reserved, like my good friend Anthony, who never boasts about his wins.'

'Please ignore Lorenzo, he is incorrigible,' said Anthony, laughing. 'After the presentation, the usual practice is to spend the next few hours answering questions on anything and everything from the crowd and the press, and then it's the after-race party. Not sure where the marshals are, though. They are usually out here ready to greet the winner.'

'They all disappeared into the director's box after Oswald Hepplewhite went stomping up to them earlier,' said Lorenzo. 'They've not come out yet. I wonder if they're sorting out the error with the lap scoring system? That was an outrage!'

'Hum; wherever they are, they're showing very bad form,' murmured Anthony. 'Oswald should be out here accepting the plaudits for being second and congratulating the winner. It's the done thing, you know. Always be a good loser.'

'He was always a bad winner, never mind a good loser,' muttered Lorenzo. 'Always gloating over the other drivers after beating them.'

'Ah, there they are,' said Anthony, nodding his elegant, silver head in the direction of the director's box. The marshals and the two Hepplewhites, father and son, had appeared and were moving to the podium.

'*O, là!* He looks nasty,' observed Lorenzo, noticing the twisted smirk on Hepplewhite Junior's face.

Poppy looked at the group as they approached and felt a seed of apprehension take root in her mind. The Hepplewhites certainly seemed exultant, and the other marshals wore stern, self-important expressions. Why weren't they simply congratulating everyone and handing out the prizes?

Hepplewhite Senior reached the podium and climbed up to the microphone at the front. He tapped it a few times, sending a ringing tone out across the

351

racetrack, and glanced over at his son before he started speaking. 'Ladies and gentlemen, thank you for your patience. We have an important announcement to make. Thank you all for your splendid appreciation throughout the day and your unwavering support for us. Without you, there would be no motor sport. Your support keeps us going, in every sense.'

'What is he doing?' demanded Simeon, appearing at Poppy's side. 'He doesn't usually butter up the crowd like this.'

'Today we have witnessed some splendid driving and real race drama,' continued Hepplewhite Senior. 'Every driver out there deserves applause for their sterling efforts and we recognise that. However, much as it pains us, we must always remember the principles of fair play, and we must ensure it is upheld at all times, for the benefit of all.'

Hepplewhite looked round, trying to gauge the reaction of the crowd who had suddenly gone extremely quiet. He coughed nervously and licked his lips. He had intended to keep talking for some time but his next batch of platitudes withered away in the alarming scrutiny of several thousand spectators, leaving him to blurt out the race marshals' decision far more bluntly than he had intended. 'Car number six has been disqualified from the event.'

The roar of disapproval that followed seemed capable of shaking the entire racetrack to the ground. Questions, statements, queries and inarticulate cries showered down on the assembled marshals, who all paled considerably as they realised they were surrounded on all sides by a huge mob of dirty working-class ruffians.

'We have not ...' began Hepplewhite Senior, but his voice was weak and scared. He coughed and tried again. 'We have not taken this decision lightly, I assure you. We acknowledge the novelty that Miss, Miss, that the driver of car number six has brought to this year's event, and we acknowledge her car also. But the rules are the rules and they have been broken!'

'How have they been broken?' demanded several voices.

'The driver was not properly registered.'

'That is a complete fabrication!' bellowed Simeon, who was close enough to the platform for his voice to be picked up by the microphone. 'I have here the registration form, made out to P. Orpington, signed and stamped by you, Lord Hepplewhite.'

'In any case, petrol cars are not eligible and hence cannot race,' bleated Hepplewhite, ignoring the inconvenient form being waved in his face and the roar of disapproval from the crowd.

'There are no rules governing petrol cars because no petrol vehicle has ever been entered into a race!' yelled Simeon. 'And if petrol is not eligible, you should have said when we registered the vehicle last month. Your argument is again invalid.'

'The argument is irrelevant. Your driver,' Lord Hepplewhite glanced at Poppy, unable to bring himself to use her name, 'crashed into another competitor, car number twenty-three, thus breaking the rules and disqualifying herself.'

'Number twenty-three ran into me!'

'And we have proof of that on film,' added Amy. 'The cameras will have picked up everything.'

Lord Hepplewhite paused. It had appeared from his vantage point in the luxurious observation box as though Tindal had deliberately swerved into car number six, but such an idea was ludicrous; it could not possibly have happened that way, and thus it had *not* happened that way. Even so, with the threat of film playback hanging in the air, he decided to move on. 'Also, there are no rules to allow prosthetic support,' he said, glaring at Poppy's shining hand under her coat sleeve. 'A driver should use nothing more than his own strength and grit to win. The driver of car number six had an unfair advantage in her mechanical hand and arm.'

'Please show me, Geoffrey,' interrupted Anthony,

his face going red with anger, 'where in the rule book it specifically prohibits prosthetics?'

'It is an artificial aid,' snapped Hepplewhite Senior, aware that there was no such prohibition in the rules, though he was determined to write one in at the earliest opportunity.

'This is an outrage,' spluttered Lorenzo. 'Miss Orpington has won fair and square!'

'This is shameful,' agreed Anthony. 'We need to encourage new ideas and new racers, not slam the door in their face.'

'The rules are the rules,' interrupted one of the marshals nervously, 'and we must abide by them, otherwise what is the point of racing at all?'

'And which rule is it that you're using to deny Poppy her victory?' demanded Amy in fury. 'You've just given us several which have all been rejected. You're making up the rules to suit yourselves!'

'The decision has been made,' snarled Hepplewhite, unused to being publicly questioned. 'We are the authorities of motor sport and that is final.'

'And are the authorities looking into the lap display?' bellowed Amy. 'Your son only completed nineteen laps. He's not even technically finished yet.'

'If the decision has been made, I for one will abide by it,' said one of the drivers, secretly infuriated at being beaten by a woman.

'I also have faith in the integrity of Lord Hepplewhite and the other marshals,' announced another driver, George Warrington, seeing an opportunity to ingratiate himself with the rulers of the sport.

'I haven't,' snapped Lorenzo. 'I came in fourth, with this young lady first. That is the simple truth. If they insist on this shameful disqualification and present me with third place, I will hand the prize money over to Miss Orpington at the first opportunity.'

'Agreed,' said Anthony. 'I will hand over my prize money also.'

'Yeah, good on yer,' shouted a voice in the crowd.

'The decision has been made,' repeated Hepplewhite. 'And I know it is the correct decision and will be supported by everyone. I see it in the faces of this … wonderful crowd of workers. Workers from the surrounding factories, including my own vast and extensive mechanical and engineering plant which relies on orders from the motor industry for its very existence.' Hepplewhite looked round. When he spoke again, his voice was cold and grating. 'And the existence of your wages. Your jobs. Your continued jobs.'

Another silence fell on the crowd. Many of them

were employed at the numerous engineering works in the surrounding area and they understood the threat against their livelihood if they continued to protest against the result. Hepplewhite gazed at the crowd in savage satisfaction, knowing he had faced down the working-class oiks and their filthy insurrection. They were all the same; when faced with a firm hand, they capitulated.

'Ladies and Gentlemen, I give you the winner of the race, for a record fourth time, Lord Oswald Hepplewhite,' announced one of the marshals, holding up a huge silver cup. Reluctant cheers echoed out over the ground, and although there were a substantial number of jeers also, they were now in the minority.

Oswald Hepplewhite waved at the crowd, holding aloft the cup and smirking wider than ever. He looked over at Poppy and shouted, knowing his words would never be heard over the noise of the crowd. 'You lost. *You lost!*'

Poppy stared in anger but she knew she was powerless to do anything. The racing authorities answered to no one but themselves, and they had the support of the crowd even if it was gained by indirect threats.

'Don't worry about the money and the contract, Poppy,' said Simeon in fury. 'We'll find a way forward, even if we have to take them through every court in the land!'

'Absolutely, hear, hear,' said a voice. The group looked around at the seemingly vacant face of the Honourable Cuthbert Gilmore. 'I just told them they should be ashamed but they say the decision is final. Which is why it's called the final decision, I suppose.'

'It's an absolute disgrace,' snapped Helena, her jaw flexing with anger.

'There is some good news, at least,' said Cuthbert, a gleam of intelligence peeking out from behind his monocle. 'Having nearly caused a riot with their truly rotten decision to disqualify Miss Orpington, I doubt they will risk inflaming the situation by refusing to honour the new lap leader agreement.'

'Gosh, I forgot about that,' gasped Amy. 'Poppy, you led the race for fourteen laps. How much do you get for each lap?'

'Thirty pounds,' announced Anthony, while Lorenzo grinned in pleasure next to him.

'That goes some way to helping with the costs,' squealed Amy in happiness.

'Geoffrey!' bellowed Simeon, again making sure the microphone picked up his words. 'The lap leader winnings, Geoffrey. They rightfully belong to Poppy because she was the lap leader for fourteen laps.'

Members of the crowd shouted out in agreement. Hepplewhite Senior shrugged before replying with a sneer. 'Yes, yes, you may have the chicken feed. I'm sure it will be more money than she has ever seen in her entire life.'

'And there is also the bet made with Lord Oswald Hepplewhite for five hundred pounds,' added Cuthbert, leaving Poppy wondering, despite her rising anger, how he had overheard the bet being made; he'd been some distance away at the time.

'What bet?' snapped Hepplewhite Senior, looking in displeasure at his son who glared in nervous disdain before realising he had no choice but to explain things to his father.

'But that bet is void,' snapped Hepplewhite Junior after mumbling his way through the self-pitying explanation. 'She has been disqualified! She didn't win!'

'The bet was not that Poppy would win but that she would cross the line before you.' Cuthbert smiled. 'I was there and stand witness to the exact terms.'

Hepplewhite Junior looked staggered, while his father grew purple with rage, but in front of the impeccable witness that was Cuthbert Gilmore, there was no way either could deny the validity of the bet. Neither was there any way of avoiding paying out, for it was an article of faith with Hepplewhite Senior that a gentleman always honoured his wagers.

'You had better write a cheque,' hissed Hepplewhite Senior to his son.

'Ah, well, truth is, Papa,' squirmed Oswald like a small boy, though his face was white with anger at his public humiliation. 'I am a little short after the costs of, um, costs of entering the race and, you know, other costs, so if you could see your way to a small loan?'

'A cheque will be posted,' barked Hepplewhite Senior, his expression making it clear he would raise the matter with his son at the earliest opportunity. 'The day is over,' he snarled into the microphone. 'Please make your way out of the track in an orderly manner. Thank you and goodbye.' He turned and stomped away, followed by the other race marshals, his son and their various devotees. It was possibly the angriest victory ever seen at a sporting event.

'There is another positive here,' gabbled Simeon, hoping to calm Poppy down with a soothing flow of words; her anger was still in danger of breaking out and doing something regrettable, and quite possibly illegal. 'We've got what your father wanted back in the beginning, what he saw as being essential for his plans to sell *Thunderbus*' designs; publicity! Look at the crowd – they're all talking about Poppy

Orpington and *Thunderbus*. The newspapers will be full of it. With the added scandal of the disqualification, done to protect the race marshal's own family, this will be talked about for a month, and I wouldn't be surprised if it even reaches the continent. This is going to be huge!'

'And don't forget what I said about endorsements, Poppy,' added Helena, who was also alarmed at the anger on her young friend's face. 'You're going to be swamped with offers soon. If we proceed with care, you should make more than enough money for the immediate future, whatever that may bring.'

'Now, we have a private supper laid on for us, so let's go and get cleaned up and enjoy the rest of the day,' concluded Simeon, physically ushering Poppy away before she did something understandable but foolish, such as pounding each Hepplewhite – and their supporters – into unconsciousness.[44]

---

[44] It is a shame that Poppy's greatest weakness – her temper – curtailed her formidable intellect at this point. She was surrounded by genuine friends rather than sycophants, and she had won far more than the Hepplewhites for she had proved both herself and her father's engine in an intensely hostile environment. Her anger, alas, meant Poppy was oblivious to the truth of the situation for some considerable time.

EPILOGUE

For the next three days Poppy took her rage out on the little steam car loaned to her by Simeon as she thrashed it along country roads at all hours of the day, sometimes speeding aimlessly in random directions, sometimes driving to see her father at the hospice where he still lay under sedation. She was alone as Amy, despite enjoying their much delayed private 'celebration', had left for a visit to her parents in Stourbridge.

On the fourth day, *Thunderbus'* gearbox having been rebuilt and the wing restored, Poppy returned Simeon's runabout and drove the now-famous car out of Pallister Hall and accelerated hard along the country road, feeling the last of her rage dissipate under her enjoyment of *Thunderbus'* speed, power and terrifying noise. She drove for miles, alone but no longer feeling lonely, until she felt a pang of guilt and turned *Thunderbus* towards the hospice. As she parked in a free spot at the front of the building, the doors opened and a nurse ran down the steps.

'Miss Orpington, Miss Orpington!' cried the nurse in excitement. 'Your father has just woken up! I think it was the noise of *Thunderbus* that did it!'

Poppy gasped in delight. She gave the nurse a hug

362

before heading up the steps, moving easily in her racing clothes which allowed much freer movement than the constrictive corsets and heavy dresses women were expected to wear. She was in her father's room in less than a minute.

Mr Orpington looked fuzzily at Poppy, a puzzled expression on his face. The tall figure was familiar, yet somehow a stranger. He squinted at the mane of red hair tumbling over the shoulders of a long leather coat, the beautiful face, the steel and brass hand coming out of one sleeve, and his disconnected mind made the link. 'Poppy? Is that you?'

'Yes, Dad, it's me. How are you? How do you feel?'

Mr Orpington looked weakly at his daughter, the frown of puzzlement pulling deeper on his face. 'Feel … strange. Where am I? What happened?' His expression clouded as Poppy quietly explained his illness and how he was now being cared for in a private hospice. She had to repeat herself several times before her father could take in what she was saying.

'How, how long have I been here?' he coughed.

'Over a week, now. Almost two.'

'What? No, no, I can't have been, the race! I have to race!' He stirred feebly and Poppy had to quickly and gently push him back down onto his bed.

'It's all right, Dad, we got another driver. *Thunderbus* took part at Purley. It was brilliant, Dad – the car never missed a beat! Each lap, regular as clockwork, and on one lap it was recorded doing ninety-two miles an hour! That's a record at Purley, and all down to you.'

Her father smiled, simple happiness washing over his face and easing his strain. 'You mean *Thunderbus* won?'

'First over the line, Dad,' whispered Poppy, feeling a stab of shame that she should be less than honest with him, but she thought it justified. The news was clearly a tonic to the sick man, vindicating his decisions and design.

'Are, are we free, Poppy? Are we free of the contract?'

'We've got more money than we could ever have imagined, Dad,' said Poppy, grimacing as she told another slight untruth. Technically they had not cleared the contract as her disqualification at Purley had denied her the full winnings, but advertisers had been bothering her daily to endorse their products. Under Simeon and Helena's guidance, Poppy had agreed to some and discarded others. The money she was promised in return for her image on advertising boards, as well as attending events as a spokesman – spokeswoman – for various companies would be sufficient to pay off Simeon completely.

'We're free, free,' muttered her father. His face relaxed and seemed less haggard, but then his hand tightened in hers and he looked in alarm at his daughter. 'Poppy, don't make my mistake,' he whispered, forcing the words out. 'Don't let that car take you over. Don't define yourself by *Thunderbus* alone. If you do, it will destroy you as it destroyed me. You'll hate it, Poppy, hate it as I do!'

'You've not been destroyed, Dad,' said Poppy, vehemently. 'You're too strong. You'll be back on your feet soon and then we'll have a new life to look forward to.'

'Don't define yourself by it, Poppy,' he insisted. 'Don't … my little girl, all grown up, look at you, new clothes, new arm, don't define yourself by the car, don't …'

'I won't, Dad, I won't,' replied Poppy, kissing his brow. He didn't speak again but he opened his eyes once or twice and smiled each time he saw his daughter there. Then he drifted off into a deep sleep and the nurse tactfully suggested that Poppy should come back tomorrow. Poppy dried her eyes as she walked away, happy her father was conscious but dejected to see him in such a poor state. Yet there was hope that one day he would fully recover. She truly felt the worst was over.[45]

Poppy strode across the parking area towards *Thunderbus*. As she walked along the side of the car, she ran her flesh-and-blood hand along the huge bonnet, feeling the cold steel, the panel-beaten metal, sensing the huge and powerful engine within. She assured herself her father's fears were groundless; *Thunderbus* certainly got her noticed, but there was much more to her than just the car. *Thunderbus* was simply an added bonus in her life. Nothing more.

Poppy slipped into the driver's seat, smiling as she turned the key in the ignition and flipped the switches to start the flow of petrol and to warm the ignition coils. Needles quivered and lights flashed on and off as *Thunderbus* awoke from its sleep. As the last needle finished trembling and held its position to show that all of the systems were working properly, she pressed the starter button.

With an explosion of red flame and a roar that shook the ground, *Thunderbus* blasted into life. Poppy rested her hand on the gear lever, feeling the power of the engine throbbing through her arm and into her body. She adjusted the fuel flow and the

---

[45] This, sadly, was not the case. The worst was yet to come, but for now I will let Poppy finish her story in her own inimitable style. Thank you for joining me at the start of her journey. James Henry Birkin.

power subsided into a soothing purr.

She engaged first gear, released the handbrake and guided the long nose of the car out of the parking space and onto the driveway. She teased the engine and herself by keeping the revs and speed low as she approached the gates. The road ahead was clear, apart from an elderly couple driving a small two-seater car up the long hill about half a mile ahead of her.

Poppy swung out after them, feeling the wind brushing her face and relishing the power of *Thunderbus* under her hands, hers to control and hers to use. She stamped down on the throttle, feeling the surge of acceleration before changing quickly and skilfully up through the gears, *Thunderbus* roaring and gobbling up the road in joy.

The half mile between her and the steam car was gone almost before she could blink. She was simply a huge blur of orange flame and black bodywork, gone so fast she never even heard the shouting from the other driver – she only saw him as a tiny figure receding in the rear-view mirror as he stood up in his little car and shook his fist at her, yelling in outrage.

'I've seen you in the papers, Poppy Orpington. I'll have the law on you, you maniac! Why don't you act more ladylike? Damn girls these days, they think they can do anything they want!'

For more information about Accent Press

titles please visit

www.accentpress.co.uk

26104351R00221

Printed in Poland
by Amazon Fulfillment
Poland Sp. z o.o., Wrocław